ANILA'S JOURNEY

Mary Finn worked for years as a magazine journalist with Radio Telefís Eireann, the Irish broadcasting service. A particular pleasure was dealing with children's books, their authors and illustrators, and the very keen readers who always insisted on knowing where ideas came from.

"My fascination with India began when I was about eight," says Mary. "There was a story at school that I now know came from the *Mahabharata*. It was rich and strange, packed with lotus flowers and princesses and birds that were twice as wise as humans. So, for me, it was a pleasure to avoid the usual advice offered to writers (Write What You Know) and instead go for the alternative version (Write What You Want To Find Out). I recommend this. As a time travel device it's the only one we've yet discovered and it's one hundred per cent eco-friendly. But having a true regard also for Writing What You Can See With Your Own Eyes, I confess I did get to go to India too."

Mary lives in Dublin with her son and works as a freelance writer.

ANILA'S JOURNEY

MARY FINN

WALKER BOOKS
AND SUBSIDIARIES

LONDON · BOSTON · SYDNEY · AUCKLAND

Acknowledgements

I owe a great debt to Bunny Gupta in Calcutta, for her interest and encouragement throughout and for her keen historical eye. Thanks also to Dr Robert Prys-Jones of the Natural History Museum at Tring in the UK, who mailed me the mythological story of the sarus crane. Colette Edwards of the National Botanic Gardens Library in Dublin was assiduous in digging out many a tree and plant fact for me. I am grateful to Assadour Guzelian and Armenag Topalian for Armenian references. Any errors are mine.

Thanks, too, to my editor, Mara Bergman, and my agent, Sarah Manson, friends now, enthusiasts always.

First published 2008 by Walker Books Ltd
87 Vauxhall Walk, London SE11 5HJ

2 4 6 8 10 9 7 5 3 1

Text © 2008 Mary Finn

Cover image based on *Sarus Crane, painted for Lady Impey at Calcutta,*
c. 1780 / Shaikh Zain ud-Din / Bridgeman Art Library and
A View of Calcutta from a point opposite to Kidderpore, 1837, engraved by Robert Havell the Younger (1793-1878) / James Baillie Fraser / Bridgeman Art Library and
An Indian Lady (oil on canvas, 102x127cm) / Thomas Hickey (1741-1824) /
National Gallery of Ireland Collection / photo © The National Gallery of Ireland

The right of Mary Finn to be identified as author of this work has been asserted by her in accordance with the Copyright, Designs and Patents Act 1988

This book has been typeset in Bembo

Printed and bound in Great Britain by
Creative Print and Design (Wales), Ebbw Vale

British Library Cataloguing in Publication Data:
a catalogue record for this book
is available from the British Library

ISBN 978-1-4063-0659-0

www.walkerbooks.co.uk

For David

In memory of
Gloria Rodriguez Finn

HOW TO
BEGIN A STORY

THIS IS MY STORY and I think there is merit in setting it down, even if I am not a princess, or a magical bird, or a gentleman who has lost his ship and found a new land. When I am old I can shake my head at it. But it will still be true.

The only thing I would choose to change, and it is impossible, is that my mother be the storyteller, for she told the best stories in the world. Hers would begin with a stolen ring or the monsoon in its black cloak and boots coming, not in summer but in winter, everything out of order and impossible to put right. But they'd end with a wedding feast in a palace and all the devils tumbled backwards into the deep blue sea.

Ask her about our own story, however, and those devil horns would poke out of the water again, just high enough to trouble me. Life is different, she said, it's just a line painted on an egg and if you think it has a beginning or an end you are bound for a fretful journey.

She took up my pen one day and drew a line on one of the smooth white stones from the fountain in the garden. She turned the stone round and round again, drawing all the while, until the line made fine bands all the way from top to bottom.

"There's the end!" I said to her, triumphant, for she could go no further now. But she turned the stone again and I saw she had made a loop back to where she had set out, so that her line had not simply come to a stop.

"You see?" she said. "There is no place here you can say is the beginning or the end. That is the way our life is too, Anila."

She believed in the wheel of life, absolutely. I was not so sure about that, not even when I was little, but especially after I was eight or nine and there were enough beginnings and endings around us for dozens of stories. I was impatient when she would not see this.

"But I began when you met my father," I said to her. "And if that was an egg in your hand, not a stone, what if you broke it? Then you'd have a top and a bottom and a beginning and an end and a middle you can just pour away. Or turn into something sweet for eating."

She held up her hands as you do to play Ikri-Mikri-Cham-Chikri with a baby but she was trying to stop my words, not to play. By that time it was a rare thing to see her smile. She feared for me because of my boldness, and my thunderclapping, as it was called in the house with the fountain. But I only had a child's desire to understand what was happening all around me.

Yet when I try to begin my own story, to write it down, all in order, in this notebook, I find that my mother's belief in the wheel makes a lot of sense after all. How is it possible to cut into the line of life and say, here it is, this is where it begins? It is not possible but surely a writer has to stab at it, like a baby bird seeking the softest part of the shell.

THE SCRAP OF NEWSPAPER

SO I SHALL BREAK my egg and choose to open my story here. Not with the ring or the storm, but with the scrap of newspaper that dear Miss Hickey, my guardian, put into my hand the day before she took ship from Calcutta for Madras.

She came into the salon where I was sitting on the old fainting couch, my legs tucked up under me. It was the only piece of furniture left now in that huge yellow room and it felt like a raft in the emptiness, with my cast-off slippers for fish.

"Anila! There you are, my dear. I've made myself hoarse calling for you in the garden. Look, see what a blessed find I've made in just the last little while, going through the packing cases."

She stepped through the wide sun stripes cast by the windows where the dust hung, turning over as slowly as honey. There was a blaze of excitement on her face but all she had was a crumpled piece of newspaper, which she held out to me.

"We've had this in the house for a week or more," she said, "but I've only now seen it, stuffed as it was inside the coffee pot, if you don't mind, and smelling of camphor balls so horribly besides. Imagine how my father's coffee will taste! Here, read it, child, don't let me ramble on, let me sit beside you on that battered old thing. You look very comfortable."

She sat beside me and smoothed her skirt. I could smell her English lavender water but also the strong whiff of camphor from the newspaper. It was a notice from *The Gazette*, torn from the pages that carried news of ships' landings and departures and the city's theatricals and balls. No wonder then that Miss Hickey had not seen it. She never read the notices.

AN APPRENTICE DRAUGHTSMAN

or similar type is required to accompany a scholar on an
upriver expedition to record avian life in Bengal.
Board will be found over a period of three weeks to one
month, conditions depending, and materials will be
supplied. A testimonial must be furnished.
Replies to Edward Walker, Master in Arts, Cantab.,
in the keeping of The Asiatick Society.
Returning to Calcutta in early January.

I read the piece twice and I must still have been showing the whites of my eyes to it because Miss Hickey started to explain.

"Avian means birds," she said.

Well, I knew that much. After all, I was the Bird Girl

of Calcutta, according to Mr Hickey, the Famous Painter of Calcutta.

"And draughtsman means an artist, a professional kind of person. Apprentice, alas, means that there is not much to be expected in the line of fortune out of this. But never mind that, Anila. Here is an opportunity for you above all others. I know my father would write a testimonial for you if he were here, so I shall do so in his place."

She sat back and I had to turn a little to see her face. My brown sparrow of a guardian had a sweet little puckered mouth at the best of times, a butter-wouldn't-melt mouth, her father called it. But when she was intent on any matter that mouth settled into a straight line the way a monkey's does when it has a plan. It was settled now.

I hardly knew what to say. The day I found the courage to tell Miss Hickey that I would not travel south to Madras with her to join her father, she told me I had broken her heart. She still said these words, yet several times in the weeks since then she had astounded me with her practical ideas for my future. I could not see any such thing on this scrap of paper.

"But it says draughts*man*," I said, "so we can know for sure that this Mr Walker is not looking for someone like me. I'm not a man and I'm not English and he is surely looking for both of those things."

"Draughtsman is just a word like any other word, so it can be turned inside out like a suit of clothes. Never be outfoxed by a word, child. This Mr Walker may not yet be aware that he is looking for someone of your particulars, but he will be when he sees the birds you can pluck out of the air with a pencil and a piece of paper. It will be our business to convince him."

Miss Hickey's mouth softened a little from its monkey lines.

"My word," she said, "when I think of you at your mother's feet, biddable as a lamb you were then, and drawing away with your little piece of charcoal..."

She stopped. In our household we were accustomed to talking easily about my mother but perhaps Miss Hickey felt that this was a dangerous time to call her to mind.

"Think, Anila," she said, very quietly. "You have not just your natural talent to support your claim but there is undoubtedly a certain liberty in your situation that I believe can aid you in this matter just as well as it might undermine you in other ways."

She took a breath. "That is, of course, if you will not finally reconsider and come with me in the morning."

The sly thing. This was the reason I had stayed all morning in the salon, though of course I had heard Miss Hickey calling me.

Her eyes were on mine, gimlets, though someone watching us might have said no, hers were blue and frank and pleasant while mine were the whetstones. I stood up from the couch and nearly fell, for pins and needles started to attack my poor legs.

Oh, but it was hard enough as it was! Ever since Mr Hickey had decided that there were too many new painters arriving every month in Calcutta and that he would make more money in Madras, my mind had had no peace. I could see every reason why I should go with these dear people who loved me, and only one why I should stay.

There was such sense in leaving. The Hickeys were my protectors and I had no others in Calcutta who truly cared whether I lived or died. We had all seen the truth of that when Miss Hickey finally bowed to my mutiny. She began to trot me out then among her lady acquaintances, looking to find me a position.

How Miss Anila Tandy could read and paint and sing, goodness, every English child in Calcutta would cry himself to sleep if he could not win my company to his house as a teacher. And Mrs Panossian of the great store near the Bowbazaar, with her famous coffees and syrups and preserved fruits and flower waters all the way from Europe? She had to agree that those goods needed clever Anila's tending as surely as if they were goats on the road to perdition.

She sold me very well, Miss Hickey did, but there were no takers, not really. There was a promise from Mrs Deering that I might come and look after her little girl whenever the ayah would declare her weaned. No ayah existed who would be that stupid, of course. Mrs Panossian, who knew my story long since, leant across her gleaming dark counter and said I was welcome to come and work a day with her so she might judge if I were as good a totter as I was a dauber. Everyone else smiled sweetly at me, the jackal-coloured girl dressed that day in a frock, her braids tied in matching ribbons. One for her father, missing, one for her mother, dead.

Except the rector of St John's, of course. He saw through that frock so clearly I might as well have danced into his study wearing my mother's old bangles, and bells round my ankles. He stroked his long beard, brown and grey underneath the snuff stains, and looked me up and down the way soldiers look at horses. Finally, the rector turned to Miss Hickey and asked her whether, as my guardian, she had a record or a witness to my baptism. This request made her turn so white I thought she would faint on the spot. But she stood up and told the reverend sahib that she had not yet stooped to stealing their faiths from other people and so we would bid him good-day. I was proud of her then, proud to have her fierce affection.

It was even better when she turned back to him at the door.

"Moreover, sir," she said, "I dropped my own baptismal name long since, when I was Anila's age. Helena is my own choice from my favourite of Shakespeare's plays and your church can claim no hand, act or part in it."

We had not seen him since. But of course he would have spread the story among his parishioners. At any rate, there had been no other offer that, as Miss Hickey put it, addressed my talents. So she had made her own secret arrangement with me. That was how things stood, I believed, but as the time for parting came nearer I felt as weak as a bird in a storm, and she was not much better, pushing me one moment, pulling the next.

So, what on earth should I think now about this Mr Walker and his expedition?

I began to walk the length of the salon, keeping my steps within the boards. Such strangeness the room had now, without any of its chairs and little tables, its rugs and tapestries and the pearl-coloured blinds. All the good furniture had been taken away in the week past by coolies and wagons.

Those things had just vanished but the cherry harpsichord had left its claw marks on the floor, like the sulky monster it was. When the rains came not even Miss Hickey, who was a pretty player, could make music with it.

The walls too, bore traces. All Mr Hickey's paintings, both his own works and his collection, had been taken out of their golden frames and rolled up like rugs. I had helped with that, carefully wrapping the canvases in further rolls of stuffs, so they were safe as babies. Now you could see the different pale shapes on the walls where each picture had hung. But the two paintings I remembered best had never lived in this room at all.

"Anila, stop pacing like a creature in a menagerie!"

Miss Hickey stood up and caught my arm as I passed her again, holding me from my march.

"It seems impossible," I said to her. "But the drawing work is something I would enjoy. And you are right. I can do things that English girls might not."

"Child, there is nothing at all to lose by trying. Go and get your drawings collected now so that we may arrange them to best impress this Mr Walker. I am going up now to unpack some of my writing paper to write a testimonial for you. Truly, I feel something might come of this and it makes me feel a little more hopeful about your staying behind in this city of scoundrels. Think, if you can do this work, a recommendation from this gentleman might get you appointed as a drawing mistress, or a proper governess, such a position that I have not found for you."

That was my Miss Hickey, my dear mashi. For that was what I liked to pretend she was, my aunt, though I had none. She always spoke in long and perfect sentences like a book, unlike anybody else I knew and not at all like her father, whose few words came out in explosions.

There was indeed only one reason why I would not go with them. As long as I had no news of my father, I would believe him to be alive. And if he was alive, he would return to find me. He had promised that, even though it was so long ago now. He knew nothing of the Hickeys or their kind of people, so if I were not in Calcutta how would he find me?

His words had left tracks as deep as the harpsichord's. As faint as the picture frames.

THE IRON
TEA HOUSE

I WANTED TO REMEMBER the view from my window for ever.

"Why my father never painted this, I cannot begin to think," Miss Hickey said. "It makes such a fine picture all on its own say-so."

She stood beside me. Our work was done. My bird paintings were sorted and packed in tissue paper. Even the stitched sketchbooks made from my father's old Company papers were wrapped and put safe into one of the tin-lined drawing cases she had purloined for me. Then, sitting on my stripped bed, Miss Hickey had written her testimonial note.

The garden stretched away down, sloping to the river. Today the river was just a grey line under a huge pale sky. In the new year, when the sky brightened, the water would turn the colour of golden mud. Then, on a late afternoon like this, all the ships and boats on it would look hugged by the water, as if the water was their mother. Today they were just painted puppet ships, gliding past. Even the great ones going down-river had only a baby swell of canvas in their rigging.

We stared until two ships had crossed the window frame from right to left.

"My ship is moored so far downriver," Miss Hickey said, "it will take I don't know how long to reach her, with all the hazards and shallows."

She sighed.

Outside the evening crows were shouting.

Anila, my little bird, the crows begin to make dusk before great Surya himself feels tired.

Our garden was full of trees, over thirty different kinds, Mr Hickey said. Our neighbours grew neat grass instead, for their cricket games and garden parties. Their trees were prisoners in pots. They hid their dhobi washing tanks and their servants' huts behind stands of bamboo. Our garden had its own proud little village surrounded by flowering plants. It had a lily pond and a huge silk cottonwood tree that dropped enough cob-web-soft down every summer to stuff all our pillows and cushions.

But it wasn't always a peaceful place. The tall palmyras and neem trees groaned like devils when the storms came up the river or over the salt marshes. The winds snapped boughs off and threw hard fruits around until the doob grass had holes like bad skin.

Our house did not lie at the fashionable end of Garden Reach, where people kept their own boats to travel to and from the city. The Hickeys did not care to do this for the expense was great, and so our garden was enclosed and separated from the waterside by, first, an iron fence and gate, then by a hedge of red olean-ders. Abdul the cook claimed that all this protection was a good thing because, far downstream where we were, ghosts left the river every night. These were the ghosts of drowned people who tried to save themselves again and again until the dawn forced them to slip back under the water.

It was down there at the hedge that Miss Hickey's and my secret lay, so far down I could not see it from my window. The first time I saw the secret, I could not believe how it had escaped me before. I who knew the garden as well as every thieving mynah that came for our prickly plums, our mangoes!

"Well then, Anila," said Miss Hickey, one afternoon. It was a week or so after our unhappy visit to St John's. "If you are determined to stay here in Calcutta, we shall have to find you a house."

"A house?"

She was smiling her clever-me monkey smile which told me nothing, but in her garden basket she was carrying a couple of the syce's horse tools. She would say nothing more but hooked that firm little arm through mine and led me all the way down to the oleander hedge. She right-turned us there like soldiers, over to the corner where the greenery was thickest. She put my hand on it and I felt the softer growth. These weeds and fronds were scrambling upwards to cover something.

"Think of the Reverend's unpleasant facial hair trimmings," Miss Hickey said. "Then we'll have some pleasure in chopping them, don't you think?"

That made me giggle. Most of the growth could be pulled away without cutting, though when I had to slash some vines I thought of dirty snuff-brown whiskers dropping off. But Miss Hickey's words proved clever because as the greens fell away we found bones underneath, though they were neither human nor animal remains.

"Oh," I said. "Oh."

What could anybody say to something so perfect?

It was a tiny house made of iron that stood clear of the ground on six legs. Once it had been painted dark blue but now it was mostly rusted. Two boxy steps led up to a tightly closed door. This door had glass fitted into it, very dirty glass, smeared and sticky except at the top where it was cut into odd shapes in jewel colours, greens, ambers, crimsons and deep, deep blues. Tatters of faded cloth hung down in the window frames instead of glass. Six spikes on the pointed roof matched the six legs underneath.

It reminded me of the fat rocket firework that Mr Hickey had brought home during last Kali Puja when the city was ablaze with lights and excitement.

"Look at it," Miss Hickey said. "All those sharp points and the glass lozenges and trefoils. Somebody pined for a Gothic fancy on the banks of the Hooghly and so here we have it."

"But nobody has ever had tea here, have they?"

"Well, not us anyway, dear, not in all the time we've been here. I let it go, there was so much else to be doing here. But this little house might be a godsend to you, Anila, if you do not find a position before my father and I leave."

My dear and proper Miss Hickey was saying such a thing about a house that looked like a firework?

She told me then that she had asked the syce to let loose his pet mongooses around the bottom of the garden so that the area should be free of snakes.

"Zakar will be staying on here as horseman, you know, so that should be a consideration for you. He's no stranger and I believe he has a good heart."

I thought about glum silent Zakar, who loved horses more than humans, and I wondered.

Miss Hickey took a key from her drawstring waist purse. It could not have belonged to any other building but the little blue house because the top of the key was shaped into points just like the roof. She fitted it and it turned easily.

We stepped in.

Something skidded by us and out the door and there was a scurry that we couldn't quite follow in the half-light. I jumped back but Miss Hickey just poked her head outside again and said quite calmly, "That will be one of the mongooses. It must have taken up abode here."

I was not so certain myself that it had been a mongoose though the little creatures do move close to the earth, and fast, in just that way. I hoped it was, and nothing worse. But I was trying to understand what was happening under our feet. The iron floor seemed to be heaving. Miss Hickey made a disgusted noise and stamped her little slippered feet down like a horse.

"The place is teeming with insects," she said. "Take care they don't go up your legs."

Now that my eyes were used to the twilight inside I could see that the floor was crossed over and over with highways of ants and beetles, fleeing our feet. A spider the size of a lemon skittered into a corner. There was a strong smell of mice but I supposed the mongoose had taken care of that job already.

"Well, indeed, it's not exactly the garden house of Eden, is it?" said Miss Hickey. "I shall have to send Zakar on a little expedition down here tomorrow. But look – what pretty drapes these were once."

On the torn strips of brocade you could still make out flowering trees, swallows and ladies and gentlemen in strange costumes crossing little humped bridges.

"I had a bedroom made up with chinoiserie like this when I was a girl in Dublin," she said, almost as if to herself. "It tells a story of two lovers. Do you see them there?" She laid a finger on one of the lady figures but the stuff came apart in her hand and crumbled, just like Mr Hickey's dried tobacco when he crushed it to fill his pipe. She dropped it.

"As you see, Anila, it's not perfect. But for a bolthole you could do worse. Nobody comes down here from the house and the oleanders conceal it."

"And I can sneak fresh water from the well in the garden."

She looked at me and her mouth suddenly twisted up.

"Oh, child," she said. "Do you really, really believe that your father will ever return to Calcutta? Else all this –" and she gestured around with her hands – "makes no sense, you know, and you should continue to be with us."

I could say nothing because my throat was dammed with a lump. There was such weight and certainty in Miss Hickey's kindness. I made as if to shrug my shoulders but she reached out her arms and embraced me. It was a very perfect action because neither of us could see whether the other was weeping, and that was fine with me.

"Promise me just this thing, child," she said, letting me go at last. "You must follow us down to Madras within the half-year if your efforts to discover news of your father prove fruitless. Or at any time if your situation here gets parlous. I will leave a fiduciary note at the shipping offices for this very purpose."

All I could do was nod.

We left the little tea house then, locked the door, covered up our secret again with some of the Reverend's chopped green whiskers. Let *him* do some work for *me*, I thought. We went back to the house and set down again to the work of packing and labelling the best house goods and setting others aside for the servants.

But that evening Zakar was called into the house. He stood stiffly to attention in the pantry, smelling of horses, his stormy brows meeting in a line across his face. Miss Hickey told him what she wanted done at the bottom of the garden.

"Remember, silent actions breed the biggest rupees," she warned him at the finish.

Miss Hickey normally spoke quite well in Bangla, our beautiful language that the English call Bengali. But that evening I wondered if she knew that her warning words to Zakar sounded like something a dacoit might say in a fairy tale. I tried to picture tiny Miss Hickey as a thieving brigand holding a dagger. The strange thing was that it was not impossible to imagine this.

I quickly explained to Zakar that Miss Hickey considered that he was bound to secrecy. About cleaning and outfitting my little house, and above all about my presence there. For this he would be paid. But he had understood, he told me. And then, when he was leaving the room, he winked at me, an unmistakeable wink under his black caterpillar brow. Zakar!

We were all dacoits in our separate ways, I thought. Miss Hickey with her fierce words and her belief that I could live like Mr Robinson Crusoe. Zakar with his thundery wink. And there I was now too, with my den down by the riverside.

Now, weeks later, looking down from my window, I knew exactly what was inside the little iron house. We had hung fresh curtains all round the window frames. They were not at all pretty ones as the China patterned drapes must once have been. They were made of heavy oilcloth to give me some protection from the elements and were a murky green to blend in with the oleanders. The floor was spread with clean rushes and there was a small round of woven coir matting laid on top of them. A string bed hung high off the ground from two of the iron supports, a red satin cushion from the salon making it bright as a bird's breast.

Miss Hickey had instructed Habdi, the kitchen boy, to find a clay oven in the bazaar and a basketful of charcoal and good firewood. When he looked confused she told him she wanted an oven just in case her ship should lack its own.

The only smells inside the tea house now came from the oleanders and, fresh on the breeze, the waterweeds and the river itself. I had placed my mother's little Durga altar on one of the windowsills. For years the old clay goddess had sat on my bedroom sill and had shared my high view of the river. I thought she deserved to have no less in her new home. There was also a tiffin box with some cooked dal, a bag of rice, some eggs and a jar of English arrowroot biscuits. That was all, until I should carry down my bag of clothes and the drawings from the bedroom. I would sleep there tonight. Miss Hickey had insisted on that.

"So then at least I will know the first chapter of your new story," she said. But her tone was dull, not keen.

MY MOTHER

MY MOTHER WAS PURE BENGALI, not half and half like I am. She was very beautiful. When we used to walk together down the lanes behind the houses, the birds sang louder. That is what I thought then. I was little and she laughed when I first said this to her. That night she told me one of her bird stories, about a bird that had no songs at all. It was the raven, who lost his singing voice when a demon locked him in a mine for nine hundred years, but his bravery never left him.

However, it was not only birds who thought my mother was special. My father followed her one day – this is before I was born – and asked if he could paint her. Of course she said no. She was a boatman's daughter and he should not even be seeing her as he walked by that morning when she was casting off the ropes for her father. He should have passed on by. He should not be there. He should not look at her. He should never talk to her. So he had to go away and think again. He came back a week later and told her father, my grandfather, that he had bought her a house.

She was fourteen then. Her father said she should go, that her life would be better. Without a mother, brothers or sisters, she would be on her own when he died. He feared famine more than anything and girls and women were the first to perish in famines. He had no money to have her married to anybody, even though she was so lovely. She said that the day she left him the tears in his eyes were like the river in monsoon, overflowing and unstoppable. She could see her red sari in his tears, her mother's bride sari he had kept for her. But she was not a bride.

Annapurna was her name, but my father called her Anna. Or rani, or queen. He liked those words for her but he was no king himself, no rajah. He was an Irishman and he never married her because it was impossible for somebody like him to marry an Indian woman. I found out later that that was not true but such was the story they told me, both of them at different times and in their different ways. And in their different languages. My father spoke to me only in English. My mother always spoke Bangla to me. She said English was like dry meal in her mouth, though she knew it well enough by then.

She called me Anila, which means the never-ending blue of the sky. My father thought the name sounded like "little Anna" so he was happy with it too.

I called her Ma or Mago. To her I was minnow, pearl, pipit – whatever small thing she was thinking about. She loved me and she was always gentle with me. What made her sad beyond everything else was that she could never go upriver with me to show me to her father, who still lived, she supposed, in their old cane house by the river. That was impossible. She had left that world behind.

It was not quite true that my father had bought a house for her. Many things about my father were not quite the way he said they were. But I think that he believed they would work out to his plan in the end, that perhaps the gods would respond eventually to the click of his fingers. Of course they did not; they laughed.

The little house was there, yes, down a lane near an old temple on the high road leading towards the bazaar area of the city. That was where I was born. I can remember the house. It was square, with a pink wash over thin bricks held together with pukka mix, and a roof that you reached by steps at the back. A flame-blossomed gulmohar tree stood across from it. When it was in flower its petals would fall in front of our door and when we came out it seemed that someone had scattered bright Holi colours just for us. But the day my mother arrived there with my father, dressed in red, and, surely, her heart beating with fear and hope, she discovered that she had to share her house with two other women. My father had rented the space from a man he knew. It was really a very little house, with only one room that the other women had already divided with screens, so they were not best pleased by my mother's arrival. And then she was so beautiful.

The two women were Malati and Hemavati. Like my mother, they were bibis — Indian women who belonged to white men. But unlike her, they were dancing girls and much older than fourteen. Malati was kind enough. When I could crawl she let me play with her anklets. My mother told me that I loved to shake them and make their hundreds of tiny bells lift our dull room into paradise for a moment. But the anklets were too heavy for me to lift out of the brass box where Malati kept her costume and clothes and I would have to flop down onto the floor again. Every time this happened my mouth would make a disappointed O, my mother told me. She had to run to pick me up before I cried.

"Then I would take you out to listen to the birds instead," she told me. "You tried to talk back to them. You made a very good little pigeon!"

When Malati danced she told stories with her feet and hands and smile – not with words, like my mother's stories. I loved her dances. She must have loved them too because she did not mind that her audience was just a little girl clapping her pudsey hands together. Or that the floor she danced on was not made of marble, just earth with reed mats to cover it. Or that she was hungry, or that there was shouting outside in the lane. Hers were love stories. Malati's man was a soldier, handsome enough in his rough red coat, but I don't think he understood her stories.

Hemavati was different. Hemavati was more light-skinned than my mother, with high cheekbones. She was from the mountains, far away to the north. We found it difficult to understand her at times, her speech was so throaty and different. Hemavati told us that she had been taken away from her home by temple dancers when she was about nine. It was hard to know when Hemavati was telling the truth. She stole kajal from Malati to paint her eyes, and paan from my mother, who used to chop the nuts, roll them in lime paste, wrap them in dark betel and sell them to the traders on the high road. And, before I learned to hide them, she stole chalks and pencils from me. She threw stones at the baby monkeys who came in the windows, as eager to steal as she was. Nobody else did this.

Hemavati would stroke my hair, and braid it when I grew older, but she would never neglect to pull it hard and painfully before she finished. If I lay down beside her when my mother was with my father, she pinched my arms and stove her dark dirty nails into my skin. I learned not to cry around Hemavati. Once when my mother was away with my father Hemavati pressed chilli seeds into my tears and rubbed them back into my eyes. I could not see for two days. But for those two days, Hemavati herself could not stop crying. She ran to the watermelon seller and brought back two slices for me and stroked me gently while I sucked them, my eyes stuck together tight and my body shaking.

Hemavati's two children were dead, my mother told me, and she could not have any more. Her man was a sailor, a merchantman, but he stopped coming to her when I was a baby. Some said he had drowned. Malati said he had probably found another girl, a girl who smiled. Hemavati went to dance in the river taverns at night and sometimes she did not come back for a day or more, which was like a holiday for us. But she never saw her man again or, if she did, she did not tell us.

"There are plenty of men who are foolish with their money," she said. "Better many fools than one."

That was the harsh way Hemavati spoke.

If my mother was disappointed in the house, in the lie my father had told, she kept it to herself all the years we lived there. She cleaned and swept our corner every day and took our sheet outside into the air and shook it so that it flapped like a heron. Then she brought it back in and stretched it so that it was neat and tight on the bed. She plumped up the two small silk feather pillows, one for her and one for me. They were my father's gift.

Our quilt was one my mother had begun to make as a child, and she was so very proud of it. Its top and bottom layers were old white saris as fine to the touch as a queen's muslin. Its warmth and its thickness came from the inner layers of old cotton, my grandfather's dhotis. All the layers were sewn together with silk threads and so was the band of birds down the centre. A peacock with his proud tail, a golden woodpecker and a fantastic purple dove lay on top of us every night. The dove had a gold ring in his beak.

When I grew a little older the quilt seemed to shrink and so *she added another length to it. She stuffed that piece with a rectangle of blanket that she bought from a wandering kambulia for a few coins and a smile. On top of those new layers my clever mother fashioned a darter from green and grey threads. No one could call this final fellow a dainty bird but his long neck stretched over the end of our bed and it seemed as if he were fishing from the floor.*

"See how your good grandfather made sure to keep us both warm," she would say on winter nights when we snuggled together and kept the edges of the quilt wrapped tightly round and under us.

By the bed we had a green basket shaped like a bowl and there she kept the big bright feathers I collected on our walks.

"Your altar," she told me. But she had her own altar as well, for her Durga made of clay. This little goddess she had brought with her from her father's house. Durga stood on our trunk inside a cave my mother had fashioned with palm fronds. Every day she was given fresh peepul or tulsi leaves or some frangipani, and some papaya or coconut that my mother cut carefully into pieces as small as a baby's fingernail.

Our screen was made of cane wood and my father was begged to bring pins so that she could stick my pictures to it. My first pictures were made on palm leaves, but after a while my father liked to bring me ruined ledgers that his Company no longer had use for. There were always pages left blank that I could work on. He brought me chalks and pencils too, and one birthday, my last with him, a pen with a fine nib and a bottle of the blackest ink.

Hemavati never found that.

THE CITY

WE WERE AS BRAVE as it was possible to be next morning, at dawn, Miss Hickey and I. We met halfway, she coming down the garden, I ascending.

"We are like men meeting for a duel, Anila," she said, "and if I could win the encounter I would bear you away with me now."

I could not look at her or she would have won our duel in that moment.

"Tell me everything as we walk. The palki has come."

She asked me how my new bed was and I told her it was light and comfortable, which indeed it was, like an infant's cradle swinging in the air. She asked if it had been noisy in the garden in the darkness and I told her that I loved to hear the owls close at hand and after them the early birds. These things were true.

When I dreamt, my father stood on a rock on the river path, peering over into the garden. But as I reached out for him he grew smaller, small as a stork, then shrank flat like a lizard. I thought he was in my hand, but when I gasped myself awake it was only the stable iron, hot as flesh where I gripped it.

Now, finally, it was time.

At the front of the house Miss Hickey and I looked at each other's tired eyes and that was that. A quick embrace and a velvet something pushed into my hand, a God bless you, sweet girl. Then she stepped into the waiting palanquin. The four bearers raised her tiny weight up on their poles and she was gone down the Reach at a trot.

Thomas Hickey Esq. and Miss Helena Hickey...

She had written the Madras address yet again for me – this was the third version I had. She had stuffed it into the velvet purse, wrapped round ten gold mohur coins and a small gold ring. This last was such a miniature I guessed it had belonged to Miss Hickey when she was a child. I had never seen it before. Two golden hands met and clasped over a heart of gold with a little crown sitting on top of them all. I slipped it onto the little finger of my left hand, the only one that could wear so small a ring. It gave me comfort to have such a precious token of affection.

Miss Hickey had left a breakfast out for me, prepared by her own hand. But all I could take was a sweet wafer and a glass of water for my stomach was dancing with nerves. I took these into the salon so I could sit down and check again my drawings and my testimonial for this bird lover of Calcutta, Mr Edward Walker.

There was no mirror left in the house but my dress was spruce and clean. I knew that. Miss Hickey had said nothing ill about it. I wore my best turquoise scarf, my blue tunic and a green shawl – for the river might be cold – and under these the trousers of white twill that I had fashioned myself. My slippers were blue brocade. All my precious belongings were inside Mr Hickey's case and I had lengthened its strap so it fitted over my shoulders like a soldier's kitbag. I touched it and felt a little stronger. Perhaps soldiers found their courage in such ways too.

I walked out the front entrance of the house and down the route that Miss Hickey had already taken, to the landing stage. But she had set sail south. I was waiting for a humble ferry-boat to take me upriver to the city.

When it pulled alongside, the early pedlars scrambled off with their bazaar baskets on their backs, calling out like crows. The clerks got on then, all black bags and silence. Some looked at me curiously. I just handed my piece to the boatman and watched the riverbank fall away as we cut along by the Reach and past the great fort.

Our destination was the Esplanade, in the English part of the city. Mr Hickey had told me that in London, Calcutta was called the city of the white palaces, as a snare to catch speculators. But it was true that the ghat where we landed was fit for a palace, with smooth wide steps that the coolies swept clean of everything, even of water.

I had never been up and about the wide streets so early before. Underfoot the street bricks were only half warm, half awake. But further upriver at this hour I knew the giant was already at work.

See, Anila, see how the giant leans from the sun and

stretches his great arms down the high road. Then he reaches
out and pokes his fingers and toes into the lanes and under the
temple stalls. That's how he stirs them into life. He's tapping
at our door, Anila. Wake up!

Some carriages clattered along Chowringhee, heading for the Esplanade. It was the Christmas season but it
was too early for the ladies to show themselves and so
there were no palanquins abroad yet.

Lots of noisy delivery carts and wagons were rolling
by in the other direction, piled up with goods for the
houses of Alipore and Garden Reach. I saw a new
pianoforte standing up smartly on one, tied down with
many ropes. Two small boys in dhotis were sitting on
top of it. Their feet just reached the curved keyboard
top.

"Anila! Anila!"

Someone was calling out behind me. I turned but
my eyes were suddenly full of sun and I could not see
for a moment or so who it was. Then I did. Her limp
slowed her down, but her smile ran ahead of her like
warmth.

It was Anoush.

I waited for my friend to catch up, my back against
the smoothness of one of the painted houses.

"Anoush!"

We hugged each other. Anoush had tiny bones like
a child. Her amber sari, as usual, was too long for
her so she'd folded it over in a double bind.
Anoush liked to wear saris even though she had no
Indian blood, not a drop. She was Armenian, with pale
skin and tiger-coloured eyes under her tight cap of
dark hair. Her face was thin and clever but it was never

those things merely because it was entirely ruled by her smile.

Like me, Anoush was an orphan, but unlike me, she had not been left the gift of good health by her parents. Her left leg had been shrunken with a disease when she was young and she used a stick to walk in the streets. Anoush worked in Mrs Panossian's shop and I had known her almost as long as I'd known Miss Hickey.

"Are you coming to work at Auntie's?" she asked me now. "Oh, do say yes. I'm going there now, as you may guess," she said. "And you, if not yes, where are you going, so early?"

"I'll walk with you," I said. For it was early yet. I told Anoush that I was delivering a testimonial from Miss Hickey in response to a notice in *The Gazette*.

"There is a position for a person who can draw birds, can you believe it? I imagine that only a boy or a man will get the work but I'm going to try."

"Oh, then you should hide your hair in a boy's silken puggree and wear a long dhoti and tunic," Anoush giggled. "Not your funny trousers. But I don't think that pretty nose-stud you have today would convince anyone!"

I had forgotten it, though I had scrubbed my face hours since in the dim light. Anoush giggled while I took the stud out and wrapped it with the coins in the bottom of my case.

We left the white and pink and ochre houses of the Esplanade behind us and turned off in the direction of the Bowbazaar, up the small busy streets that led through the old butchers' area. I hated the sounds and the smells around here. But almost immediately we were at the great glassed doors of Mrs Panossian's shop and the waft of roasting coffee beans was in my nose instead. In the window, boys with long irons tumbled the beans over and over in a great iron bucket oven heated from below by a charcoal fire bowl. The rich aroma squeezed out through every gap in the window frames. Behind this morning work I could see the dark shelves that reached right to the ceiling all round the shop.

"I have an idea, Anoush, a plan. For you, too…"

A clatter came from inside, a loud voice. "Anoush!"

"Call in when you are finished and tell me how it goes," said Anoush, quickly. "You can talk to Auntie then too. Something will work for you, Anila, I'm sure of it."

She patted my arm, then pushed through the doors and was gone.

THE RING

BACK AGAIN ON THE ESPLANADE I dipped between the palkis and the buggies and dodged a holy man covered in ashes who was shuffling along with his eyes closed. The long building ahead that looked like a temple was the Supreme Court. That was where the Asiatick Society did its business, Miss Hickey had told me.

A barrier ran between the building and the pathway and when I found a gate it was locked, with a sentry in a sentry box in front of it. The soldier's hand rested on a musket that stood as upright as he did. Behind him in the box, a large brown dog with matted curly hair was stretched out. The dog opened an eye to look at me and then closed it again.

"Sir, I have to deliver a letter to Mr Edward Walker," I said.

Minutes seemed to pass before the soldier moved his eyes from the far distance to my face. But he said nothing. Behind him the dog sighed like a human.

I held the letter up so that he could see the address in Miss Hickey's fine script.

He said nothing but suddenly put two fingers of his left hand into his mouth and whistled as loudly as a boy with a fat blade of river grass. Behind him two men ran forward and pulled on the spears of the gates. They made an opening that was just wide enough for me.

"First door at the river end of the building, then ask," he said. "You're in luck. Mr Walker has just come back to us since yesterday. He woke up old Curly Dundas here this morning first thing, remembered to bring him a buttered bit from his breakfast, as he always does. He's a good sort, Mr Walker."

I made to move but he spoke again and jabbed his thumb at my hand.

"Your ring. Where did you get it?" he asked.

Did he think I had stolen it? I caught a breath.

"It is a gift from my guardian. She is an Irish lady."

"Yes," he said. "She must be, to have a Claddagh ring."

He reached into a pocket of his uniform jacket and took out a ring just like mine but twice, no, three times as big.

"It's no good to me in the heat over here," he said. "The fingers swell up so I can't wear it. I have this from my sweetheart back home. But look. You should turn yours round with the hands and heart facing in. Wearing it out like that means that you've got a fancy man – and you're a bit young for that, aren't you?"

I blushed. But he was being kind so I thanked him and smiled my best smile at him. He slammed his heels together and straightened up and then his eyes returned again to the fascinating space ahead. I felt encouraged by this encounter. But I wondered. If the soldier had not seen the ring with its hands and heart facing out to him, perhaps he might not have been so helpful. I would leave it facing out for now. For luck.

Yet what had he meant about Mr Walker returning? *The Gazette* had said: *returning to Calcutta in January*. That was at least nine days away. I had thought to leave my letter at the right door and then make my way back to Mrs Panossian's store. I wanted a quiet word with Anoush.

But perhaps this was luck too.

I went past the sturdy passageway arches of the great courthouse. The last door was open. It led into an enormous hallway floored with black and white slabs. A stairway curved in two directions, an elegant shape like the hands in my ring. A single flight then vanished to the dark floors upstairs.

"Yes?"

A man stepped out from a room on the right of the hall. I had never seen anybody who really looked white before. Most English people were pink or red though some turned quite yellow under our sun. But this man's face was as white as a shirt. He was dressed completely in black and a huge bundle of keys hung from his belt.

"I was told to ask for Mr Edward Walker, sahib," I said. "I have an important letter for him."

He picked the letter from my hand and held it out far from his face, squinting at Miss Hickey's clear writing.

"Give it here," he said. "Mr Walker arrived back unexpectedly in Calcutta yesterday, it is true, but I have not seen him yet so I imagine he is resting from his journey at his home. Go along, then. It's safe with me."

Until I had spoken with the soldier, this was just

what I had been expecting, that I would leave the letter with somebody in charge and go on my way. But now I was disappointed.

"But I thought, sir," I said, "well, it's just that the sentry soldier seemed to think Mr Walker was here today, and I would very much like to hand this letter over myself because of its nature."

The man was staring at me with his forehead puckered in a puzzle. I knew he was trying to make a place for me in his divisions of people. I could almost see the wheels of his brain turning over like the wheels in a timepiece.

Here is a girl who looks half-bred but she speaks English well enough. She must have an education of some sort. She's got strange clothes, she must not have a mother who shows her the proper ways. People noticed these things first. Then there was usually a division, just as there was in the stairs ahead, in the way they behaved towards me. One way went: the unfortunate child, I'll hear her story out. The other way went: she's got right little airs, this one, for what she is.

I could always tell when this last was the conclusion. It mostly led to a poor outcome for me.

"Go on your way, girl," he said. "Whatever this is, it hardly concerns you, and I'll have some words with that sentry about his loose tongue. Mr Walker is not to be bothered..."

"Who's talking about me being bothered? I'm always being bothered, Mr Minch, and uncomfortably often it's by your good self."

The deep voice was coming from the dark at the top of the stairs.

"Send the young lady up to my room since she's good enough to arrive in person."

The man in black stood back and made me a mock bow. There was no expression in his face, though, and he vanished back into his room without a further word.

I started up the left arm of the stairs. Then the voice boomed out again.

"And bring some tea up, Mr Minch, please."

MY FATHER

MY FATHER WORKED FOR the East India Company. He was a Writer. The Company had lots and lots of Writers, young men like my father who travelled in ships all the way from the river in faraway London to the river in Calcutta. My father was only eighteen that morning he met my mother on the riverbank. He was not much more than a boy, just four years older than she was.

A Writer was not a poet or a storyteller. A Writer was a clerk. Or a scrivener, my father said. That was a word with a thin, mean feel to it. Writer sounded better, I thought. Every thing that the Company officers did or owned, the Writers wrote down.

"Cottons and silks, spices and diamonds. Fresh minted rupees. Horses and camels and elephants. Pinnaces and palaces and palanquins. Soldiers and sailors. Princes, merchants, farmers, weavers and bearers. Battles and burnings. Spies!"

He loved to sing all these things out for me and then hiss the last word in my ear like a snake.

Everything that happened in India was on a page somewhere in the Writers' Building, my father told us. For a long time I thought there were magic books in my father's workplace from which, if you took them down and opened them, tiny elephants would march and princes would stumble out, searching in their pockets for their diamonds.

"We came all the way across the world to make our fortunes," my father told me when I was old enough to understand a story that didn't have birds or princesses in it. "But I am the only one of the Company to have found the best of all fortunes."

He meant my mother and me. His face was glowing and happy and he squeezed us tight in his arms. I always felt excited when he came from his Writer's lodgings in the city to our little house, which was not so often, not more than once a week, and sometimes not even that. When I thought he was coming I would go up on the roof to wait so that I would see him turn in at the top of our lane. Then I would shout to him.

"Papa!"

That is what he liked me to call him. His name was Patrick Tandy. He had amazing eyes, for one was green and one was blue. Like a lucky cat, he said, but for a long while I believed all white people had eyes of two colours. He had light brown hair that was fine and straight, unlike our wavy black hair. My mother liked to cut and trim it for him, which she did as well as any of the expensive hairdressers in the city, he told us. I liked to rub my face against his cheeks before he shaved. He called this rub a chinchopper because of his bristles. It made us both giggle.

My father worked so hard, sitting at a long table with all the other Writers, he told us, copying neatly with his pen, until his eyes and his hand hurt. He showed me the blisters on his first finger, his writing finger. I would kiss them. Then my mother would rub them with neem oil, to soften the skin.

The blistered finger was also his drawing finger. Because he could draw so well, the Company paid him extra to make plans of new buildings and warehouses they wanted to raise down beyond the river landing places, the ghats. He saved this money, he told us, so that one day we might all live together in our own house.

But, for all his drawings, my father never did make a painting of my mother. I can remember how he tried to. He would take us away from the house and we would walk down the lanes quite a way until he found a tree he liked. He liked willow, he liked tamarind. They made a fine canopy, he said, and my mother would look like a queen resting on a journey.

"Tamarinds are dangerous," my mother said. "Ghosts live in them. And they make people tell lies."

But she sat down, happy to be with my father, happy to be away from the house. Out of his big camel bag – that's what he called it – he took everything he needed. He set my mother on a fold-up stool and fixed her arms and her head and draped her sari just so. Sometimes he brought along a beautiful purple scarf for her head and shoulders. He never left it with her when we went home again but always put it back in the bag and took it away. He was afraid Hemavati would steal it.

When she was sitting perfectly, just like a rani on her throne, he told her not to move.

I was little then so I had to stay beside her or him and not wander out of sight. If it was a tamarind tree I walked round it and stared up, looking for the ghosts. I could see ants and beetles walking up the trunk. I could see leaves shaking in the breeze, turning their backs and dancing. Once I saw a small spotted owl, asleep on a branch, close to the top of a tall tree beside the tamarind. But I saw no ghosts.

"Stay still, Anila," my father said. "You're distracting me. When you're a big girl I'll paint your picture too."

So I came and sat on the ground beside him on his picnic stool. He had sheets of light-blue paper, held together by a pin that rested on a stiff square of leather. His pencil strokes were very fast. I watched my mother appear, always her body first, turned just the way he had placed her. The folds of her dress he drew like folds in cream when it's whipped. Then her neck, slender as a stem. He left her feet and her arms until last. On the page they grew on her and held her together. But her lovely face, that was the difficult part.

I looked at my mother, who was only feet away, and at my paper mother. The face I touched every day was soft and full and its eyes were merry, sad, dreamy, different things that I could see with my own baby eyes. The mother on the page had a thin face that would not fatten or, some days, a fuller face that, no matter what my father did with the little cross-strokes of his pencil, he could not slim down into the face that we were looking at. Her paper eyes remained dark, with no lights in them.

"I can draw anything, any palace, any shopfront, any redcoat with his sabre and pistol," he said to me one day, "but your mother escapes me."

He sighed. "Maybe the tamarind ghost takes your mother's soul away from me while she sits under his tree," he said. That frightened me, and my mother scolded him.

He told us that these were only sketches and that what he planned was a big — he made a shape in the air — painting in oils of my mother. These oils were not mustard cooking oils he told us, but oils that you mixed with earth or ground-up stones to make bright colours. He would show his painting of my mother to a gentlemen who knew about paintings. If he liked it they might show it in the Company Hall, along with paintings of English ladies, and soldiers on horses, and palaces from faraway parts of India, and even paintings of the Company's fierce Indiamen ships with all their guns blazing.

I wondered how the painters made the ships stay still while they sketched them, and where they sat to make their drawings while the guns fired. Even ships that were moored at the ghats moved all the time, not like my good obedient mother who stayed absolutely still.

My father never made the oil painting or, if he did, he never showed it to us. But he saw that I liked to pick up his pencil and make shapes on his papers.

"Look at Anila," he said to my mother. "She can draw a perfect leaf. She's even put the sawteeth in."

I never tried to draw my mother, or my father. I don't know why. Perhaps I was afraid that it was not the tamarind but the paper and pencil that had the power to take a soul away. Perhaps I was afraid that I would fail, as my father did, so often that there were some afternoons he became so cross with my mother and me that he left us without his usual warm hug. Perhaps it was just that I could see my mother's face every day around me, and that when I wanted to see my father I could close my eyes and there he was in my head, with his crooked smile and his dancing eyes.

What I wanted to draw was what I knew I would not remember unless I put its shape and colours down onto paper. I began with leaves and trees but my mother told me that, from the beginning, every one of my trees had a bird in it, and not just a pretended bird like her lovely purple quilt dove, but a bird that really belonged to that tree. Possibly that owl was the first, but then owls are quite easy to draw. Not their feathers though. If you want to have a proper owl on a page to remember it, then you must be able to show all the different shades of brown in one long wing feather, the light bands running across the feathers, the swell of its chest and the soft wisps round its legs.

My father could do this, only he didn't draw birds. But when he drew a building, a real one or one that he was inventing, he made you see hundreds of shades in the stones. You could see sharpness and even softness, because my father's buildings looked almost alive. If he showed glass it shone like eyes. Besides this, somewhere in every drawing there was a door that was not quite closed or a window flung open, even in the palaces, like an invitation to enter. You had to look. There would always be a way in.

So, that is the gift my father left me. Drawing. But somebody else painted my mother.

MR WALKER

I WENT UP THE STAIRS. The testimonial in my hands seemed to get lighter, as if it wished to take off and leave me with nothing to say for myself. I patted my bag, to feel the sturdy form of my work inside. But this Mr Walker would surely laugh at the crazy notion of employing me and never ask to see my drawings at all.

He was standing at the beginning of a long passage-way. Doors led off this on both sides but only one of them stood open, and now he stepped back inside it.

"Come along in and tell me who you are and why you have been sent to me," he said. He truly had an extraordinarily deep voice, but it was not unfriendly or frightening. It was almost musical. He rolled his *rs*.

I followed him into his room.

"Leave the door open for Mr Minch," he said. "I hope he has the redeeming grace to bring two cups."

Now I could see that the man talking to me was per-haps about thirty. Older, anyway, than my father the last time I saw him.

He was tall and thin, and though he seemed poised he was edgy too. He reminded me of a hunting dog, the still, clever kind who find things. Deep lines ran between his nose and his wide mouth and his forehead had four wavy furrows like the sea in a sea–picture. His sandy hair was bound into a pigtail, but everywhere there were bits escaping. At least it was not a wig. So many English gentlemen wore those hanks of dead hair on their heads.

He was standing on a rug in front of a desk piled with papers and books. A silver elephant sat on the tallest pile of documents, pressing them down. The room was quite in shade because drapes covered its one large window but I could make out shelves of dark wood. Their feet stood in troughs of water to protect them from insects. There were more books stuffed together on the shelves, but also, like creatures in a dream, there were birds.

Large and small birds were piled up on these shelves. The big ones stood on their own. The little ones perched on twigs inside small cages. All the birds were staring out with glassy eyes. They were dead birds, sad birds.

"Now," he said, "you must tell me who you are, young lady, and what your business is with me."

I had not yet spoken one word to this man but somehow I knew that he was not busy making judgement on me. Suddenly I wanted him to see me in a whole and proper way, the way Miss Hickey did.

"Sir, I have come because of the notice in *The Gazette*," I said. "I can draw birds and animals and plants. I have a testimonial here, and also samples of my work."

He let out a slow breath, almost like a whistle. But

before he could speak there was a clatter outside and Mr Minch made his way into the room bearing a large tin platter. On it were two white china cups, a beautiful pale green teapot and cream-jug and a tiny silver bowl filled with dark sugar crystals.

"Thank you, Mr Minch. A proper wake-up for duty is needed, after all."

"Can I get you something to eat, sir?"

Mr Minch seemed to have put himself back in good humour, I noticed. Perhaps the sentry would escape his tongue-lashing.

"No, thank you. My stomach has still to custom itself back to Calcutta after its visit to the south. Unless Miss…?"

They both looked at me.

"No thank you, sir," I said.

Mr Minch put the platter on the desk and went out, closing the door behind him.

"Now, you could show me your drawing-room skills and pour, or I could play host and pour – which is it to be?"

He smiled, so I pointed a finger at him.

"You pour, sir. It's a very pretty pot. I would hate to break it."

"It's a very ancient pot indeed. That's well observed of you. It's pure China porcelain, with a celadon glaze. My late aunt's bequest to me. Mr Minch is under pain of death not to break it and certainly not to lend it to any of the other saints or scholars who work here. And above all never to a gentleman of the law, not even a judge."

He poured tea into the cups and we sat down, he

behind his desk, I on a leather stool in front of it. He shot me a glance.

"There's a common bird in these parts that has just such a rare green in its feathers. I wonder if you know the one I mean."

Well, but of course I did. If this was a test I could pass myself off reasonably.

"I don't always know the English words for all birds," I said. "But it's a kind of duck. A small duck that we call the whistler."

"Very good. But now, to first details. What is your name?"

I told him.

"And — I am estimating here — you have an English father and an Indian mother?"

I nodded. Then I shook my head.

"My father is Irish."

Sing it loud, sing it proud, the princess Anila of Calcutta has not a drop of English blood!

"Is it either of those who have supplied this testimonial?"

He had the thick envelope in his hand but had not attempted to open it.

I almost laughed. What an idea!

"No, sir, of course not. It was written by Miss Helena Hickey on behalf of her father, the artist, Mr Thomas Hickey. I have been boarding with them for these few years past. I was an assistant to Mr Hickey. But indeed it was my father who taught me how to draw."

He looked at me with some respect, I thought.

"I understand that Mr Hickey is celebrated in

Calcutta for his portraits," he said. "But it is quite another skill that I am looking for, you understand."

"Yes, sir," I said. "And I can show you my work that suits your requirements. I have it right here with me."

He told me to take out my drawings while he read the testimonial. I turned away, and struggled to get the leather case out of my bag. I knew what Miss Hickey had written because she had shown me the two closely written pages yesterday and I had read them while she was out of the room. That had been extraordinary. There were my circumstances laid out as if they belonged to a character in a story. And then at the end:

Miss Anila Tandy has rare ability to extract from Nature nothing more and nothing less than what is given. She does not embellish or decorate on the page, she recreates the diversity of creation and the beauty of line... In addition to her natural genius for draughtsmanship she is an honest and thoughtful young person and has an original cast of mind in two languages, English and Bengali. I would much have preferred that she should remain in our household. But we move to Madras and Miss Tandy prefers to remain in Calcutta.

"You are quite a paragon, it seems," said Mr Walker. But he said it slowly and without any trace of mockery. "I must admit that I would give a lot to have met with the writer of this missive. Though I would naturally fear for her opinion of me."

He reached across for my notebooks. He turned the pages, slowly, without looking up at me. Sometimes he turned back and looked over a particular one again. I wondered if I should explain the order I had made, and the names I had given the birds. But I knew that the drawings had to speak for themselves, and that they must speak louder than all Miss Hickey's kind words.

Mr Walker got up and went over to a shelf by the wall. He took down one of his dead birds and brought it back to the desk. It was an oriole, a black-headed one, and its legs were nailed onto a small log. My notebook was open at a painted sketch of an oriole I had made last year, on a picnic with Miss Hickey and her friend Mrs Hadley. A storm had appeared like bad magic, with rains that soaked us through while we ran back to the carriage, laughing and spattered with mud. I had finished the oriole from memory back in the house. It was a good likeness.

"You have caught the curve of the bill perfectly," he said. "And goodness, what sharp eyes they have!"

I did not point out to him that the poor bird on the desk had only brown buttons for eyes and that insects had gnawed its bill to dust.

He left the oriole back and returned to the desk with a little garden bulbul. It had only one leg; the other was supplied by a twig.

"Your bulbul has just the outraged look that I have

observed in every one of these creatures," he said. "Look at this fellow. He has it too. They remind me of farmers' wives asked to give the parish a few eggs and cabbages at Christmas-time. But perhaps you have painted your one a little more of a red rump than he deserves."

"But that was exactly why I chose that bulbul," I said. "You see, I knew him."

Anila, he's back again, the little red bottom bird. Our own dancing bulbul!

"I liked him because he was much more garish than most. He lived down the lane where my mother and I had our house. He used to take baths in a dish of water we kept outside the door for him. That is one of my oldest drawings. I like it for all those reasons, but it is not as finished as one I would make now."

He gave me a sentry's look.

"Miss Tandy, your correspondent here has not sold you short, not by any means, but she has not explained how you acquired your affinity for nature and that I really look forward to hearing about you from yourself."

He stood up. All at once he had so much energy that he crackled.

"But I must leave you now. I have an engagement. What I propose, if it is agreeable to you, is that you and I take a walk in the city Gardens tomorrow morning. Bring your paper and pens. Then we can discuss how we might proceed and whether this might be at all a proper arrangement. But certainly on the evidence of these pages I cannot imagine I will find your equal in all of Bengal."

He paused at the door.

"Ask Mr Minch for directions. He's not as dour as he looks. And come early."

MRS PANOSSIAN'S SHOP

"BUT ANILA, HOW CAN you think Mrs Pan will ever agree to your plan? It's quite impossible. She will be so cross she won't want to look at you again. Then you'll never ever have any work here."

It was dinner-time. The white city had closed its doors and shutters and gone back to sleep. There was nobody in Mrs Panossian's huge shop room except myself and Anoush so she felt free to come out from behind her counter. She stood beside me, biting her lip.

She had heard my story of meeting Mr Walker, and the birds and Mr Minch and the green china teapot, and she was pleased for me. Then she'd tried on my ring. It fitted her slender third finger perfectly and she turned the arms and heart out as I did.

"Fancy man, where are you hiding?" she giggled when I told her what that meant.

"If it was from anybody but Miss Hickey I would give it to you, I promise."

She laughed and squeezed my arm and put the ring back on my little finger.

Then I told her about my idea.

"Just for the English Christmas, Anoush, you must come and stay with me. My little garden house will hold two string beds, I know it will. We can have our own holiday with nobody beckoning and you need not have to clean up and mind children when you should be free. We could even walk abroad in the evenings like two ladies."

"Like two ladies," said Anoush slowly. Her dark eyes were huge as a baby's.

We both knew that that was just my talk. Ladies did not walk abroad in the evenings on their own. But I had lived for years in a house that had no men in it and it seemed entirely possible to me that I should do that again. Poor Anoush had no idea that there might be such a world.

She was kin to Mrs Panossian, she called her Auntie, but there was no bedroom for Anoush above the shop. She lodged with a tea merchant's family. Every morning she had to dress and feed their children, pick up her bedroll from the floor and put it away, and then make her way to the shop. She felt trapped, I knew that.

Why, even standing inside Panossian's store was like being inside a giant coffee bean. There was the glorious smell, yes, from the coffee roasting oven. But more than that, everything that belonged inside the shop was dark brown: the shelves, the drawers, the thick over-jackets or long pinafore aprons that the assistants had to wear over their clothes. Even the glass jars of preserves seemed stuffed with dark things: sugared plums, browned peaches, berries, juniper fruit. I thought of the bazaars in our city where fruits were huge and bright and tumbling over each other, ready to grow again where they fell. Was everything in Europe so very dull coloured, so small?

Yet Miss Hickey loved this shop. And coming here with her, after all, was how I came to know Anoush.

"Mrs Pan would never let me leave the Seropins. They pay her a little so I can get Vard, Liza and Mariam up and out in the morning and back to bed at night. And help Vard with his letters."

"Oh, Anoush. That is such an injustice. For all that you do, you earn that money, not Mrs Pan."

"But a free bed and free meals – and to get all this arranged for an unmarriageable orphan? That's what Madame would say from the top of her high mountain of fruit and coffee beans. How I'd love to…"

Anoush stopped speaking and swiftly moved back behind the counter. She picked up a piece of madras cloth from underneath it and started rubbing down the wood.

"Well, my dear Anila. And are you buying something or did you come to call on me? I believe the Hickey household left Calcutta today, am I correct?"

Mrs Panossian's voice had a high pitch, like a child's. Somehow it was a little menacing to hear this sound coming from a body that was anything but a child's. She had enormous bosoms and her face was pale and moon-shaped. Anoush said she was proud of her tiny feet but I thought they looked badly on her, as if a doll maker had run out of stuff at the end of his task. She always wore a bonnet with white streamers and a bow on its top and her dresses were black bombazine. Yet Mrs Pan never looked hot or bothered, never the smallest bit *loolally*. That was what Miss Hickey called English ladies who became strange in the heat and dust of India.

"Yes, Mrs Panossian. Miss Hickey left for Madras on the morning tide."

"And you, Anila, where are you staying? Have you decided to be sensible and come and work here with your little friend? I can always use a hard worker and I pay a fair wage."

She turned her head like an owl, to see what Anoush was doing, but clever Anoush was still polishing, her head facing towards the windows.

"You are very kind," I said. "I think I shall have a position soon but it is not going to be for long."

Before she could take another run at her questions I decided to be brave.

"Mrs Panossian – I have a place to stay just for now and what I wonder is, do you think Anoush could be free from her lodgings to spend Christmas Day there with me? Just one day and night? Or perhaps two?"

Anoush's head was so low down it was practically polishing the counter on its own. Even the shop seemed to be holding its breath in the moment that followed my plea.

"A place of your own? And where would that be, child? For I could not send my own kin to a place that might compromise her, you know."

Her small round eyes bore into me. The words were cruel but I do not think she actually meant to be so. She was being plain. I guessed what she thought – that I had somehow returned to live again in the little house of long ago, with Malati and Hemavati. Mrs Panossian knew all about that part of my life and I wished she did not.

I took a deep breath. I could not afford to have Mrs Pan as my enemy.

"It's just a little place that Miss Hickey arranged for me. She wanted me to be safe until I became settled in a position. I would dearly love to have Anoush there for English Christmas Day, so that she can have a holiday too. And I have money left to me to buy some festival food in your store, Mrs Panossian."

I looked sideways. Anoush was approaching us, her face flushed.

"Oh, Auntie," she said. "Just this once. Please?"

Mrs Panossian looked from one of us to the other. Then the door opened and its bell pinged. Two bearers approached the counter with a long list and Anoush moved away to serve them.

"You are too close with your story, girl," Mrs Panossian said to me. "You must tell me whereabouts in the city you are staying."

"It's in Garden Reach," I said, looking straight at her. She would probably have sent a boy after me anyway, her curiosity was so roused. Mrs Panossian was not one to leave questions sticking in her head overnight like hairpins.

"It's in a little garden tea house that Miss Hickey saw restored for me. I shall not be there for long at any rate. I hope to have news of my position tomorrow. But the day after that is the English Christmas Day."

Mrs Panossian raised her eyebrows at that, as well she might.

I hardly knew why Christmas mattered so much to me. As the Reverend suspected, and Mrs Pan knew, I had not been baptized. My mother's devotions still beat in me like a pulse and I truly loved the way our gods were close to us, with all their adventures and their moods. From them came the music and colours and excitements of our puja festivals in the misty season. Miss Hickey never made any difficulties for me. But she believed that I should go to church services with her nevertheless.

"It will help you, Anila," she'd said. "People will assume you are one of us. For myself, I am only interested in the kindness suggested to us by religion, not in its show."

So I went, and they were dreary affairs, those services, with ladies and gentlemen pressed into their pews like sticks of cane in a box. The rector climbed into a little tower and talked to us about God's mercy until our teeth hurt. The only service I liked was Christmas.

"Very well then," said Mrs Panossian at last. Her high voice had something in it I could not quite make out. It was hardly a smile because her face was still.

"But my Anoush must be back with us for the day after the holy feast."

Poor Anoush was still reaching up and pulling things out of drawers but I was sure she had heard the good news because she was smiling at the bearers as if they were not one but two Krishnas come to visit. Then Gabriel, the old shop boy, came through the door at the back of the shop with his brown coat bursting open after his lunch and Mrs Panossian told him to help Anoush with the big order. The doorbell pinged again. More customers.

"You run along now, Anila," she said. "Tomorrow night you can come back for Anoush. I'll tell her the news myself."

STORIES AND
TRINKETS

MY FATHER DID NOT really care to spend time in our house down the lane. He wished he could afford better and he was unhappy about Malati and Hemavati in many ways. Most of all, I think, because they were so different from my mother, who would never have danced for strangers, whose voice was gentle, who was little more than a girl.

"That hyena," he called Hemavati. Poor Malati and her soldier, he thought them stupid.

But they bothered him, more simply, because they were there all the time, or most of the time anyway. He wanted us to have our own house but he could not yet pay for one on his own, he told my mother, even though he had got a promotion in the Company. Houses in the English part of the city were very expensive. She would have lived in a bamboo house with a thatched roof but he would not have that. So she had to share, that we might have bricks round us and a firm flat roof over our heads.

In monsoon we stayed indoors when my father called, even though my mother and I were both itching to run out into the lane and stand under the rains, laughing until we were soaked through. He could not understand this. He never travelled out during that season without his tall black umbrella and even though it was so warm, he would button up his jacket in the rains.

"This is what we do in Ireland," he said sternly when we teased him. "You can catch a chill from the damp even in summer. My poor brother died from a summer chill."

So we stayed in our corner of the house, behind the screen. My mother cooked for her little family which she loved to do. She liked the way my father would not eat until she joined us, though she told me this would not be approved in her village.

One year during monsoon when I was four or five my father decided to teach me to read. It was a long business that continued over many afternoons.

"Ask your mother for a story," he would say. She would tell me a story — about the squirrel who helped King Rama build a bridge to rescue his stolen wife, about Hanuman the monkey god and his daring monkey army, about the golden birds of Ayodhya. No matter if food was smoking or rice was sticking in the pot, she had stories.

I had to tell him the story in English. Then he would take out the pages he had brought with him and start to write the story down. He was clever because he made the written-down story mostly of very simple words, and he drew pictures alongside the words that looked difficult. Then he got me to read the story back as he had written it. When I could do that, he wrote me out a picture key.

"This is your alphabet," he said. "Your ABC. You must learn to write as well as you can draw, Anila. Practise."

He told me some stories too but he did not have my mother's gift for relating them. My favourite was the story of the great flood and the animals that were saved. Together we drew a picture of the ark filled with all the creatures I knew:

mongooses, elephants, horses, toddy cats, monkeys, storks, vultures, parakeets, bulbuls. Two of everything. My father added a couple of black river shrimps sitting in a bowl of water and waving their long feelers through one of the ark's windows. I tried to make my Noah look like the vendor of sweets who came down our lane, a kind man who gave us children his broken crumbs.

When we had eaten our meal, and my father had gone back to his lodgings with his umbrella over his head like a storm cloud, I folded the alphabet key and put it into my peacock-feather bowl. Then my mother and I rushed out into the rain with our dishes to wash them off, and ourselves too. We never caught a chill.

But I did learn to read and write because of monsoon.

The rest of the year, we left the house when my father visited. Unless Malati and Hemavati were both away, of course, but that was rare enough.

On his special drawing days, he brought a buggy to the top of the lane and walked to our door and dipped his head in.

"Anna and Anila – we're going on a picnic! Come along, quickly, before the horse bolts!"

He always said that though the poor buggy horses were too slow and too stupid to dream that they could ever do anything so exciting.

Then my mother would turn quite pink and she rushed to dip a cloth in the water bowl. She rubbed my face and hands, then her own, and dipped a finger into her jar of red sindur, to rub some of the vermilion powder into her hair parting.

"We're ready!" she said. And she sounded like a child. Her voice sounded, even in my ears, like mine.

We went up the lane and my father lifted me into the buggy and then handed my mother up, as if she was an

English lady getting into a carriage. When I was little I sat on my father's knee. Later I sat on the tiffin box he had packed and brought with him for our picnic. The buggy driver flicked his whip and the horse and buggy trundled towards the city. Then we looked out for the turnings that led to the loading ghats where the ships were supplied with goods.

It was so busy there, every time we went. In the terrible heat of summer it was always a little cooler by the water. We covered our heads and my father held his great umbrella up to shade us. All along the stone ghats were barrows stuffed with mangoes, guavas, green bananas, yams and all kinds of gourds from fat pumpkins to baby potols. There were coconuts mounting like bricks in a temple, and baskets of chilli pods whose heat you could sniff on the salty air. Gunny sacks spilled over with dark betel leaves, green cardamom seeds, papery sticks of cinnamon, shiny nuts of different shades – honey-coloured, bunting and darkest brown. There were piles of huge lopsided jute cushions stuffed with grains, with fat husks spilling out of the loosely sewn seams. Not like my mother's neat sewing! Sometimes we smelt a strong smell that my father said was tobacco, dried brown leaves also packed into sacks. Ropes lay coiled on the polished stones along the edges of the ghats. They looked like brackwater snakes, only thicker.

There were bamboo cages with ducks and guineas and bantams. I liked to pick up some grain seeds and fling them into the cages but mostly the birds ignored them and did not bend their sad necks down for a snack. Pigs and sheep and goats were fenced in or tethered to posts waiting to be harnessed and lowered onto boats: when the men hoisted them into the air in harnesses they kicked like babies, and squealed too. Much further down the river – we did not go so far as it was dangerous – were the great bales of calicos and stuffs waiting to be lifted onto the biggest ships.

I liked to watch the work on the ghats, and the great-beaked birds that stalked and swooped and stole what they could, the storks and gulls and kites. But my mother was happiest watching the boats.

The first time we went there, the first picnic I can remember, she was quiet for a long time. Then she pointed at a long stately boat, set deep in the water in front of the ghat.

"Look, Anila," she said. "That's a budgerow. My father thought they were the best boats in the world. We would watch them come up the river past our landing. Oh, but he'd love to see these great ships with their own trees on them to hold the sails."

My father told us that there were much much bigger ships miles further down the river, ships too big to come up to the city waterfront, ships that had travelled all the way from England or from China. Our huge wide river Ganga that he called the Hooghly wasn't deep enough for them.

He had to settle to his sketch work, even in summer, even when the skin on his face wore the angry rash he called prickly heat. But one year my clever mother cured him of that. She rubbed sandalwood paste on his face. He looked filthy that day, like a madman, but he never suffered from the rash again. After that treatment his face turned a pale gold every year instead as the summers lengthened.

So, after we had settled on the day's viewing place, he would put on his funny sunhat made of hard tree pith and go off with his scrolls and pens and the flat top to support his papers. We were left to sit on the folded cane seats that he always brought in the buggy. Those times we kept the umbrella. He told the buggy driver to tie up his horse and watch over us so that none of the ghatsmen or boys would bother us. He paid him a little too, to bring us a jar of drinking water. We dipped our scarves in it and tied the damp cottons over our foreheads. You could tell whether it was April, May or June by how quickly they dried out again. But we both kept our eyes busy with the river traffic and somehow that kept us cool too.

Then, when my father had finished his sketches, he would come back to us with his tiffin box of green cane, bound with leather straps. It was safe with him, he told me, but someone might snatch it from us while we were on our own. Always he made us guess what was in it before he opened it.

"Mango," I shouted. "And sugarcane and gur and sweet fish curry and cooked eggs."

"Duck meat and sweetmeats," my mother said. "And ginger beer."

We were rarely wrong because he always brought fruits and a curry of some sort and ginger beer. He bought everything in an English chop-house near the Writers' Building he told us. It sold the kind of Indian foods that the young men liked though he knew we ate very differently at home, plainer meals but spicier, and sweeter too. Sometimes my father brought the bread that he liked himself, pau roti, which we could tear into strips and dip in the curries. Very occasionally the chop-house provided a jungle fowl that one of the other Writers had shot and given away to settle a toddy bill. They were tasty but I always found myself wondering what bird it was that I was eating and so I would not eat much.

But Papa always slipped in something special that we could never guess. That was because it wasn't something to eat. It was a present for each of us, something small enough to fit in the box.

Trinket time, my father called this part of our picnic. My

favourite gift was a kite shaped like a fantastic beast. "It's a Chinese dragon," he said. It flew as fast and fierce as a fighter kite even though it was not much bigger than my father's hand. It had a blue face and a smile and paper hair that hung down like a holy man's.

My mother got soap and tiny pieces of silk. Or shells, silver and pink and blue, with pearly entrance chambers. He told us they came from islands far away to the south. I got coloured papers and threads and, once, a sand timer.

"That's one minute of your life," my father explained, as the sand ran from one end of the waspy glass to the other. I kept it in my feather bowl but one morning it was gone.

SECRETS

MR WALKER'S HOUSE HAD a red door with a brass knocker shaped like a fist. It made a booming echo like a big festival drum and I shrank down into myself. What if I had woken the whole street of Englishmen up?

But not this silent house, it seemed. I was about to try again, just a tap this time, when the door opened a crack and a little man in a dhoti, dark-skinned and old, scanned me up and down. Then he reached out a hand to pull me inside.

"Quickly, quickly," he said in Bangla. "But you should have come while it was still dark. Now they will say all those bad things about the master. Come."

He led me along a gloomy passageway.

"Sit there." He pushed me onto a chair that I could hardly see and then vanished through a doorway on the left. It had no door, just a thick red curtain hung from a pole. I could smell food now, something smoky and something else milky, sweet. I had eaten nothing yet and I had been up for hours, since long before light.

How long was the walk from Garden Reach? As long as I was foolish, I would have to say, for every step was on my own account. When I reached my little house last night I had my ten gold mohurs but no small pieces, nothing for a boat ride until Mrs Panossian should be my banker. So when I woke I took Anoush's advice even though she'd intended it for a joke. I tied my hair up in a head wrap as a man does and I wore a dark tunic over my twill trousers. Again I strapped my case of drawing things safe over my chest, with my money wrapped inside it. When I stepped out along the river path, I felt invisible, like a boy on an errand.

For all that, I was glad it had grown rosy when I came to the beginnings of the city and the long street they called Burial Ground Road. Not because of all the English people who lay dead in a field there under sad grey slabs of stone. I did not fear their ghosts. But further up that swampy road there were dacoits. Everyone talked about them, those real dacoits with murdering blades. By then, though, the sun was up and all the early wagons out with it, and horses and riders too, galloping by the green open space of the maidan.

"Anila! What an early riser you are."

Mr Walker pushed his way past the red curtain. He was dressed in a shirt and breeches, no jacket. I had to struggle with my smile, for he looked just like a heron, long-legged, stooped and spike-haired, and like a heron his colours were grey-blue and grey.

"Come and have something to eat with me. You can have a second breakfast."

Breakfast! I followed him through the doorway, past the curtain that smelled of ink and smoke, men's smells.

This room was light, with walls of creamy pink, and it looked onto a small walled garden. Through an open window red hibiscus flowers and white climbing roses pushed into the room and tumbled around a little table spread with plates and dishes. Mr Walker pulled out a chair for me and we sat down. The little man scurried out again, muttering.

The dishes on the table held fish and rice, curds, preserves, nuts, persimmons and some round rough cakes.

"Have an oatmeal cake," Mr Walker said. "They're Scottish. Chandra makes them to my grandmother's receipt, as best he can. I would prefer to breakfast outside, but then Balor would be jealous of the garden birds."

Who was Balor?

Mr Walker smiled and pointed to the top of a bookcase behind me. He kept his finger stretched out. I had hardly begun to figure the grey shape up there for what it was when it suddenly changed its size, took off from its pinnacle and landed in a flurry of feathers on Mr Walker's finger. Great black beak, black claws firmly folded round a hand.

The huge grey parrot waddled sideways along Mr Walker's hand, walked up his arm and kissed him on the mouth with the top of its head. I laughed and so did the bird, a booming deep laugh. This must be Mr Walker's laugh which I hadn't heard yet.

"Put your elbow on the table and let your fingers touch mine," Mr Walker said.

The bird came down his arm, crossed over and then I could feel the sensitive feet travelling fast up my arm. He was on my shoulder. I felt a tug and my head wrap was loosed, picked up and tossed onto the floor.

Now it was Mr Walker's turn to laugh and I could feel the parrot thrum with pleasure.

"Balor likes hair," he said. "I think he must have been a barber in a past life. If we don't stop him he'll have your braid unpicked in the same way he deals with my poor coiff."

He tapped his chair back and Balor waddled down my arm again and hopped up.

"I bought him in a street market in Spain, years ago, when he was much more of a street urchin. He's blind in one eye – if you look carefully at him, you'll see that. He can speak, like most educated parrots, but I cannot discover what his native language is. He refuses to speak English. Or Bangla, though Chandra claims that he says puja prayers. I called him Balor after an evil one-eyed god from Ireland, your father's country. Eat, Anila."

I took a cake. Mr Walker reached over and cut it in two for me and spread it with butter and a dark fruit jelly from a pot. I took some fish too, and some rice. He poured tea for me and then a cup for himself. We drank in silence until I began to fear that I had seemed too greedy, too starved. A Hemavati at her worst.

"I'll draw Balor for you."

Balor cocked his head when I said his name. He watched the pencil in my hand as it moved over the paper. But only with the good eye of course. The other he kept turned away so that I had to draw him in profile, that vain bird.

"My mother used to say that all birds have a secret," I said. "She didn't believe I could find out what their secrets were by watching them and drawing them."

"How, then?"

"She said the secrets were found in the stories people

passed on. But there were lots of birds that we had no stories for so my father and I would get cross with her about her reasoning." Quickly I looked away and began to shade in Balor's wing feathers. Purple-grey, black-grey, silver-grey. Water grey.

Little one, tell Malati why the poorest grey pigeon wears jewel colours round her neck. She might put your story into her dance.

"Those are the very kind I'm looking for, Anila." Mr Walker laid his hands, palms up, on the table. "The birds with no stories because nobody has noted them down. Let me tell you this. The reason I want to journey upriver, up the Ganga, is to find a bird with no name."

I did not understand him.

"A magical bird?"

"No, Anila. I am explaining it badly. I mean no name that we Europeans know for of course all creatures have been named by somebody, by their nearest neighbours."

He told me then that if we found such a bird – a new *species*, he called it – he wanted more than anything to name it after his sister. He sounded shy, almost, when he said this.

"Eveline was my twin. She died when she was just sixteen, of a chill. We had been swimming in the Tay – that's a river near my grandmother's place – but it was too early in the year and we should have been cannier. It was my notion, of course. She was ever so much more learned than I, so much more promising. Every day of my life I miss her."

A chill.

"Sometimes she ransacked my wardrobe and dressed

herself in much the way that you dress, I've noticed. Once she passed herself off as me to my father and went with him to Sunday Meeting, riding my horse. That was how like we were then, though she was finer looking."

He cleared his throat.

"Have you heard of Mr Linnaeus? Perhaps your father might have known of him?"

"Was he a Writer?"

Mr Walker smiled and shook his head. He reached for my drawing and turned it round.

"This is the very spit of that rascal parrot. We'll give it to Chandra and he'll forget his grizzling and be your friend for life."

There was a boom on the front door, a worse din than I'd imagined when I was outside. And, straightaway, a similar monstrous noise sounded in the room, just as loud. Balor flew up to his high perch and looked down at us, his beak half open and his purple tongue curled round itself. He looked as pleased as a child that has learned to take its first step.

Mr Walker groaned.

"He's never attempted to ape the doorknocker before. You've appealed to his devil's side, Anila. Poor Chandra!"

He stood up and motioned me to take my bag and go ahead of him. Out on the street, there was our carriage, no buggy this one but a proper four-wheeled carriage with a roof, and a horse that looked like it knew how to run. Chandra fussed around us but Mr Walker sent him inside.

"I'll tell you about Mr Linnaeus in the carriage, Anila. Now let us get on our way to the Gardens before the high-born ladies start taking the air."

THE GARDENS

THE FERRY BOAT FOR the Gardens sat in the water like a slice of watermelon. It was painted a bright green, and front and back it rose up into carved points but its middle was snug and wide and held the seats. From my bedroom window in Garden Reach, I had often seen such boats crossing to the Botanical Gardens, full of ladies in bright outdoor clothes, and gentlemen, and, sometimes, their children. Well, this day I had joined them and some of those ladies wrapped up in warm shawls could not take their eyes off me, even though there was surely so much else to look at as we moved away from the ghat.

I was no longer a boy. I had draped my tunic more becomingly and now I wore my scarf in the usual way, loose round my head. Mr Walker got his share of hard stares too, though he did not appear to notice. I sat on a seat and looked over the edge at the little waves that lapped round the boat. The sun was throwing gold spangles at them and they danced. Under my feet the boat swayed like a cradle.

We passed behind the end of a ship that was chained

fast in the water, like a watchdog in Garden Reach. It had many little windows cut into its great height and a bright pointed flag hanging out from its tail. Two sailors leaning over the wooden rail saw me stretching my neck back to look up and they waved down. I could feel the eyes of the other passengers on my back.

"This is my first time going across the river," I told Mr Walker.

He smiled. In the bright light I could see he had freckles starting across his nose, the sun dots the English ladies feared as much as snakes.

"This boat is rather like a gondola from Venice," he said. "A little showy, not like the craft I have in mind for my trip."

He did not say "our" trip I noticed. But we had covered quite a few points about that business already. Mr Linnaeus, I discovered, was dead and so had nothing to do with us, not really. But he had invented a clever way to name animals and birds and plants so that everyone all over the world could understand which creature was intended, even though the world contained so many different languages. This man from the cold north of the world used a language that nobody on earth spoke any more and he used it to give every animal and plant a personal name and a family name.

"If you find a new creature you are allowed to choose its personal name, you make it sound a bit like Latin, and then it goes into the Book of Knowledge for all time."

To my mind, that made Mr Linnaeus a Writer, for sure, but I said nothing. It would be a fine thing to have a beautiful bird named for you, as Mr Walker hoped to do for his sister, but what if you found a new jheel snake or biting bug?

He told me that there would be no women on his boat, only men. As well as himself there would be his manservant, who was English, his bearer and the boatmen.

"That would be a difficult situation for any female, in any country," he said. "But I do know a couple of ladies who have such a passion for knowledge that they find themselves in constant conversation with awkwardness. They are definitely not ladies of the salon."

I thought of Miss Hickey and her plain dresses and her books.

"I know ladies like that."

"Well, if you do you will know that they tend to have other useful weapons against society, like money, or an old name. Your situation is a delicate one, Anila, as I understand it from everything you have told me. This river journey is only a short one for I shall be returning to England in the new year. I cannot guarantee that you will make any progress as a result of having made the trip with me. Indeed in many ways I think you might suffer because of it. Do you understand?"

He did not want me after all. I would be too much trouble. I clutched the straps of my bag until my fists felt hot, hard as stones.

"Mr Walker, I can take care of myself afterwards. The English ladies that you are talking about do not want me even now, and I have done nothing awkward yet. But I would love to travel up the river because of my mother and I would love do this work for you because I am able to do it. And then I would return to

Calcutta and perhaps be a little braver. Perhaps I was too young before but you see all this time I have done nothing to find news of my father, though Miss Hickey did try at the beginning. When he left he promised to return and I know that only something serious could have prevented this."

Mr Walker had made a sympathetic noise to that but he did not enquire further. That was all.

Now we came alongside the Gardens' landing beach and everybody stood up at the same time so that the boat started to tip over slightly. Some of the ladies squealed. They had to be lifted out by their gentlemen and placed onto the sand, where they smoothed down their big skirts and made silly faces. I jumped out, splashing my slippers in the water. It felt wonderful.

Mr Walker and I walked up the pebble path towards the thick planting of trees that faced the river. Parakeets and drongos dashed from one high branch to another, shouting in excitement. I saw a flash of blue that was so light and airy it seemed to come from a dream. I had never seen such a colour on a bird before, not even on a kingfisher.

"A flycatcher, surely," Mr Walker said. "But not one I know."

There was a bench beside the path and I sat down and took out my notebook and pencil. Mr Walker continued up the path and out of my sight. I think he wished to leave me to work in peace. Or perhaps he was curious about what I might choose to draw, left to myself.

The Gardens seemed to be one big bazaar for birds. There were rollers and hoopoes, different from the ones I knew. Two koels were having a singing competition, one pitching his notes higher than the other. I could see a woodpecker resting on a branch, fat and redbreasted, digesting his feed.

I saw the flycatcher again, a tiny perfect shape. I wrote "Malati's Radha sari" and "peacock eyes" beside my sketch. That would remind me how to bring the little bird's beautiful colour to the page.

As if to say I was on the right track, a peacock stepped out of the bushes near my bench, and spread his tail for me. Away behind him, another of his kind shrieked.

I loved the mad, sad sound of peacocks. My mother had hated it, though she liked to help me gather up their dropped tail feathers.

In our village there was a boy who was cruel to peacocks. He tore their feathers from them, even from the hens. He drowned one day and all the night that followed the peacocks screamed for joy.

I started to draw some of the trees too. Many had strange shapes and colours and I had never seen them before, but there were plenty of common neems and acacias.

"Come this way, when you are ready, Anila."

Mr Walker had come back and now stood in front of me, looking down at my open page filled with tree shapes and branches.

"Anila, you are a true artist," he said, "and I am not. So – while you have been so engaged I have done an even more important task. I have arranged something for us to eat."

He took my materials although they were not heavy

and we set out. The plantation had swallowed up all the great-skirted ladies and their husbands, it seemed, for we met none of our fellow passengers.

Mr Walker told me that the Gardens were not very old.

"But in India all plants grow fast in the heat and the rains. If this were the king's gardens outside London you and I would still be taller than many a tree the same age as these. Look at that banyan."

I stepped over to the tree. Like all banyans it had sent down shoots from its own body into the ground. But this was an odd one, for they were forming a perfect ring.

"This is a clever tree," I said to Mr Walker.

Then I saw what he had arranged inside the circle and I had to laugh.

One of the garden boys had laid out some food for us, on a log, in among the pillars of the banyan. He stood there beaming at me, standing guard over some roti, palm fruit slices, shells with cordial in them, just a little of everything. There was a cloth spread for us to sit.

I told Mr Walker how the banyan tree got its name. I think he knew the old story already but he pretended not to, to give me the pleasure.

The first people in the world thought the banyan tree was no good because it had no fruit and no flowers. Even its wood would not burn well for fires. But a wise man said that the tree should be left to grow because the gods must have put it there for their own reasons. So the tree grew up without any name. It grew out, and then it grew down until it made more shade than any other tree in the world. Then the banians, the merchant sellers, came to set up their stalls underneath it. People called it the banyan tree and in every village where it decided to grow, it had the place of honour.

"Hoy! Walker!"

An Englishman in dark clothes was approaching the banyan tree. His face was red and hot-looking and when he came into the shade, he took off his hat to wipe his forehead. I saw that he wore a wig, a poor one with a pigtail that seemed to be made of donkey hair, it was so grey and coarse. It hung crookedly round his face, one side too far forward, the other too far back.

"Crocker! I would not have taken you for a botanical man," said Mr Walker. His voice had no welcome in it, I thought, but he stood up.

"Oh, I have my secrets," Crocker said. "Like any man." His eyes passed over me, up and down, then slid over the boy and the remains of our food. He leant forward over my bag and scooped up some of the broken roti with his damp fingers. "Are you not going to introduce me?"

Mr Walker muttered our names so fast that all I noticed was that he said Crocker's name first. Jeremy Crocker. Then mine. That was what Miss Hickey would have done. That order meant that I was grown-up, a lady.

Ladies have the advantage in introductions, Anila. Remember that. We have few enough fiddle-faddles that go in our favour.

"Miss Tandy is the finest artist from nature that I have seen in Calcutta. I have been very impressed by her drawings this morning."

"I'm sure you were, Walker, I'm sure you were," Crocker said. "Miss Tandy, indeed. I wonder now, after all."

He did not say what he wondered but he kept staring at me. His wet eyes made me think of leeches and I did not want them to look at me. I pulled my scarf over my forehead and looked down at my feet. But he had more to say.

"Well, that's one for the books, I daresay. The dedicated scholar finally falls for native charms, just like the rest of us…"

Mr Walker moved towards him, and, thin as he was, his fists were up like a fighting man's.

"Damn your filthy impudence, Crocker. You were ever a disgrace to the Company and to your country. Clear off from here, and make sure you do not journey back in our boat or I'll have the ferrymen pitch you out in mid-channel."

Crocker moved away. When he reached the path he turned and offered me a small unpleasant bow. I looked away. I felt dirty. But straightaway I felt more sorry for Mr Walker than for myself. He was banging the poor banyan shoots so hard with his hand that it must surely bleed.

"That ditch-born weasel, that apocalypse," he said at last, spitting out the words. "I apologize for his boorish behaviour, Anila. Crocker is known from here to Madras and beyond for it. He has been in charge of the Writers for many years and I pity the young men who have to humble themselves to such a character from the day they arrive in India. I'm sure he sends them down all manner of crooked paths."

What did I remember, suddenly?

Yes, Anila, you're right, that is an ugly face I've drawn in the gutter spout. That's a real face too, and I'll you about its owner sometime when we're far far away from him.

I also understood properly Chandra's cross words about what might be said about his master, having me turn up on his doorstep.

Our picnic was finished, now. Even the birds seemed to have hushed above us. Mr Walker paid the garden boy for what he had done and we started back towards the river. He was quiet until we saw the cheery shape of our boat ahead.

"Now, do you see what I mean?" he said at last. "But do you know, that encounter which has so angered me has also served to firm up my mind. I feel I would be a coward if I were to allow the attitude of Crocker and his kind to prevail. After all, I *do* know several here who are not narrow at all, nor inclined to be twisted. I would vow to promote any work you do for me among the scholars here, the ladies included. If you feel bold enough to serve as my draughtsman on the river trip, that position is yours, Anila."

BLOOD GIFTS

ONE PICNIC DAY WITH *my father was different.*

That day the trinkets were not in the box. My father took two folded-up leather pouches from inside his jacket. He didn't offer them to us to open, as was his usual way. He unwrapped them himself. Inside one was my mother's purple scarf, but instead of shaking it loose he folded back its layers as if he were peeling a fruit made of silk. At the heart was a ring, a ring for my mother, a gold ring with a dark crimson stone set into it. When he put it on her finger it sat there, a tiny cushion. Then he arranged the scarf round her neck while she looked up at him, huge eyed. My pouch on that day had gold too, a locket shaped and engraved to look like a peacock's tail.

My father had tears in his eyes when he put the ring on my mother's finger and then fastened the locket round my neck.

"I have to tell you something," he said. We stared at him, my father, always strong-voiced and funny, but now his words were trapped inside him like chickens in a cage, and his breathing was strange. He told us that he had to return to Ireland, that his father had died, that his mother and sisters needed him, the only man in the family. He said that as soon as it could be he would come back and bring us to Ireland on a

ship, and then, no matter what anyone said, he would marry my mother. Ireland was different from India, it was different from England, even, you could do that there. Meanwhile she should have money.

When the last of his words had escaped from my father's mouth my mother stood up and moved towards the steps of the ghat. She just stood there, for a long time, saying nothing, and I could not see her face because she was staring out over the water. A small boat was making its way out to a goods ship in the middle of the channel. Goats, five or six, no more, were standing in the space in front and behind the boatman. All of them were facing the ship except him but he steered perfectly, dipping and dropping his oars like wings.

She turned and said to me. "Anila, go to the buggy driver and tell him to leave us now. We'll walk back, you and I, we know our way."

My father stared at her miserably. I didn't move.

"Go and do it!" she said, almost shouting at me.

When I looked at my father to see if I should do this strange thing, me, a little girl give an order like that to a grown man, he just nodded and gave me some coins to give the man. I went over to the buggy, feeling very important and did as I was told.

"We know our way," I said to him. But when he had clipped the horse with his whip and trotted off over the stones I was sorry he was gone. I could still see the buggy swaying, getting tinier and tinier.

I was really too young to realize why my mother was so angry. I had heard my father's words of course but I was not yet nine then so I didn't understand what he meant when he talked about us coming to his country. That is – I understood what he said. But what I didn't know then was that, as my mother saw it, he was describing a dream, an impossible dream. To me it sounded like a plan, like something he and I could draw together on a piece of paper and hand over to somebody in the Company to make real. Like a building.

But my mother, still white, was furiously trying to pull the ruby ring from her finger. She was shaking and couldn't get a proper grip on it. Perhaps it was too tight even for her slender hand. Her knuckles were too clenched or her poor flesh was too swollen and the ring was trapped.

"You'll take it back," she said. "You'll take this blood gift back."

I had never heard my mother sound like that, spitting words out, each one a snake thrown at my father. She would have scared demons away. She scared me.

She was speaking in Bangla of course. But my father understood every word. I could see that.

"Anna," he said. "I can do nothing to prevent my leaving India at this time. I promise you that I will return. It is a solemn promise. I would swear to write to you if there was a point to that, but where would my letters go?" He stopped for breath, but he had found an idea as well.

"This is what I'll do, Anna."

He reached out to take my mother's hand. She slapped it away but he spoke his thought anyway.

"I shall write to you in the care of Robert Sedge, Malati's soldier. He will bring you my letters and Anila can read them. You'll have money, you'll know how things stand."

"And your daughter, how will she live as she grows up?" said my mother. "You think I can make a marriage for her? You think the English will take her? You think your sisters will do that much for you?"

He started to say something but she grabbed my hand, and

pulled me away with her, away from my father, away from the river. I looked back and he was following us, slowly, but then he stopped. Next time I looked he was just standing there.

We were walking fast but then she made us run, on and on over those stones until I cried out to her to stop because my side hurt. She was glad to stop. Her breaths were pushing in and out, hurting worse even than mine, I could see. She hunkered down and pulled the purple scarf over her face, not touching me, not looking to right or left. She sat there like a beggar, all alone.

We had taken a turn from the ghat in our rush and now we were on the great street that ran alongside the river. In the middle of all the traffic there were some cows and while we took our heaving breaths I noticed one of them in particular, a lovely old cow with a brown stripe down her back. She was batting her calf into the centre of the road, keeping it safe, nosing it with her head, blowing on it with her breath.

My mother was like that until today, I thought. Now I don't know what she is like. And because I was tired and sore and afraid that something terrible had happened, I began to cry. Without looking upwards, my mother reached out her arm and pulled me down beside her. She stroked my back until I stopped sobbing.

"Oh, Anila, Anila," she said, more to herself than to me. "What will happen to us?"

People passed by and paid us no attention. Why would they? All over the city people sat and squatted and turned away from the bustle. But my mother had never joined them until today. Here we were beside the river and just feet away from us carts and carriages thundered past, churning up the soft earth. Crows dropped down immediately to see if anything new and tasty was uprooted for them.

We sat there for a long time. I began to think of the tiffin that my father had brought and wished we had eaten first, as we usually did, before he produced today's trinkets. My mother stood at last, and reached out her hand to pull me up. Only then I saw that something had happened to her stubborn finger. In our frantic dash or perhaps during our rest here, that finger must have shrunk thin again. The gold and crimson ring was no longer sitting proudly on her left hand. There was just an angry red and white mark in its place. I was afraid to ask her if she'd lost it.

But the lovely purple scarf survived that day. I wore it for a long time, wrapped round my waist under my sari. When my mother saw it afterwards she wanted to shred it but my cries were so terrible she let it be. And for once, so did everyone else in our little house.

AN EXTRA BED

MR WALKER INSISTED THAT his carriage would take Anoush and me back to the garden house.

By now he knew most of my circumstances. That was my fault in the main, for once we had made our bargain I felt so easy with him that I wanted him to hear my story. But it was also his fault because he listened as well as a woman and did not interrupt. He agreed with me that Anoush deserved to be liberated for Christmas but he would prefer, he said, that we two should spend the night in his house, for it had many rooms. I told him that in that case Anoush would be compromised.

"Really? You are quite the alarming Mademoiselle Decorum, Anila."

For a moment I thought I had offended him, but no, he seemed to be struggling to keep his mouth stern. That did not take him long.

"No, but to be so close to the riverside, so unprotected, I cannot like it. You will let me inspect this strange home before I relinquish you to it."

It was almost dark when we drew up on the Esplanade. A fog had spread a smoky shawl over all the streets that led down to the river. The carriages that were about already had lanterns lit, front and back, white and red ones. They looked festive, but ghostly too, swaying in the gloom. I thought of the akash pradip, the friendly lights that people hang on bamboo poles to guide wayfarers during the misty months.

Mrs Panossian's shop was cosy inside, browner than ever. There was no sign of Anoush but Gabriel and his son Mesrop were still serving a couple of bearers. Gabriel raised his thumb to say "upstairs". Mesrop stared at me with his large slow eyes. This boy, who was really a man, years older than I was, made me feel uneasy. I never knew what to say to him. But Anoush was kind to Mesrop, always. He was not allowed to write an order in the big ledger book but she would write down every item he called out to her – figs, sultanas, jams, wines, flower waters, patent medicines – and then read them back to him. She said he could remember each order for weeks.

Now his face blazed with pleasure. Anoush burst through the inner door, two cloth bags hanging from her arms. Loose on her head she wore a beautiful gold scarf that I had never seen before.

"I'm ready, Anila! Ready to go with lots to bring!"

She took my arm. "Let's go."

"But Anoush, I was going to buy some…"

"No need. Mrs Pan has made up a food parcel for us. Here, take this bag. She wouldn't tell me what was in it but now I feel I would do just about anything for my dear old cousin."

She reached for her stick which stood on its own in the great monsoon umbrella stand by the door. Mesrop rushed forward, something I had never seen that slow boy do, and he bowed good night to us as if we were Mrs Panossian's best Company customers.

Outside it was now completely dark. I led Anoush towards the Esplanade, a small walk for us. I had convinced Mr Walker it was the best arrangement. If Gabriel and Mesrop were to see us getting into the carriage outside the shop, Mrs Panossian would surely have the story in a moment.

Anoush was in a trance, completely silent as long as it took us to climb inside and settle ourselves on the cushioned seat. There was no sign of Mr Walker.

"Anila," she whispered. "Did you pay for this with your precious money?"

She stroked the old velvet of the seat and then turned round to look through the little square window behind us. "Someone is coming," she said.

Mr Walker opened the carriage door. A curl of fog had settled on his hair, covering it in shiny droplets. He made a little bow to Anoush.

"Anoush, this is Mr Edward Walker, my employer," I said, trying my best not to sound grand, though I truly felt like Lakshmi, the goddess who brings gifts to the good. "Mr Walker, this is my friend Miss Anoush Galustaun. Anoush, Mr Walker is kindly driving us to Garden Reach."

Mr Walker said he would sit up with the driver and not discommode us. I fancied he shot me a look when he said that, but quickly he stepped down and banged the door safe. The carriage buckled as we felt him clambering up to the seat on top. Then we were off, turning wide at the top of the Esplanade to trot down the road towards Chowringhee.

All of that long journey Anoush was quiet, but it was not a worry. She was full of wonder she said, at the speed a person could travel sitting down, while all the time the city unrolls itself by your side like a great carpet. She had never ridden in a carriage before.

"It's like flying," she sighed once, almost to herself.

When we reached the white houses of the Reach, they glittered with their hundreds of chandeliers and sconces and lanterns as if a piece of starry night was laid across the earth. Our carriage had pulled up at the only dark space.

I led Anoush and Mr Walker round by the stables and down the garden, through the oleanders, to my little door. When we left the paving stones behind he held an arm out for Anoush to lean on, and he took her bag from her. I felt mean for thinking of myself then, but I did, just for a moment. I wanted to drop the two bags I was carrying and dance on the velvet doob grass.

The riverbank was full of noises but after two nights in the open I could recognize most of them. Water splashed and sucked at the sand, frogs blew air from their bellies, reeds rubbed together, water birds were loud and cross with each other like children. There were slithers and scrabbles in the undergrowth, shouts from the ships in the channel, owls calling in the gardens of the Reach. I could explain all of these to Anoush. But I hoped she did not fear bats.

"Allow me, Anila," said Mr Walker.

He took the key from my hand, set it into the door

and went inside, banging his feet down on the floor.

"Have you a candle?"

I had a candle lantern and a flint inside and he busied himself with making a light.

Anoush came up the steps just as the light took. My round room was suddenly dark gold and full of our moving shadows, with the night sky cut into lozenges round the top. I think we all gasped. The others because it was so beautiful, I think. I because of the clean charpoy bed that was newly in place alongside my string bed. And the two fine nets that now hung over both.

"Zakar! How kind he is."

Or was. I felt sure that Zakar was gone.

"Anila, your house is bigger inside than it is outside – how can that be?" Anoush asked.

She sat down on the bed and drew its net round her. Then she peeked out again. Her scarf had fallen and her curls showed golden lights. Her smile was wonderful.

"Mr Walker, you must have hospitality with us," she said.

She reached for the bag I carried and began to take items from it, unwrapping each so that we could see.

There was a small fruit cake, the English kind. "From last year, but Mrs P says they get better with age," Anoush said. There was yellow almond paste and long sticks of dark cane. Small red and green apples. Wet buffalo cheese, wrapped in muslin. A coconut and a squash fruit. Dark flat bread that felt fresh and soft.

"This is our Armenian bread. And see, I have green walnut jam to spread on it. Mrs Seropin gave it to me today. I'm still disappointed. When I saw the walnuts on her table I was hoping she would spend the day baking me the pudding that has my name, Anoushapur. It's the most delicious thing in the world!"

Mr Walker took my clay oven outside to brew some tea. Then we had our little meal, we two sitting on the bed, Mr Walker on the steps with the door open, his long heron legs folded and leaning in over the threshold. The fog had lifted and the air was fresh.

Mr Walker told us that he admired Mrs Panossian's clever mind.

"This plum-cake is proof. She takes care to stock every item that will remind us northern strangers of our home cooking, our childhoods and our festive occasions."

He looked lost for a moment. I was certain that he was thinking of feasts with his sister Eveline.

Anoush had lost her shyness with Mr Walker.

"Will you be very glad to go back to England?" she asked. "Mrs Pan says that all the English people become homesick after a while in Calcutta."

He laughed.

"I have a lot of work to keep me busy. And I'm not English, I'm a Scot. But to answer your question, Anoush. I *must* go back to London to deliver my reports and findings in person. It's not a question of wanting to. However, if the outcome there is good, well that would mean I will be able to return to Calcutta again. So that is the real question I think about – do I want to come back to India? And the answer is yes. Definitely yes."

Anoush beamed at him.

"And do English people really think our birds are so

important that they will send you back to find more of them?"

Anoush admired my drawings but she had no interest in birds or trees. She always wanted me to draw people instead. Practise on me, she'd laugh, and then she'd pose like a dancer, or a haughty salon lady. I truly doubted that she knew a stork from a crow.

"Goodness, no," Mr Walker said. "The birds are all my own hobby-horse. No, my work here has been to find good teachers and writers of Indian languages. Not just Bengali, you know. There are many different languages spoken from Madras all the way to the great mountains in the north and it would be a fine thing to set up a school for Indian studies here in the city, at Fort William. My task in London will be to convince people of this."

All this day in his company and I had not known this!

Mr Walker looked over at me before I could fix my face.

"One of the reasons I was so pleased to discover Anila is that she is not only a fine artist but she speaks both Bengali and English. And so very well. Now I was so taken with all this genius that I believed her to be a mind-reader also. Anila, I believe I neglected to tell you my true business here. I apologize."

What could I say? Anoush laughed and gave me a dig with her elbow.

"But I can speak three languages, Mr Walker! Armenian, Bangla and English. You must offer me a job too!"

He chuckled and stood up, then wished us a good

night and a good holiday. He said he would expect me at his house two days after Christmas. Then he fished about in his coat pockets and laid some cowries and some small coins down on my bag.

"Take this small money, Anila, so you can take a palki or a boat to the city. You and Anoush both."

He paused then, framed in the doorway. Like a sentry, I thought, except that he was outside and we were in.

"Anila, I freely admit that tonight at any rate, the attractions of your little house surpass all its insecurities. My grandmother also had a little summerhouse, as near to the river as this is, and though we were not allowed to, my sister and I would sneak out and spend a summer's night there, watching for otters and getting up with the dawn."

He gave a little knock to the roof, for luck, he said, and then he was away, striding into the darkness of the garden. Anoush and I settled into our beds to tell our stories of the day. But I know I had not got even as far as Mr Crocker and his leechy eyes before we both drifted into sleep.

I never found out what the bats did that night to get into or out of my little house.

HEMAVATI

IN THE MIDDLE OF *bad times people sometimes surprise you. It was not cheery Malati who was kindest to us in the fearful weeks after my father left Calcutta. Or at least we supposed he had, because he had not called on us again and it was the month when the great Indiamen ships were at their busiest, taking the quick winds for Europe. He had taken his passage, my mother was sure of it.*

No, it was Hemavati who bought food for us at the stalls, using her own small supply of money. She sat beside my mother as if she were her very own mashi, washed her, and made her eat and drink a little each day.

"Annapurna, you must take this," she would say, forcing my mother to sit up and pressing a cup of fresh ghol drink up to her mouth as if she were a baby. "Take it for the child's sake but take it for yourself too, for your strength."

The rest of the time however, beginning a week or so after that cursed picnic, my mother lay on the bed, not seeing any of us but playing terrible scenes over in her mind, dreaming bad dreams with her eyes open. We knew this because she would call out words, though these made no sense to us. She did not have a fever, her forehead was not hot or cold, but otherwise she had all the signs of wasting. I woke up beside her every morning and she was just as she had been the night before, turned on her hip, bony as a dog on the high road. My mother who had been softness itself!

Hemavati had taken the screen away from round our bed so she could watch my mother for signs.

"Good or bad signs," she shrugged when Malati asked what she meant. "There's always a time when the person you're watching over decides which it is to be."

Every morning Hemavati made me go outside and find company with other children in the lane.

"Help them with their chores," she said. "You are too much on your own now but you're no tiger. Not yet, anyway."

I didn't know what she meant. But it was good, somehow, to leave the little brick house that was full of sadness and make my way down the rutted path in search of something else. Our lane joined one of the great old roads into the city but it was a noisy busy world of its own. My father always said that when he stepped off the road he was stepping into an India that his fellow Writers never knew was there.

On the lane there was only one other strong house like ours, which was owned by a palanquin builder and his sons. Long clean planks of wood were always lined up against the front walls of this house. Round the back, where the earth was covered with wood dust and chippings, the boys hammered and sawed all day long, turning the longwood into the box-carriages without wheels that the English had come to love. They lined the most expensive ones with pith to keep the worst of the sun's heat away from the passengers. The smells of wood and paint escaped onto the lane. The paint smell I especially liked. It went up my nose like oven smoke.

I loved to slip into the yard and watch the eldest son painting the finished palanquins. He had a fine talent, I thought, able to fill in, using just a thin brush, fruit and vines or chains of tiny elephants or monkeys. Sometimes he simply drew the plainer decorations and lines that you would find picked out in stone on the big buildings in the city. He knew I was watching but he let me be. I think he liked an audience. I always hoped he would give me an old paint pot but he never did.

The other houses were thatch over bamboo, or mud houses. Some of the mud houses were splashed with indigo dye and I thought they were beautiful, blue like jheel water on a thundery day. Monsoons were hard on these houses though, ones that were not pukka-built like ours. In bad years some were swept away by the rising waters and people had to splash down the lane, up to their knees in the brown floodwater, in a desperate search for their cushions and beds, boxes and ovens. Once from our roof, I was thrilled to see a swan float past with its big black feet on an English table top.

"Goddess Saraswati will be proud to see her faithful friend on a royal raft," my mother had said when I told her. But that was long ago.

Everybody worked outside. Women came from the bazaar with huge baskets of rice, bananas or mangoes to sell, balancing these fat pyramids ever so delicately on their heads. They each had a place to sit and sell, a chosen tree that was their destination. But for us children, it was their slow walk down the lane that was important. If they put a foot down carelessly a fruit might topple off its pile. It didn't often happen but when it did those hardworking women could do nothing but shout after us when we snatched the fruit from the ditch and ran.

"Devils get you, little thieves!"

A Mussulman tailor sat on a rug next door to our house, a quiet hunched little man whose needle flashed faster than a slant of rain. He kept hens and a cock, the only ones at our end of the lane. The cock called him to prayers every morning but everyone else nearby also had to rub their eyes in the darkness when that fellow hopped up on the dung pile to shout. I admired the bird, his bright colours and the bossy walk he had. He thought he was a maharajah.

On the other side was a potter who made large brown earthenware water pots that were fired and then sold in the bazaar. He had left his own district and people whispered that it was because of a murder. At any rate he lived on his own. He shouted when children came near his row of pots and we were afraid of him. The clay he used smelled quite strong, as if it had been freshly scooped from the river. But if you could lay hands on a piece of the soft dark stuff that had fallen in the grass you could make little animals and birds and leave them to bake in the sun. So we dared his shouts.

My usual companions were Varsha and Bashanti, who were sisters, and Dinesh, their cousin. The girls' father kept three goats in their little yard and their job was to see that the animals got safe feeding during the day and rice water from those who would give it in the evenings. We wandered after them, keeping them out of houses but all the time watching everything that happened in the lane, collecting stories to bring home. I was desperate to make my mother smile again but even a cackle from Hemavati was a reward.

I told them about boys who left dirty footprints on newly washed clothes spread to dry on the ground and the rocks by the water. I told them about the sadhu, the holy man dressed only in a string, who stood on one leg under the peepul tree for a whole day until sunset came. He kept his heavy matted hair off his shoulders with a trident that looked sharp enough to kill, yet a tailorbird had landed on it and picked straws from his head. I told them how Bashanti's father beat her when she tied nutshells round her ankles and started dancing outside her house. I even told lies about the monkeys, just to keep Hemavati happy. These were little brown monkeys, smaller than cats, that lived in the ruined temple up by the roadside. They took turns swarming down one lane after another. I told her about babies bitten and pots of rice carried off into the trees. But really the monkeys were like children, like us. The harm they did was very little and most people felt they were lucky creatures. I thought they liked to see what we were doing just as much as we liked to watch them.

I soon noticed that Dinesh made his own journeys, ones that were not mapped out by goats. Every day he went past the last house and beyond, heading for wherever there might be stands of trees left, away from the lanes. His job was to gather neem and tulsi twigs and other leaves for the apothecaries in the bazaar. Dinesh had the most beautiful white teeth I had ever seen. This, he told us, was because he cleaned his teeth with the very thinnest neem twigs. He gave me some for myself.

My teeth were fine, I thought, but I envied Dinesh his long walks by the river channels. He would see birds, I thought, though he never mentioned them and I was too shy to ask him what else he saw besides trees.

I was getting tired of the goats and of never leaving the lane. I missed the trips my mother and I used to make, and not only the ones we shared with my father. Sometimes I went round the back of our house before Varsha and Bashanti had left their yard to come along towards ours, and I climbed the steps to our roof. I could hear Hemavati shouting through the open door at them.

"She's gone, ages ago! That one rises early!"

Kneeling so that I was hidden from below, I could see all the way up the lane. It was here that I used to wait for my father's visits. Underneath, I knew the two girls would trudge along by the sluice ditches, after the goats-with-no-names. There would be washing and cooking and babies to watch but I had a taste for something different, something further away.

Those mornings, when I saw Hemavati leave to go up to the stalls, I would come down again and slip back inside the house. I sat beside my mother on the bed, and stroked her arms or her hair, glad to have her to myself. I would take out my book of stories, written in my father's clear hand, and read her one. They were all her own stories, of course, but now she was taking no pleasure in them, none that I could see anyway.

I was just a child. I thought that if my mother stirred, and was herself again, then surely our life would soon fit back into the picture I could recognize, with everything in the correct proportions. The people who used to be big – my father, my mother – would be their proper size again, not shrunken, not invisible.

And Hemavati? That was a difficult question. Hemavati had turned into a larger person than I had thought she was. I would have to find a new place for her in our picture.

But did I believe then that my father was gone? Not truly, not yet.

ANOUSH'S
CHRISTMAS

"HALLELUJAH! HALLELUJAH!"

At first I thought the choir was singing out Miss Hickey's word, loolally, which did not seem right for church. But no, all the little boys who were standing in front of the altar stalls had their mouths open on a lovelier word, a word that sounded like birdsong. The boys were dressed in loose white lace kurtas and long red skirts. They looked like little Christian angels and their high voices sounded like my mother when she sang panchali or her father's boat song.

Anoush and I were wearing our favourite saris, she in pink and I in my blue, sitting in a pew at the back of the church. We were squashed in with the English maidservants and some of the wives and daughters who were half-Indian like me. So Anoush and I were not the only ones to smother a giggle at the bosomy dresses that flounced down the centre aisle after the service.

Outside, in the shade of the wide yellow-stone porch there were groups of officers and soldiers, men in sober black suits and others in breeches and coats of every colour. But there was no Mr Walker. I surveyed every face.

I saw the reverend though, reaching dutifully for people's hands and petting children's heads. He was as hairy as ever, which was a disappointment, somehow. I did not want to catch his cold eye so I whispered to Anoush that we should squeeze through the crowd and slip away. As we left, the bells in the steeple began to peal and everyone seemed to shout louder. There were a few sympathetic eyes for Anoush and her limp and some greetings too, but she took a firm grip of my arm and marched us through the gates of the church.

"This way I can walk as well as any cavalry wife in a frock," she said, squeezing me.

She steered me towards the grassy stretch in front of the Esplanade where we would take our picnic and watch the horsemen and the carriages, the children running with their kites and all the others who were celebrating their Christmas out of doors in the winter sunshine.

"Let's sit close to those people," Anoush said.

If I was the one to spot birds, Anoush could spot people. She had picked out an English family party. Two ladies in dark wool dresses and a grey-haired man in a plain black suit had settled themselves on cushions round a rug. On the rug was a beautiful baby girl with fair curls, playing with a doll that was bigger than she was. Two boys were playing leapfrog close by, with one of the family's bearers helping the smaller boy clamber over his brother. Another bearer was unpacking food from a large tiffin box and putting it out onto china plates.

"I'd like to see who they are," said Anoush. "I've never seen them before but they look like a comfortable family. If I can hear their name then I can tell Auntie about them and she can send them a card."

"Anoush, you mustn't think of work today! It's your holiday."

"Don't think for one moment that I will not remember that, Anila." She smiled. "And I'll remember the river always. But it's good to look at people too."

Earlier this morning Anoush had squealed with horror when I suggested we wash ourselves in the river, which ran clean and cool just beyond the fence. But when she saw that my feet were standing firm on sand and not on the back of some monster of the river, she bent some reeds over, sat down and dabbled her toes in. Then she leant over and scooped up water to splash her face and neck.

"It's got salt in it, like soup!"

She took so much pleasure out of that simple wash in the river water. I thought how my mother would have been proud of me.

Now I was thirsty.

We spread out our own picnic on top of my cloth bag. Rice with spices, Armenian bread, bananas, cake. A green coconut that we would have to break open somehow, for its juice, for I had forgotten my knife. Otherwise it was a long walk over to the Chowringhee tanks and the guards there might turn me away, for badness.

"Anoush, I'm going to see if I can find something to crack this open."

The family near us had also begun to take their food

but I had noticed they had only small tea knives. But a little way off, behind some trees, a new wall was going up, and surely I might find a sharp stone or stray piece of metal there.

That was where I was when I saw the beginnings of what happened.

I turned round, first because of the noise, the loud pounding of horses in the distance, galloping very fast, tearing up the earth as they moved. Two soldiers chasing each other, or chasing something else, and shouting, holding long sticks out by the sides of their horses.

Then I saw him. The smaller boy just stepped away from his family, the way a baby goat does, or a fawn. Nobody was watching him to make him stop. He had a funny, stout walk, almost a run, and he too was chasing something. He was heading straight into the path of the horses as if he did not hear the thunder of their hooves. And the riders were looking away, they must have been, because they did not rein in or change their course. They came on.

But Anoush had seen him. I heard her call. "Stop!" It must have hurt her throat and chest so very much if I could hear that cry so clearly where I was. But nothing stopped. Everything just continued, horribly, as if it was a dream. Why did nobody see him?

I dropped the silly coconut and hitched my sari up to run but I was too far away to be useful. That small boy was going to die, I could see that. I shouted too. That was when I saw Anoush push herself up from the ground with her stick. She couldn't run of course, but she dived forward onto the ground instead, she spread herself flat out and shot forward that long stick of hers so that it fell like a spear between the little boy's legs.

Down he came, flat on his face, only a few lengths of his little body away from the cruel hooves. I could see his mouth opening but there was no cry I could hear.

The father and the bearers were running now too but I was the first to reach the little boy. I picked him up and felt the harsh gasps and gulps as his chest rose and fell. He was a pretty one, fair-haired with curls, but his face was streaked with dirt and tears and his little white breeches were quite torn away in front. I handed him to his father who stood, rocking him, petting his face, kissing his head. The bearers looked grey and shaky. I glared at them. Why was everybody here so foolish?

Just beyond the trees the horses were pulled up now, with shouts, and then turned to trot back to us. The two soldiers jumped down and while one stood holding the reins, the other ran after me to where Anoush lay. Her legs were twisted to one side and she was breathing hard. He helped her very gently to her feet and then went to pick up her stick.

"Anoush, are you all right? Are you hurt?" I whispered, holding her.

She shook her head but she kept her hands folded over her chest and there were tears in her eyes. I lifted her hands away and there it was, her beautiful pink embroidered sari in shreds down her front and every part of her covered in earth and grime.

"It's not the sari, I promise you," she said. She clasped the torn cloth again. "That doesn't matter. It's just that it was such a difficult thing to make my stick fly like that. It might not have worked."

She began to tremble and I put my arms round her.

"Miss, you saved the little boy's life," said the soldier standing with the horses. "We didn't see him until the very end, he was that low down and you can't see that patch from the saddle. And we were all wrapped up in our mountainy game – we saw nobody until you fell forward."

"Anoush, you are wonderful," I whispered.

"That she is, my dear, that she is," said the father, who came up beside us. The mother and the other woman now had the little boy between them and they were hugging and kissing him, while the older boy held the baby.

"My younger son is deaf," said the father. "We think he saw something he wanted and he went after it when we were all occupied. He never saw the horses and of course he couldn't hear them."

The other soldier came back with Anoush's stick and handed it to her. He clicked his heels together so hard that the spurs on his boots jangled. Anoush flashed him a smile then, a shaky one. He was a very young soldier, so young that he looked as if he still had growing to do. He had black hair and such very pale skin that I guessed he had not been long in India.

"My dear, you must tell me your name," said the father to Anoush. "We have so much – no, everything – to thank you for. You must come home with us straightaway, for I am a physician and can attend to any injuries. We will of course replace your damaged garment."

Anoush made a little gesture as if to say, no, no trouble please, but I was not going to have that. My friend should have her due.

"Her name is Miss Anoush Galustaun and after Christmas is over you will be able to find her in Mrs Panossian's emporium off the Esplanade. That's the favourite store for the English in Calcutta, you'll discover very soon."

The father looked at me in amazement.

"We are just lately arrived in the city, but you seem to have divined that. Please let me introduce our family. I am George Herbert. And this is my wife, Mrs Charlotte Herbert, and my sister Miss Sarah Herbert. My sons John and Christopher, whom we call Kit, and my infant daughter, Georgiana."

His wife grasped Anoush's hands as if she would never let them go. "Thank you, thank you, thank you," she said. The little boy, Kit, kept his face buried in his aunt's neck but then he looked up at Anoush and smiled.

"I'm so glad I was here," she said.

The two riders apologized again for their lack of care and made to get on their horses. I could see that the young soldier desperately wanted Anoush to look at him and acknowledge him but she was busy playing peep with little Kit. She turned though, as they trotted off, and gave him a little bow, with joined hands, a true namashkar, something I had never seen Anoush do before.

"I see the carriage coming now," said the doctor. "Our driver, at least, knows his business. You must come and be attended to and then I will have you returned to your home."

The women nodded and smiled and the aunt said something about having a dress that would fit Anoush. But Anoush looked at me, her eyes huge and urgent, and she gave a tiny shake of her head. I knew then that she wanted us to return to the garden house, to be on our own, to be quiet after this alarm.

"We live a long way distant, in Garden Reach," I said. "But if you could take us to the Chandpal Ghat that would be a great kindness, for we might take a boat there."

That then was how we finished our Christmas Day picnic on the green. We rode to the river in a carriage, a plain brown one, with two brown ponies pulling it, each of us with a child in our lap, except for poor Anoush who was still sore. Mrs Herbert passed a flask of lemonade around, filling the one cup, which went from child to adult and adult to child. No distinctions were made. That was the kind of good people they were.

FRUITS FOR DURGA

ONE MORNING, AND I cannot say how many days or even weeks she had lain there, my mother got up. She was thin as a twig and her hair hung like dry leaves, unbrushed and without any of its gloss. But even I could see that whatever Hemavati had meant when she talked of good signs, those signs were there that morning.

"Anila!"

She called me to her — I was sweeping the floor and Hemavati and Malati were out — and she hugged me. I was then only as high as her chest but that morning I could feel that I had more weight than she had. She asked me to go to the tank for fresh water. She said that she wanted to wash at home with nobody looking at her.

I ran down the lane to the tank with our biggest jug and dipped it in several times to make it brim over. My mother washed herself all over and her sari clung to her poor bones so that you could count them. Then she took some of Malati's soapnut for her hair and I ran again for more water.

She came with me then, up the stairs to the roof, to dry out, and also, she told me, so she could breathe good air again. No matter that most of the smells were oven fires and mustard oils burning, and the fresh dung of animals and people. She said she could smell the river on the air and the fragrance of trees.

"Now I must find work," she said. "But what can I do?"

Before, my mother had earned a few annas in the week by preparing paan for the stallholders on the high road. But that was in addition to what my father gave her and now even if she chopped nuts and rolled leaves all day there would not be enough to live on. Perhaps she could sew more quilts, I thought.

"Hemavati was kind," I said to her. "She didn't steal, she gave us things instead."

"And Malati?" my mother asked.

"Oh, Malati says she is marrying before monsoon, but no one believes her," I said. "But perhaps she will because she has gone away. We haven't seen her for quite a while."

My mother smiled and shook her head. Her beautiful black hair lifted in the warm morning breeze and strands of it crossed her face. I drew them back and saw there were tears in her eyes.

"At least I never said that," she whispered. "Even if I do put sindur in my hair like a married woman." Then she laughed until she began to cough.

So I told her about the goats and the girls and Dinesh, about the potter and the palanquin maker's son. Before, when I had left the house, it was always in my mother's company. She did not want me running wild on the lane, she said. But Hemavati had told me that my mother feared in case other children would say nasty things, or reject me.

"They won't do that if you're tough enough," she'd said. "I had to learn that for myself when I was not much older than you and just as pretty, I can tell you. Besides everyone on this lane has something to hide. If you can find what it is, what each person's secret is, then you'll be the toughest of them all. They will fear to cross you."

Hemavati made daily life sound so interesting, like the everlasting battles between gods and demons. It really was not like that at all. But I learned one thing. Although the girls' father was not so happy about the dancers in our house, Bashanti and Varsha themselves thought it must be wonderful to share a house with such exotic people. They envied me that, while I did not envy them their goatkeeping. Was that being tough?

My mother decided to cook a meal to make a thanksgiving to Hemavati for all her care.

"I have a little money hidden," she said. "You go out and buy for me. I don't think I will try to walk that far today. Not yet."

We went downstairs. The statue of Durga was the hiding place, and the money was still there inside her clay body, though my mother was shocked that none of us had thought to put offerings out for the goddess all the time she had been ill.

"Anila, my golden Anila," she reproached me. "You above all people know that Durga is treasured in our family. What will she think of us? Get some fruit for her and some fragrant leaves too. A garland if there is enough left."

I ran out again, this time in the other direction, up to the stalls on the high road. When I came back with my basket full of good rice, fresh ginger, chillis and greens, ripe figs and some yellow puretti fruits for Durga, my mother was sitting outside our door talking to Varsha and Bashanti. Already she looked so much better, with colour in her face and even in her poor famished arms, but that was not what surprised me.

It was to see her enjoying the girls round her. I don't believe she had known their faces before, and certainly not their names. Now she was listening to what they were saying and, yes, even teasing them a little. She looked up at me and drew me down to her lap, gently removing the garland of yellow marigolds that I had placed round my neck.

"Anila, I have made one big decision while you were gone. Varsha and Bashanti tell me they cannot swim and they are afraid of the water. So I am going to teach them and you too, of course, how to swim. The goats can watch! And if anybody else wants to come along, a mother or a child, well that would be very fine too."

Bashanti was staring at my mother with adoration. Varsha was jigging up and down with such excitement that she didn't notice that fresh pellets of goat dung were squeezing up between her toes. As well she might feel that way. Even I didn't know how to swim, though I always loved going down to the washing bank with my mother. But I had never seen her swim before. Only the boys swam.

My mother must have read my thoughts because she said, "I was telling the girls about my father and the life we had on the riverbank with the boats. He taught me to swim when I was much smaller than any of you. All these years in our house I have gone without it and now nothing would give me more pleasure than to show you how to become a fish."

She made a twisting-fish gesture and the girls collapsed in giggles. She told them to go home and ask their mother's permission.

"Tell all the mothers to come too," she said. "If they don't want to swim they can do their washing. They can do both, tell them!"

She said it would be some days before she felt able but that I would come and let them know when. They skipped off then, like little goats themselves, and we went inside to prepare the feast. Only Hemavati and ourselves were there to eat because once again there was no sign of Malati. She had never been gone from us for so long before. Perhaps she really had got married before the monsoons.

I thought then that my mother had learned to become tough. It was a different way of being tough from the way Hemavati had proposed and to me it seemed a much better way. When we started making our trips down to the little creek I soon discovered the joys of learning to belong in the water. In a little while Bashanti, for one, excelled even my mother at swimming. I think it was because she was always competing against Dinesh, her cousin.

But at that time what I liked most of all was this: that my mother could wake up and shine like a sun again after such a darkness. Knowing that she was able to do that, even once, even for a short time, always gives me hope now when it's hope I'm searching for. As for herself, she said it all came about because Durga was watching over her, anxiously waiting for the only person in the house who would provide her with gifts of flower petals and fruit.

HERA

"ISN'T THIS A BEAUTY?"

Mr Walker was almost whispering, as English people do in churches. But we were in his carriage, clattering along the fine street surfaces, heading for the boat that waited for us north of the city.

I looked at what he was holding up, a gun, a golden gun, like a smaller brother of the guns you might see poking out through the sides of some of the ships on the river. It was made of brass, a fat barrel of brass. I could see no beauty in it except that it was shiny, and small too, at least for a gun, and that it had its own neat brown case.

"Are you going to shoot birds with it?"

He looked at me as if I were mad.

"This is a Gregorian telescope, Anila, one of the finest of its kind. You will love the power that this will add to your perceptions of the world. When we are on the boat I will show you how it brings the most far-away thing close, even the moon and the stars."

If only the barrel could work that magic on my father, I thought, then I would be impressed. No, what

I preferred to trust was in the large tin box at my feet.

Mr Walker had been busy around the city suppliers since I had seen him last.

When I came from the ferry stop that morning, as early as I could be, he was outside in the street helping two men load his goods onto the roof of the carriage. All manner of bulky items were piled up there and the men were on top, laying them out and tying them down. Mr Walker waved at me and straightaway went inside his house, shouting out for Chandra. The fair-haired Englishman did not stop his knot-making to look at me as I came close, but the little dark-skinned bearer beamed at me from the top of the carriage.

"I am Hari. Sahib's man. Give me your bags."

I lifted up my canvas bag with my clothes and my combs but I patted Mr Hickey's case to show him that I was keeping that one to myself.

Mr Walker and Chandra came out of the house. Chandra was carrying a neat tin case sized like a card-table top.

"Show Anila her box of tricks."

Chandra opened the lid for me and I gasped. Inside, the box was divided into portions. One had coloured chalks, another pencils and crayons, and a long narrow section held a number of brushes, each one tipped with gleaming fur. The centre portion had dear little watercolour cakes set into it like pendant jewels: emerald, ruby, topaz, jet, as well as every other shade a bird's plumage might demand. The box lid was hollow and there were a couple of large notebooks strapped into it, tied safe with crossed leather straps.

"Now you will make more fine pictures of Balor," said Chandra. His smile was a fierce one, for he had no teeth in front, but his eyes made such fine nets of crinkles you had to smile back at him.

"Even Mr Hickey has nothing like this, so perfect to travel with," I said to Mr Walker. "I have never had such fine things of my own to work with. Oh, thank you, thank you."

I felt eyes on me and turned. The fair man was kneeling on the carriage roof, looking down over us. He had a rope in one hand, a stubby knife in the other. I caught his glance but he did not look away, and continued to stare boldly, at my new present, at my face and hair, at my trousers. His eyes were blue as the sky above and his skin clear and clean as a child's. He waited until I closed the box and then reached his legs over the guard rail and jumped down, slightly brushing me as he stepped past. The knife was still in his hand.

"Anila, this is Carlen," Mr Walker said. "He's been storming Fort William for me these past days, finding all our provisions. He has much experience in making camp so we'll be in good hands."

Carlen put his knife into his belt holder and nodded his head, but did not bother to notice me further now that his feet were on the ground. For my part, I had never seen a grown English person with such smooth fair hair. It was clipped in layers, neat as feathers, and shaped round his ears. He wore brown kerseymere breeches and a clean white vest, no jacket but a waistcoat with many pockets. He wore these things as if they were a hide he had been born with; they moved on him like muscles.

"Your maps, sir," he said to Mr Walker. "You'll want them inside?"

He went into the house and came out with a leather case like mine, which he placed inside on a seat. When everything was packed inside the carriage, or on the roof tied down, Carlen checked the harness and traces, taking his time. He stood in front of the two black horses and spoke to them as if to encourage them, stroking their muzzles. Then he swung himself up to the roof again and sat beside the driver, who glared at him. Hari stood on the step at the back and Chandra waited anxiously while Mr Walker and I stepped into the carriage. He waved until we had gone down the street and turned right onto Chowringhee, heading north.

Mr Walker must have been disappointed with the welcome I gave to his telescope for now he reached for the leather case.

"I'll show you where we are going," he said.

I had seen maps before, for sometimes my father had used them while he was drawing up his plans for this or that building, but I didn't understand how they worked. Maps were not pictures of anything I could recognize. I looked down now at the one Mr Walker had taken out and opened up. I saw a shape like a large piece of ginger root with a dark line snaking up to the top of the page to meet a thicker black line travelling across it.

"This is Mr Rennell's masterpiece," he said proudly, smoothing out the sheet. "A map maker who knows India the way the eagles do. The rest of us are only worms on the ground."

He placed his finger on the thick black line.

"Look, this is the Ganga rising to Benares," he said. "And this here is our Hooghly, which as you know is really just another branch of the great river. And this," he planted his finger on top of the ginger root, "is the Sunderbans, as jungly a place as anyone could wish for. Hari is from that region and I had my own adventure there last year. I tell you, Anila, we would surely come upon the giant bird from the Persian tales and more like it if we were to travel downriver to the Sunderbans. But unfortunately the place is full of tigers and crocodiles and we'd need a shooting party. So, we're going up the Hooghly instead and we'll see what rare creatures may be waiting for us along the riverbanks. If any."

"Is Carlen good at finding birds? Did he shoot the birds that you have at the courthouse?"

I thought of Carlen sitting on top, as easy-limbed as a monkey in a tree, his blue eyes sure to be fixing on everything we passed, no matter how the coach swayed and rattled. Now that we had begun to leave the good city streets behind our way was full of holes and wheel ruts. We could hear poor Hari groaning from time to time as a wheel dropped down into one and bumped out again.

Mr Walker laughed.

"You're set on guns today, Anila. No, Carlen is a countryman all right but he has no proper feeling for any beast other than a horse. My birds... well, let's just say I acquired them before I knew better. People knew I was looking for this one and that one, and there'd be a knock at my door one day, a hand stretched out to relieve me of considerable quantities of annas, and another poor bird taken out of life's reckoning. I learned to keep my mouth shut."

The buildings we were passing now were ever more rickety and when we brushed against their thatched roofs they felt like rags. On the streets people were rushing, pushing and pulling things, and shouting. Our house on the lane could not be far distant, I thought, but I could not figure where it lay. Then at last we were following the river over quiet soil where tal trees and feathery bamboos ran alongside us.

We drew up alongside some bamboo houses grouped in a huddle and set back from the water. The houses actually looked like boats, at least like some of the boats tied up at the riverbank. These were lean as knives with messy thatch dropping down over them like wigs on Englishmen. One was different.

"It's not hard to guess which one is your boat," I said to Mr Walker. He laughed.

"We should be comfortable on her because she's made for these waters," he said. "She's like a very small budgerow. And we can take sail or scull, depending on conditions."

Small? The boat was almost as long as our salon in Garden Reach, though of course it was not so wide. It seemed to have an entire room sitting on its deck, the walls made of glass windows on all sides, all topped with a flat roof of dark wood. There was a green paint trim all round the boat and it had a name written on its side in gold, an English name, I thought. *Hera*.

Men and boys came running from the houses when our carriage rattled to a stop. They swarmed over the carriage, clambering over each other to reach the bags and things on top. The horses shifted sideways with fright and whickered as we rocked. Carlen stopped the climbers with a roar, his hands raised against them.

"Stay down and catch what I throw," he shouted at them in English.

Mr Walker and I stepped down from the carriage with our own precious bags. I lifted the painting case carefully from the floor and gripped it tight. I shook my head at the boys who came towards us, their hands out to seize whatever they could. Behind them I saw the smallest boy of all running for the boat with my canvas bag on his head as if it had no weight.

A dark man dressed only in a long dhoti came from the biggest of the bamboo houses and walked towards us. He wore no head wrap, and had no hair at all on his head, but lots on his face, thick eyebrows and a pair of curled moustaches that he obviously took good care of. His scalp gleamed like a well-oiled egg. He was taller than Mr Walker, taller than Carlen, and he stood in front of us as strong and steady as a tree coming out of the earth. I had never seen anybody like him.

Then he smiled.

"Sahib, I am Madan, your boatman. Your man, the other sahib there, he came some days ago and said make ready everything and I do. We can leave now, whenever you like."

Mr Walker took a linen cloth from his trousers pocket and wiped his brow. Already his hair was beginning to escape from its pigtail in its usual way but this didn't seem to bother him. He spoke in Bangla.

"Excellent, Madan. Your companions are myself, my drawing assistant here, Miss Anila Tandy, my manservant, Carlen, whom you've met already, and my bearer, Hari. We are a very small company as you see. And how many do you bring on board yourself?"

"Just my son, sahib," said Madan. He pointed at one of the taller boys on board the boat but his back was to us. "Benu is a good boatman too, and very quiet. Your sahib said you did not want many men so that you may see all the birds you want, in peace."

He looked at me then and clapped his hands to his moustaches.

"You have dressed for the river," he said. "I have not seen this before." He pointed at my twill trousers and laughed with delight. It did me good to hear him.

Miss Hickey had been unhappy when I began to wear my own designs. She loved my saris, she said, they were so much more elegant than any English dress. But Mr Hickey said my trousers were an old tradition and that I should be let wear them. He showed us a painting he had bought on one of his trips to the south. A handsome prince was sitting in his garden with a group of ladies. His favourite, for she was in the centre, was dressed in a soldier's jacket and a pair of pink sprigged muslin breeches that came only as far as her knees. I thought she looked as bold and brave as her master.

What I had learned, and Miss Hickey had too, was that nobody expected me to do things properly, the way English ladies did. That was fine by me. That was how I was here today on the river.

Mr Walker ushered me ahead of him towards the little plank that led onto the boat. We had to dip our heads to enter the salon, where there were seats all around. At the back there were small cupboards of polished wood built into the walls of the boat. Madan said we should stow our personal goods in them.

"If the sun gets too strong you can close these," he said. He pulled a cord and the slats of the wooden Venetians came together, just as they would in a house. For more shade there were tied-back drapes made of red canvas.

"Red like the sails. Look, Anila," Mr Walker said. "They're raising sail now. We're away!"

BY THE CREEK

MY MOTHER NEVER CAUGHT *fish down by the river. She caught men instead. Or they caught her. I wasn't there of course when she and my father met, when she was just a young girl living with her own father in the village by the river. But I was there the day Mr Bristol paddled into our lives.*

There was huge excitement when the boys first saw the long flat boat coming upstream from the main river. Only small punts ever came up our creek, and they usually stayed much further down, near where the waters met, where the men could net shrimps and other small grey fish. The boys rushed up to warn our group – the women who were washing clothes and bathing and the girls who were ducking themselves under my mother's careful watch.

My mother was standing up to her waist in the middle of the creek and she waited there like that until every child was safely out on the bank. Then she bent down into the water to swim over to the washing rocks. She had no veil or scarf and her hair stretched out behind her like silky black waterweeds.

There were two English men sitting on little chairs on the flat boat, with two boatmen, front and back, who were working their way through the water and mud with tall poles. The men were wearing broad hats because of the heat, but their jackets were dark and they sat in the full sun.

One of them called on the boatmen to stop. Everybody was out of the water on the bank now, my mother too, and they were walking quickly away from the creek over the lumpy ground. Only Dinesh and I remained, sitting on the bank with our feet dabbling in the water. I was too hot to want to leave the creek for the lane and I knew these men would soon pass on. My mother had not yet noticed that I had stayed but there was little she could do anyway when she did miss me except send one of the small boys to get me.

"Can you speak English?" the man called out to us. I could not see his face properly under the hat but he was tall and stout and his voice was pleasant. It was very different from my father's voice but I could understand him well enough.

"Yes!" I shouted back. I was proud to be able to say this because I knew Dinesh had no English at all.

"Who is the lady who was swimming out here where our boat is now?" the man asked. His friend made a noise that could have been a cough or a laugh.

"My mother," I said proudly.

"I thought she might be," he said. "And what are your names?"

I told him my name, my mother's name and then Dinesh's too, just to have Dinesh give a little jump of surprise beside me. I gave him a dig with my elbow.

There were more questions, all from the same man.

"And how might I find you if I came down your lane? Where would I take a turn from the high road?"

I thought about this for a while. I was trying to figure out which was the best way to pick our lane out from all the other lanes that also led off the road. But he must have thought that

I preferred to keep this information to myself because he told the boatman to take the boat in closer and then he spoke to me again. He had remembered my name.

"Anila, I am writing stories about Calcutta and the people who live in the lanes and the bazaars. But it's hard for me because so few people speak English. Your mother does too, am I right?"

I nodded. But I wondered what kind of stories he was talking about. We could tell him much better stories, I thought, stories of princesses and demons, magic birds and trees that talked. He could write the best tales down in his notebook, I thought, as my father had written them in mine.

"My publisher has given me a big bag of money to help me find and collect these stories. I would pay you and your mother for your help."

Well, that was the best news I could hear. Life had been very hard lately even with my mother back in good health. We had eaten nothing but rice for weeks, and of that only the dirtiest of husks, and no salt with it either. One day there had only been the cold rice water that on our lane was normally given to animals.

I asked Dinesh what direction I could offer and he said that our lane was the one just after the ruined temple. If you were journeying towards the city, not away from it.

The man heard me and gave a little bow from his chair. Then he gave another order and the boat moved off, up the creek, just as it had been travelling before. Dinesh and I waited until it was out of sight and then we slipped back into the water.

But I discovered that I could not relax there. It felt warm now, not cool and I wanted to get home and present my good news, news that seemed almost a food in itself. Dinesh was *pestering me to tell him what the stout man had said but I had no wish to do that. My mother should know first. She could decide what stories were best to tell and how we might prepare our little room for the Englishman's visit.*

I left Dinesh and ran back to our house, dripping water like a piece of washing that had grown legs. I spattered the tailor's red hens as I passed them on the lane and they squawked with rage to meet this sudden shower from nowhere.

"Mago!" I shouted when I got inside our door. "We're going to have a big bag of money soon!"

She shushed me and took off my wet sari, wrapping me in one of her own, scolding me for staying behind. Then she sat me on our bed and heard my story. I watched her face for signs of pleasure but there were none. Yet I knew that the hunger I felt now in my belly was in hers too.

At night when we were preparing our dirty rice, picking out the stones and grit and worse from it, we talked about food and what we would buy if we found a coin on the road. My mother named all the kinds of fish she knew, even ones I had never heard of. We would eat these with handfuls of sweet sticky rice mixed with seeds and spices. We would have dishes of hot dal and little purple brinjals with enough chillis to make tears come to our eyes. Then I listed all the sweetmeats we would have afterwards when our hunger pains were banished. Soft creamy balls of naru, dusted with sugar and seeds, fresh from the maira, the friendly sweet seller, who walked the high road calling out the names of all the delicious things he carried on his tray. But we would also have sweet bananas fried in oil and sugar. Melon cubes in syrup stuck together like jewels. Mangoes.

Sometimes tears came to my mother's eyes when we talked like this.

"I'm called Annapurna after the great food provider but look, this is all I can offer you," she'd say in a whisper. Then our brave little game would end and a hungry tide would wash over us again.

Now she had a very different look.

"And you told him where we lived?" she asked.

Her eyes looked as unbelieving as if I had told her that I had killed a buffalo calf.

"But we are so hungry, Ma," I said. "If he gives us the money what harm can that do?"

She turned away from me and went out the door. I could hear her feet on the steps outside and then their light tread on the roof as she paced. I could not understand why she had taken no joy from my news. If I were her, I thought, I would be up there with a smile on my face, waiting for the stout man in the black jacket to appear at the top of the lane. I would have swept the floor and put blossom in the water jug. I would have my best sari on, and my hair washed and oiled and my head full of stories. And I would have my best golden girl dressed up too, waiting beside me, waiting for the bag of money so that we could eat as never before.

CARLEN

I SOON FOUND THAT a boat was like a church. Everyone had a proper place to be and woe to anyone who strayed out of that place. Then Madan would roar, no matter who was at fault, even if it was Mr Walker doing a turn to help Carlen up front, hauling on the ropes with his long thin arms.

Benu, the shy boy, was in charge of the tiller, the wooden handle that steered the boat from the back. He kept out of trouble, mostly, with his eyes fixed ahead. He never looked at me, that first day. But sometimes he was not speedy enough when the big boats came down the middle of the river heading straight for us. When that happened his father became like Ravana calling on his demons.

"RIGHHHHTTT side, Bigbelly!" he shouted. "Do you want us to be sliced down the middle like a hairy fruit?"

Hari knew what to do on a boat and he moved around neatly, putting his feet down as if there were marks on the boards telling him just so. That was a science that took me a while to learn, especially when the big boats passing made us rock in the water. With no fuss Hari put away our bags and unpacked what was needed, setting out a water flask and cups.

I took my notebook and pencils out of my case and sat down on an upturned barrel away from the ropes and canvas. The seats inside would be more comfortable but I preferred to be out here with nothing except air between me and any birds we might see.

There were plenty, already, most of them on the banks, or else in the bays of shallow water the river had shaped out of its own sides. Ducks were fussing and crowding each other into the reeds and lily pads to get away from us. But the long-beaked egrets stood firm and watched for frogs in the mud and water. One was close enough to the smooth water to make a perfect twin of himself. He stayed still, even when the ripples from our boat broke up his watery self into a white shudder.

Buffaloes called out to each other from the water meadows. Sometimes we saw them, swishing their tails, but not when the green bank sides grew tall with growth. Kingfishers flashed past us over the dark water and disappeared.

Kingfishers are the blue arrows from Lord Krishna's bow, my little one. He shoots them up and down the river to make us wonder.

My pencil was moving quite as fast as a kingfisher, I thought. But still I saw the shadow fall on my page.

Carlen.

I smiled at him but was uncertain if I should. We had not spoken and he seemed aloof, or perhaps he was wrapped up in his own fair perfection.

"What are these words?" he asked. "I can't read them."

He crouched down, so close that his leg pressed on mine. No accident, for it followed me when I shifted. Above the roaring in my ears I heard him call out a couple of the words I'd pencilled in alongside my sketches – belly white, conch pink, mango green. But they sounded like nonsense when he said them. My words were Bangla words but my code was to write them down using English letters. For me it was a way of honouring my mother. She couldn't read or write any language yet she always found the way of telling you the precise colour of anything – birds or saris, jewels or fruits. She even had words for the different shades of rain.

Now Carlen stood, but he leaned over my book still, trying to turn the page back, to see if he could find anything else. I pulled it away from his hand and held it closed against my chest, furious. Why was this man suddenly treating me with such rudeness? I took a long breath.

"They're Bangla words," I said to him. "They're for colours so I'll remember them later when I paint."

"But you don't want anyone else to know your secrets, is that it? Or can you not write in proper English?"

When he stopped talking his mouth stayed open like a cat that sees a bird. I could see the points of his neat white teeth.

I looked around, quickly. Mr Walker was doing his best up front with the ropes and Madan. I could see Hari through the glass, sitting cross-legged on the floor of the cabin. He seemed to be praying. Benu's red head wrap was pointed in our direction but that was all I saw of him.

"I can speak your language as well as you can," I said to him. "Can you speak mine?"

He laughed.

"Jabber's no language, whatever foolishness the master has swallowed down with his whisky."

He reached forward then and, before I could twist away from him, he thrust his hand under my poor paper shield and squeezed my right breast through the thin cotton tunic. As if it were a fruit in a bag. As if it were his to handle. I managed to scratch the back of his hand before he took it away. But he laughed and held his hand to his mouth, licking the cut as if his own blood were a food.

"How old are you, anyway? Fourteen by the feel, I'd say. Nigh on fifteen. Or maybe you rice-eaters never grow anything better than that. Tell me, is that so, my black kitten?"

He laughed and made paws of his hands, pushing them at my face.

All the air had left my lungs. I couldn't speak.

"And that's no dress at all. I've known Indian dark-women, more than a few, I can tell you, and they'd not dream of getting themselves up in kit like that. What class of a creature are you, anyway? Down my way we'd call you a hinny."

He moved away then, abruptly, going forward so swiftly that I knew even before I looked up that someone was coming. My body blazed like a dirty torch as Mr Walker came towards me. "Dirty", like the word hinny, whatever it meant, lodged now in my brain.

"Anila, come forward with me and talk to Madan. I think he may have some news for you."

He picked up my notebook and read out the same words that Carlen had chosen. But he said them beautifully in his deep rich voice.

"Belly white, Anila? Is that English belly white, as in our pale skins?"

He laughed but I knew he was mocking himself, not me. I could not even force a laugh myself, but I felt my blood flowing again and the jags in my stomach grew less painful.

"It's the white a buffalo can be underneath,"

I could hear the dullness in my own voice. I tried to cover with a cough and said more than I needed to.

"That makes it not really white at all but a creamy grey with brown mixed in."

Mr Walker's eyebrows shot up. Should I tell him what had happened? I doubted I could find the words. Not in Bangla, not in English.

"Ah," was all he said.

Madan looked up as we came forward into his little domain of ropes and canvas. Carlen was there too, hands busy, but his eyes were all for the passing crafts on the river. I kept him severely out of my glance.

"Sahib tells me your mother grew up on the river," Madan said. "Where was that?"

I told him the name of the village. He threw his rope across to Carlen and came to my side.

"We pass there tomorrow," he said. "She really grew up by the river?"

What else would come to trouble my poor stomach

this day? I clutched it to ease the sudden shock and stared down into the water. Tomorrow I would be passing my grandfather's village. Yet I didn't know whether he was alive or dead.

When I looked at him Madan had a strange expression.

"Yes, her father was a boatman," I told him. "She lived there until she was fourteen. There were just the two of them and she helped him with the work like a son."

Now he was staring at me like a person does who has met you once a long time ago and is trying to remember your name.

"Was your mother's name Annapurna, whose father was Arjun?" he asked, at last.

My legs and hands were shaking and I was glad to sit down, on a cask. I laid my notebook down on the deck but when I saw there was water puddling near it I picked it up again. My throat had closed itself off so I could hardly whisper back to him.

"Yes."

Madan beamed, obviously satisfied with his good memory.

"I know Arjun," he said. "But I never knew that he had a granddaughter. We knew Annapurna had married an Englishman. Many young men wept tears into the river that year, I can tell you. So, that's the way, is it? Well, Arjun is a good man, a very good man."

There was a roar from the back of the boat, from Benu. Quickly Madan pushed Carlen to one side and dragged hard on one of the short ropes he held loose. The sail tilted sharp towards the centre, as we skimmed along just inches away from the branch of an old willow that had fallen over and stretched itself far out over the river. Another flat boat was coming down the river and the men on board laughed rudely at us for our near escape.

Madan turned his broad back to them. He looked at Carlen.

"You are no boatman," he said quietly, and this was worse, somehow, than his roar. Carlen's skin flushed red, even his hands, I noticed. I wished he was gone. Back to the city, back to England, anywhere but on our boat. I did not want this man to hear another word about my mother. That was what had taken his attention from the ropes, I was sure of it.

"Carlen, the afternoon is well advanced. I think we shall eat soon," Mr Walker said. "Will you take care of things in the cabin?"

He looked anxious, I thought, for all that he was the master here. When Carlen moved away inside, he spread his hands and sighed.

"Carlen's genius is to be a jack-of-all-trades," he said in a low voice. "Perhaps he will learn a little more mastery from today's lesson."

Madan shrugged. He turned to me again.

"Does Arjun know you are passing by?"

I shook my head.

"I have never met him."

I could feel tears, hot in my eyes. And I could see through them that Mr Walker was making signs at Madan not to question me further. I knew then he would tell him my story when he got a chance, so that Madan might understand why tomorrow we would sail past my grandfather's village and not call on him. Would he tell him also that my parents were not married, as he believed? It mattered little. In our society when an Indian girl leaves with a white man her family might be happy at her fortune, but they also understand she cannot ever come back again to be with them. Madan must surely have guessed this already, just by looking at my skin.

But it was all so close. I had not dreamed it would be so close, or that I would ever hear news of my grandfather in this way. For all that his dhotis had kept me warm when I was little, I had not felt his protection in my life since then. Now that he was there, somewhere upriver along the peaceful banks, surely there was some way that I could see him for myself, discover all that my mother came from?

THE HOUSE WITH
THE FOUNTAIN

WHEN WE MOVED INTO Mr Bristol's house it was clear
from the beginning that he was an honest man. That is, of
course, if you leave out the matter of the story collection he had
mentioned. Though he did indeed write things down, he was
not really gathering tales from anybody, we had discovered.
Which was perhaps just as well, as my mother was in no
mood to tell any at that time. But there really was a bag of
money. It was all his own, or so it seemed, and it was in the
matter of this money that he showed his honesty.

He asked if my mother could read a document and when
she said no, she could not, but that I could, he gave me the
page that he had written.

"Read it and then you can explain it to your mother," he
said.

It was difficult because there were many words I did not
understand but he pronounced them for me and told me their
meanings when I asked. I knew that it was useful for me to
learn to read such long words. My English had become much
weaker since my father had gone away.

Mr Bristol told us that the document was a contract of service. He said that he was known in London as a man of the

law who believed in justice and fair play.

"I am against all slavery," he said. "Some people consider these kinds of arrangements to be a form of slavery. I wish to make it clear that your mother is to be a paid intimate who will receive a small salary that will accrue to her, as well as food and benefits in kind, as long as this household shall last. That she may leave my household at any time and, should that be her choice, she will then receive those monies that have accumulated to her. That you, her dependant, will also receive food and benefits in kind as long as this household shall last. That any child born of this union will be acknowledged as my full dependant to be educated and provided for until its coming of age even in the event of your mother choosing to depart my household."

And there was more. Mr Bristol asked me to sign my mother's name to the document.

"But only if she agrees to everything itemized in it," he said.

Back in our little house in the lane my mother had told me what her dealings with Mr Bristol would be when we moved into his house on Old Court House Street.

"He wants me to be his bibi," she said. "But I do not love him and he knows that. He does not love me but he finds me beautiful. I shall have to sleep with him when he wants me to. That means there might be a child. But I think he is kind enough in his way. He thinks you are a clever girl. As clever as any English child he knows, he says."

But still she hung her head when I told her what was in the document.

The house in Old Court House Street had two storeys and a flat roof but apart from the roof it was not like our old house in any way. A tall brick wall ran in front of it, cutting the house and its garden off from the street. You went in and out through green gates that were opened and closed by a durwan, a paid gatekeeper.

The garden was planted with a pomegranate tree and soft springy grass. A straight pebble path led from the gates to the front door. Halfway along the path a large stone bowl sat on the ground with water in it. It was like a tiny tank. Two white fish creatures, also made of stone, reared up in the middle of the bowl. They blew water out of their mouths up into the air where it hung in a fine thread and then fell back into the bowl.

"They're dolphins," Mr Bristol told me when I asked him what they were. "The king of France had such dolphins at the palace of Versailles, I'm told."

My mother told me later that the stone creatures looked nothing like the dolphins she used to see leaping in the river when she was young.

Mr Bristol warned me not to drink the fountain water, that it was not safe. But all the songbirds in the garden came to the bowl to drink and some of them took baths in it, fluffing up their feathers and dipping their faces in the water.

The street beyond the wall was so wide that our lane would have fitted into it about five times over. But I could no longer run outside as I used to on the lane, nor were my mother and I permitted to take a walk together on our own. If I climbed the pomegranate tree I could see the carriages and palanquins hurrying by in the mornings and evenings, and the people parading all day long, but my mother begged me not to do this.

"Mr Bristol will be angry if he sees you up there," she said. "Please, for my sake, Anila, don't be so fidgety, stay still and be quiet."

She used the word ushkush for fidgety, a word that always

used to make her laugh when she heard other mothers use it. It was such a funny word, she said, and yet they always sounded so cross when they said it. But she was not laughing now.

So, the only outside life that I saw after that was the top halves of elephants, and those only if they happened to be passing on our side of the street. I could see their eyes, if they were tall elephants, and their painted foreheads and bright cotton headdresses. The mahouts and the people riding tall in the howdahs behind them could see down into our garden and into all the others on Old Court House Street. I envied them their view. The durwan always shouted or shook a stick at me if I went near his gates.

My mother and I shared a room most of the time, a room on the second storey at the back of the house. Underneath our window, alongside the cookhouse, was a long house where the women servants slept. At least we had not been put there. Sometimes my mother went downstairs to talk to the old ayah, Rupa, but Rupa was a shy woman. She was also loyal to her master.

Mr Bristol's room was upstairs at the front of the house, and he liked to stand in his window looking out at what was happening in the street outside. From the garden I could see his plump figure framed there. Sometimes he waved to me.

All the windows of the house had shutters and so, even though the windows were tall, some with real glass in them, we could make our room dark and cool in an instant by pulling our shutters closed. When my mother wasn't there, I liked to play with the shutters, opening and closing them as if they were the gates to an enchanted palace and I the durwan with the key.

We had a wide comfortable bed with linen sheets, and a pillow for each of us, a chest for our clothes and a long mirror *that you could tilt up and down. My mother had brought her Durga and the little altar with us and she talked to the goddess even more than before, if that was possible. But there were not so many other mementos remaining from the house on the lane. I had cried when my mother refused to bring the bird quilt with us.*

"That is all in the past now," she said. "We have everything we need here to make us comfortable. Besides as long as Hemavati has it, she will always remember us."

I knew then that the quilt now reminded her of my father rather than her own father.

Our clothes were new, and, my mother's especially, very beautiful, far lovelier than anything we had ever owned. Mr Bristol ordered saris, scarves and shawls from the big bazaar for her, and a dressmaker came to fit us both for sets of stitched clothes. Silks and brocades and fine Dacca muslins for my mother, cottons and one good silk for me. But we would soon be the same size, the dressmaker told us, and then could double up our clothes and be twice as rich.

She was a tiny person with grey stripes in her hair and a laugh like a magpie. She was not from Calcutta at all, she told us, nor even Bengal, but from the holy city of Kashi, that the English called Benares, far up on the Ganga. Mr Bristol said she was in great demand among the highest society English ladies in the city for making their dresses and costumes.

"In London, she would have her own shop on Bond Street, and dozens of seamstresses working for her," he said. "Imagine."

My mother admired her fine stitching and liked to run her fingers up the seams of our brand-new tunics and blouses, marvelling at the smoothness.

"If you could only learn this trade, Anila," she said to me, "you need never have a life like mine."

My mother dreamed of such things for me though I think she knew I would have been like a caged monkey with such work. She had no further dreams for herself, that was clear. Nor stories either. I was the one now who told our old stories over and over, trying to make her smile.

She attended Mr Bristol as he wished, and not always merely to his bedroom. When he had gentlemen callers to the house, persons from the law courts and the Company, or friends from the hunt, he liked her to be in the room too. She might chop their cigars with a knife, or keep their hookahs, their hubble-bubbles as they called them, watered for smoking. She cut up their tobacco, handed round their drinks, and even offered paan to those who had learned to like the taste. If they took their drinks into Mr Bristol's billiards room, she had to go in there too and pick the coloured balls out of the table nets for them and set them back on its green top.

"That Mr Percy said it's because my hands are smaller than the male servants' hands and not so greasy," she told me. "He dares say that, whose hands are the filthiest in the city!"

Mr Bristol was kind in his fashion, and respectful to my mother at all times during these occasions, she said. But several of his friends were anything but.

"They are disgusting people," she said. "They use foul language. They spend a fortune on pomade for their hair but they do not even leave the room to take their toilet. I tell you, they have a great bowl in a corner of the room where they relieve themselves. And this in front of a woman, even if I am only a bibi!"

She was supposed to sprinkle rosewater to take away the smells.

After the first few occasions like that my mother would have weeping fits for days. Later, and this was worse, she would laugh as she told the story over and over, laugh until she was taken over by hiccups and had to gulp for breath. I hated that. She sounded like Hemavati.

The strange thing was that I knew Hemavati would think our present life was wonderful. That if I could slip away to the lane for an afternoon and tell her about the silken saris, about our airy room, and the garden with the fountain, about all the foods we ate now that were putting flesh back on our bones and gloss in our hair, that Hemavati's eyes would grow huge with wonder, or envy, or both, and that she would not laugh at all.

Of course there was no question of doing that. All I could do to amuse myself was read. Most of the books in Mr Bristol's glass-covered bookshelf were dull law books, bound in leather, which I hated to touch. But there were some cloth-bound books too, mainly travellers' tales, which interested Mr Bristol most, he told me. Of course that reminded me of the lie he had told me by the river but I said nothing. My favourite of these was by a man whose ship had left him in countries ruled by giants, and madmen, and horses who could talk wisely. Mr Bristol told me that the story was all make-believe, that there were no such countries as these and that as far as he was concerned India was the strangest country he had ever travelled in.

I must have looked cross to hear this for I wanted to believe all stories were true. He told me then that I made a face like a thunderclap and I should banish it smartly, for he liked to see sunny faces in his house.

CAMPING

"THIS BIRD WILL TAKE the fish from my hands, clever one!"

Madan was admiring my new drawings. In his hands my large notebook shrank to storybook size but I noticed that he turned the pages over as carefully as a scribe. He paused over a heron that I had taken some time with.

"See how patient he is, this fisher bird. His legs will hold him there till Hanuman throws a bridge across the Ganga."

Yes, I believed I had captured the heron's secret, as my mother would say, for all the while I was staring at the grey bird it could not see me, nor indeed any of us, as we set about our separate tasks. Benu had steered our boat into a tent of green coolness under a willow tree.

While I drew, Madan and Benu landed fish from the end of the boat, Carlen fried them and Hari laid out scoops of delicious rice for each of us. Mr Walker insisted on his tea then, but the rest of us drank water that Hari had drawn from a tank in a field behind us. Carlen tipped his clay cup back as if he were enjoying the drink, but he said nothing to anyone and stared off into the big sky across the river.

Behind our tree the land stretched away in faded colours, yellow for old mustard, grey where a few empty paddy fields were still flooded and sad without their rice, brown where the fields had had their winter cuttings. There were little islands of trees here and there where the hamlets were and people moved between them like flies on a rope.

"Madan, I will show you another drawing."

I stepped into the empty cabin and went to the cupboard where my leather case was stored. In among the bird paintings that I had brought along to show Mr Walker that first day was another loose-leaf drawing on thick cream paper. I kept it between boards for safety, wrapped in oilcloth. It was not my drawing.

That is, it was not by my hand. But it belonged to me.

Madan looked at the drawing for a long time. Then he smiled and gave it back to me.

"I don't need this to see that you are very like Annapurna," he said. "She travelled on this boat once too, with Arjun, when she was just a little one. And I will tell you something. She did not have the fine clothes of that picture but nor did she have these things!"

He pointed to my trousers again and laughed so that his belly shook. But I felt a glow inside me. Madan was pleased with me, I knew; the same way that I was pleased with the kingfishers I saw that morning flashing blue fire; the same way I liked his own great size and his twisted moustaches.

"May I see it, Anila?"

Mr Walker stood up and threw the dregs of his tea over the side of the boat before reaching for the portrait of my mother.

"She is very beautiful," he said, after a long look. "I can see why you want to keep it by you. I have nothing like this to remember my sister by, alas, for my father was a strict churchman who thought portraiture was the devil's own sorcery."

His face was set hard as he said this. I passed him the heron sketch then, in case it might cheer him. Though of course a heron was not a new bird to any of us.

"You could bring this to the Royal Society in London, Anila," he said when he had finished his scrutiny, "and they would find it fit to hang it on their walls. I'm very pleased with you."

He held the page up so that Benu and Hari could see it. Hari nodded his head gravely.

"I remember what you tell us, sahib," he said. "We must all be looking for the great birds for Miss Anila tomorrow and every day we are on the river."

Benu was looking at my heron as if a star had fallen out of the sky onto the page. I reached for a piece of drawing paper from my case, sketched a quick copy for him, signed it, and put it into his hands, along with the black crayon. He blushed but folded the margins of the page to make a frame round the bird and kept it in the flat of his hand, looking at it.

I returned my two precious drawings to the cabin and when I came out on deck again, though it was only a few moments, the sun had dipped down below the far side of the river and Mr Walker was making arrangement for our sleeping quarters.

"Anila, you shall choose. Would you care for a fine soldier's tent all to yourself? I should be nearby in a similar one and the men would stay together on board. Or you might prefer to take the salon to yourself, pull the blinds down and construct your own apartment. In that case Carlen will take the tent and the others will stretch out on the deck. It is a fine arrangement either way, this beautiful night."

"Oh, I choose the tent!"

"I thought you might. Well, it's no elegant affair, take my word. But we'll steal some of the cushions from the cabin while Madan looks the other way."

Madan pretended to look fearsome but it was Carlen whose face was the study as he and Hari wrestled the lengths of canvas and poles off the boat and across to a flat mound that Mr Walker declared was dry as a biscuit.

I hadn't thought when I spoke but I realized that Carlen now had another reason to vent spite on me, whatever his first cause might be. His face told me that he had wanted the favour of being set apart from everyone else, there with Mr Walker on that little mound.

When he had finished his work with the poles and the ropes my little tent was standing up with a sharp gable on it. I thanked him though the words stuck in my throat and I hoped his scratched hand was hurting him. But he said nothing, just walked away back to the boat, his fair hair catching the light the stars threw down. There was no moonlight, only the black moon with a tiny moonbaby in her arms, ready for sleep herself.

I stepped into the tent and pulled the flaps across. Inside it was dark, though gradually I could make out a glow cast by the remains of our cooking fire. It was not tall enough for me to stand up but it felt safe and dry and cosy. Like something an animal would make if it had hands, I thought, a clever bear or a lion.

I spread the cushions and arranged the rugs that Carlen had thrown into a corner. It was quite cool now, cooler than it had been any of the nights I had spent in my little iron house. I supposed that the city, with all its palaces and houses and people, drew lots of heat away from the sun and kept it for later, like gold in a bank. Here we had just the river and the flat fields stretching away for ever. No wonder then that every night the sun would roll itself away underneath, as fast as a billiard ball.

"Are you warm enough, Anila? Have you enough of the rugs from the boat? The city is a warmer place you know. It's the same the world over."

Mr Walker must have been reading my mind. I heard him clear his throat outside the tent and then he beat on the canvas softly. I untied the ropes that bound my tent closed and there he was, hunkered down to speak with me. He looked anxious.

"I'm very fine, truly. I have my shawl too. Only one thing would be better and that would be for Anoush to be here with us."

"Ah," he said. "Well, that would be splendid indeed. But now, you must have no fears about wolves or tigers or such. There is none of them here. And any jackals that you might expect to find, well they'll get an unfriendly welcome if they dare stick a snout too close."

He patted his belt and I saw he had a pistol. This time even I, who could not tell a firearm from an optical instrument, was certain of that.

"Good night, Anila."

He started up but I called him back.

"Mr Walker. What Madan said about my grandfather and the village. I know we are travelling upriver as fast as we can. But do you think that on our way back, perhaps..."

I stopped. For what could be done?

"Of course, Anila. As for what may be the best plan when that time comes, let us leave it to Madan to be the judge. I have more confidence in him after a day's travel than I have in many of my more tested acquaintances. I wish you a fine sleep now, and no fears."

Perhaps I might have thought more about those jackals, or about which charms we might use to flush out a bird with no name for Mr Walker's sister, or indeed how I might teach Carlen civil manners or else avoid him. But after I lay down on the soft cushions and began to hear some of the familiar rushes and dashes of small water creatures close by, I forgot it all.

THE PALANQUIN

WE HAD BEEN ALMOST a whole season – winter – in Mr Bristol's house when our life began to change again. This time, it was no event, no sudden decision, that overturned everything. It was simply feelings that boiled up and over like water in a pot. They began with me and my worries.

"Ma, if my father comes back as he promised, how will he find us here? Please, can we go back to the lane and tell Hemavati and Malati about this house so that he will know where we are?"

I had been asking my mother the same thing, over and over, for weeks, though I was smart enough to say it in different ways at different times.

I was becoming a pest. But truly I felt that we had been dropped into a hole and been covered over so that my father would never find us. He had only stepped out of our lives, I thought, and one day, whenever he could, he would step back in again. All that was required was that he know where to come.

At first my mother would say very little in reply, except sensible things. She said, "Your father told us his ship spent more than half a year coming from England to Calcutta. It's not much longer than that since he left, is it? He will still be on the ship."

"But they can send letters, Ma, from wherever they stop. He probably has sent us one already, from Africa."

My mother had no place in her heart for letters from Africa or Spain or Ireland or any of the places my father had told us about. She closed her face like a shutter and she shushed me, saying she was tired. Or another time she might say that she was doing her best for both of us and that it was for my sake that she had chosen to come here and live with Mr Bristol.

I knew this was true. But I would come back again the next day with another argument.

Finally she told me that Mr Bristol believed my father was dead. Long since dead, she had told him. So I should watch my tongue in this house and remember which paddy field my rice came from.

I was shocked. She wanted to forget him, I knew that. But I wouldn't. I couldn't. On the lane I could have lived without conjuring him because he was part of that place. His feet had walked down our lane, across our earth floor, across our roof. His hands had touched everything we had and he had breathed our air. But not here, not in this shuttered house and locked garden, this place of half-elephants. Here he was not even a ghost.

Perhaps it was because I was pestering her that my mother in her turn became more of a trouble to Mr Bristol. Some nights she would plead to him that she was ill and not able to go to his room. She told him that making paan was not good for her skin. She confessed to him that some of his friends had said unpleasant things to her. He promised that they would not come to the house again.

What changed our lives most of all was that one day she asked him if we might have the use of his beautiful midnight-blue palanquin when he was not taking a ride in it himself.

"My dear Anna, why of course," he said. "I would be glad to see you out and about and have the roses back in your cheeks again."

We travelled out then on many an afternoon, the two of us, with four sturdy palki bearers to carry us wherever we wished, though we understood that on Mr Bristol's orders our journeys had to lie in the English part of the city.

"Let's go past the Writers' Building first," I would say, and my mother did not mind. We had never been there in my father's company so it was not a poisoned place for her, as the shipping ghats were.

The Building was quite close to Old Court House Street, where Mr Bristol's house was, and it faced Tank Square and its orange trees. It ran the length of the square and with its brooding size and its stout pillars it looked as strong as Fort William itself. Except, of course, it had more entrances than a pigeon-house. My father had once drawn me a picture of the Writers' Building so that I could see where he worked. He told me that the door he had left open in his drawing was the door he went through every morning to reach his working chamber. It was in front of that particular door that I liked the bearers to stop, so that I might see the young men, the Writers, go in and come out. Some of them must know my father, I thought. Perhaps they could be told our new address? But my mother refused to let me step outside the palanquin.

"I promised him that we would not do anything notice-able," she said. "The bearers would tell him if you do that."

For her part, she loved to visit the Esplanade area and look down at the great stretch of the maidan.

"It's so airy, Anila. I can breathe here. Look at the kites soaring!"

She told the bearers to put the palanquin down so that they

could rest, and then we would pull the curtains fully back, to watch the horsemen and the carriages go by, or the neat rows of soldiers marching past on their way to the Fort.

"They're like ants," I said, and she laughed.

In Tank Square there were sometimes elephants in the water with their mahouts. I loved to watch them play, blowing water at each other or showering themselves, turning from dusty brown to a full glossy black-grey. At Holi time, which was when we first ventured out, the elephants were bright with pink and red and yellow splashes, the colours rubbed into their thick skin by their mahouts. They were the only creatures in the English part of the city who knew how to enjoy Holi and its carnival games.

When the durwan opened his green gates to allow us back in after our trips, we would wait to be put down and then stumble out of the dusty palki and come inside the house to wash and change our clothes. Often our legs were unsteady and inclined to wobble after lying straight out for hours and this made us giggle. We were full of tales for Mr Bristol. My mother had begun to recover her gift for telling a story and she knew the kind of details he enjoyed.

"We saw a fine sofa running into the house down the road with the feather palms in front," she told him.

I liked her notion of the sofa running. It had made us laugh so much to see the great yellow thing moving on four human legs, the men's heads hidden underneath the frame. But though Mr Bristol didn't quite see the fun, he saw other things.

"That's Jellicoe the surveyor's house," he said. "Come from China, that sofa, I'd wager. All his good stuff does."

Another day she told him that we had seen a shop being born. My mother had been so captivated by all the activity on *the little street off the Esplanade that she had asked the bearers to stop there so that we could watch the carpenters and the glassmen at work and the crates and boxes being trundled inside.*

My eyes were all for the painter of signs who was perched on a rickety ladder propped against the shopfront. His letters, in gold paint, took him a long time because he drew shadows behind each one, making each letter stand out fat and firm. He had written ANOSS with his paintbrush by the time we left, but there was space left on the placard for more.

"I don't think it's to be a dressmaker's shop," my mother said. "They were making up too many shelves for that."

Mr Bristol looked pleased. He had a piece of information for us.

"No, my dears, it is not a dressmaker's shop. I have overseen the contracts myself. It is to be a food emporium importing and selling fine English goods. Marmalade! You must taste that, Anila. There's nothing so good in all of India. And, you know, of all strange things, the shop is an Armenian enterprise. Now what do you think of that?"

We had no thoughts at all so Mr Bristol gave us his.

"The Armenians are trading people from the east. Well, I correct myself, Armenia is actually west of here of course, but east of England, if you follow me. And my client, Mrs Panossian, is taking us on at our own game. Well, good luck to her, I say, if I can get my marmalade for breakfast."

He got up to leave us and then leant over and gave my mother's cheek a little pinch.

"You look very lovely today, Anna. So lovely indeed that I must tell you about the plan I have in mind, when I come back from dinner. I think you'll be pleased."

PINK DUCKS

ON MY FIRST MORNING on the riverbank I discovered the finest thing about a tent. You do not have to rise to look out at the day. You can lie there, snug, and when you wish it you can reach out and part the canvas to take your view. No maharani lying on furs or silken covers could be better off than I was, I thought, for I could see the sun peeking back at me from his own tent of orange and rose.

Nobody else was stirring.

The birds had been quiet since I woke. But now they started over, loud with the light and all the food that lay around them. I decided then that it was a good time for me to take my first bathe in the true wild Ganga waters, with no one to call me strange or foolish. Mr Walker, I knew, would worry about chills if he saw me, and indeed it was a true winter air that I felt on my skin when I slipped out of the tent and took to the path. I was in time to see a rat scuttle away from the leavings of our fire. Perhaps it was keeping warm too.

Then I heard a splash behind me, where the boat was, and I crouched down. The last creature I wanted to meet was Carlen. If he was a true countryman, as Mr Walker had said, then he was surely an early riser. And unlike us, he would probably take off his fine clothes to bathe.

But it was Benu in the water, striking out for the centre of the river, something I would never dare to do. He had strong arm strokes and he kept his head down in the water like an animal, so that he seemed to belong there.

I watched him swim but did not want to bother him, as I guessed I might if I made conversation. Instead I went further up, round a small bend where the river opened into the bank, making a shallow place where I dipped myself all over but did not swim. It was cool water and I felt fresh when I came out, though I had to pick off the waterweeds that clung to my trousers.

I sat on a log to drip off, and fixed my hair into a braid while it was still wet. Already I could see men and women coming into the fields across the river, and, farther away, smoke rising above groups of palms and tall trees. Two small fishing boats passed downstream, the men shouting to each other like brothers. The world was awake at last.

All these activities must have stirred the large awkward duck who chose that moment to step out from a clump of tall ulu grass and begin to waddle towards the river. His head and beak were pink, a pink like the brightest sari in the world, and the rest of him was dark and silky brown, the very colour of Mrs Panossian's most expensive chocolate.

I had never seen such a bird and my fingers were itching to paint him. But I had nothing with me, not even a pencil, and this showy fellow was a nervous bird. If I moved suddenly I would lose him. As I waited, trying to picture every feather in my mind, his mate came out to join him. She was not so brilliant as he, but she was bolder. He was still fussing about in the mud but she stepped into the water like a lady into a palki and straightaway began to reach her long neck out for food.

"Pss, pss."

It was Benu. He had made no sound to disturb the birds but he was on the path now, holding out to me the page I'd given him last night, and the crayon. Without the head wrap he looked younger, and I saw that, unlike his father, he had lots of hair, long, dripping wet hair, and his dhoti was dark with water.

"That's so smart, Benu," I whispered back.

He watched while I drew the two ducks with the smooth crayon. That was not so easy, but it was my fault for not giving Benu a proper pencil. I wrote "Mago's sari from Papa" beside the male's head and "Malati's lips" beside the female. Chocolate did not need any words.

"Will you fill in their big black feet for me while I go for Mr Walker?" I asked Benu.

He had a smile almost as wide as Anoush's.

Mr Walker was out of his tent now, dressed in shirt and breeches. When he saw me he stretched his arms towards the sun and then started raising his knees up and down, pretending he was a soldier. Carlen was bent over the fire, frying fish. He did not look up.

"I found some new ducks. Come quickly."

I grabbed my bag from the tent and then he followed

me back to the little place of shallows. Benu was standing by the log, as still as my heron. He put his finger to his lips as we came near, and then he pointed.

There were six of the pink-headed ducks now, four new ones sitting on their bellies in the clearing, while my first pair were finally together in the water. The new birds must have believed Benu to be a tree to have settled themselves so comfortably. They took no notice of us, and again I began to sketch.

"If they were humans they'd be fat-bellied men passing round a hookah," Mr Walker whispered to me.

"My mother never told me about any pink duck and she knew almost every bird on the river," I said. "So I think they must be very rare. Do you think this might be one to name for your sister?"

He shook his head slowly but his eyes were dancing.

"Alas, I think not, Anila. I've heard of the pink duck before, you see, though I never saw one until now. Last year when I was up-country beyond Murshidabad someone promised me a carcase but it never turned up. We can check the records but I cannot imagine that the glorious pink duck doesn't already have his name written into Mr Linnaeus's book."

I must have looked disappointed because Mr Walker put his hands together and made me a namashkar. Nor was he making mock, not at all.

"Anila, don't fret. Seeing the live creature is the very best reason for our adventure in the first place. I thank you for my pink ducks."

We left them then and came back for our breakfast. Carlen was still not speaking to Madan or to me, but nobody could find fault with his fish. Or with his speed at dismantling the two tents and packing them on board in neat parcels. We were sailing so soon that my two pink ducks were still in the water when we passed the little bathing place.

"Ah," said Madan. "The gulab-sir. The bird whose eggs are as round and white as pearls."

He told us he'd never seen pink ducks so far down the holy river, that they liked to live on the flatlands just before the great mountains began.

"Perhaps they've run away from home," said Mr Walker. "Like so many of us do."

He did not look sad when he said this. But I wondered what he meant.

It was green everywhere, lovely, with many fruit trees planted, some even near to the river. The villages seemed closer together as we passed, and there were many small boats. I moved to the cabin where I could do a finished drawing of the ducks. I wanted to use the chalks in my box, to find the right pinks and browns.

Towards noon, Mr Walker came into the cabin.

"Anila," he said. "Madan tells me that your grandfather's village is coming up over the next length of the river."

We came out onto the deck and Madan pointed away to the left bank.

"See there?" he said, with his great arm pointing across like a signpost. "Arjun's house is halfway between the village and the river, along by those palms, where the path runs."

I squinted and I thought I could make out the lines of a simple thatch and bamboo house where the trees stood. I saw a group of children leading buffaloes along the path from the village. Perhaps my mother had done this too when she was little, when she was not working the boats with her father.

There were a couple of fishing boats tied up at the small ghat and some of the hollowed tree boats too, but when I looked at Madan he shook his head.

"Arjun has a bigger boat," he said.

He called out a greeting to some young men on the jetty who were shaking out their nets. Then we were past.

For the first time, I wondered how my mother had come to the city to join my father. I knew she had worn her red sari and I knew that he had lifted her up and over the doorway of the house in the lane, just like a bride back home, he said. She had told me that. But how had they come there? In whose boat?

And how had he come to be here at all on that first afternoon when they met, he so far from his work and his lodgings with the Company?

Because only now, when I could see how great the distance was, did I understand what it had meant when she had given up her life as a daughter in this green place. Madan had made it clear that Annapurna was treasured here. Yet she had left it all behind to make a strange new life, and in just a short time that life included me.

I thought how brave she was and how much I missed her and I had to look away then from everybody and stare hard into the sky. But all that was up there were the kites, doing what they always did, drawing black lines over the sun.

THE PROPOSAL

MY MOTHER SAID SHE could not understand Mr Bristol's new proposal at all, but I was thrilled to hear about it. After our palanquin trips, it was the first interesting thing to come our way in this house.

We were in our room when she told me about it. My mother was standing in front of the long mirror. I was sitting on the window ledge watching her. She was wearing a pale blue silk sari with chikan embroidery, just recently delivered by our lively little tailor from Kashi, and she had a new gold chain that I had not seen before. She was trying it different ways, round her neck, across her forehead, even dangling it over her nose like a bazaar monkey.

"Why does he want to have a picture made of me?" she asked me, over and over. "He can see me whenever he wants to. It was different with your father. He had a feeling about making a picture for himself even if he couldn't actually do it..."

But then she would break off that particular thought. She would return to Mr Bristol and his reasons.

"He says this Mr Hickey is one of the very best painters who have come to Calcutta to paint all the famous English

people. But I am not one of those. Why does he not paint Mr Bristol himself, then? He's famous enough, or so he tells us."

I laughed at that thought.

"Mr Bristol is plump and pink like a plucked chicken. No one would want to look at his picture, Ma!"

She glared at me.

"He is kind to you. Don't you be unkind in return."

"I know, Ma, I know. But you will make a beautiful portrait lady. He knows that."

My mother was going to have her portrait painted by one of the best painters in our city. Why was she not excited? It was a better way, surely, to spend her time than filling hookahs or passing around paan or running round a table picking up billiard balls.

When I said that I got another angry look.

"Perhaps I don't want to be stared at. Perhaps I think it is wrong for people I do not know to be looking at me when I am not there. English people, too. You could never know what they might be thinking. Besides, I know the real reason is that it is just a kind of competition. This Mr Hickey has already painted another Englishman's Indian bibi and Mr Bristol wants my picture to outshine hers. They are so childish, men. They are worse than fighting cocks."

But she settled the chain over her forehead and fixed her glossy hair to suit it. If it truly was a competition my mother knew she would have to play her part.

"He has promised me gold drop earrings, Anila, though what I would really like is just to run out on the street and buy a simple bangle with my own money. I wish I knew too whether all this jewellery will be yours one day or not. That's not written into his famous contract, you know."

I thought again of the beautiful crimson ring that my father had given her on that last day we were together. I would have cared to have that. I touched my peacock locket for luck. Inside it was a button, a small bone button that had come from one of my father's shirts. I had found it in our house one day when my mother was ill. It was the only thing of his I had. The storybooks he had made were ruined long ago.

Days went by and it was getting to be high summer and very clammy. The bhistis who were charged with sprinkling water could not keep the dust from rising in the streets and we choked if we did not pull the shades over inside our palanquin. Going out was unpleasant. Everyone said the rains would be late.

I found another good book in Mr Bristol's library, a book about a sailor left shipwrecked alone on an island. When she was with me in the evenings, and not doing duty with Mr Bristol and his friends, I read some of Mr Robinson Crusoe's adventures to my mother. She felt he was lost for love more than anything else. Perhaps she was right. But I could find no fairy tales or romances on Mr Bristol's shelves.

Then on the first day of Asarh the monsoon arrived with a black scowl that made everyone smile and the rains started, as heavy as any I had ever seen. They fell into our fountain like hammers beating on metal. But that was not all. Something else was making a thundering noise, and it was not in the sky but much closer to hand, at our gate. I was standing in the porch, dry as a baby bird, watching the rains because I could not go out, and I saw everything. The durwan opened the gate, which took him a long time, perhaps because of the damp in the lock, perhaps because he was slowed by the rain which could take your breath away with its force. When the gate finally creaked open, four bearers heaved a square plain palanquin through it and staggered over the wet stones up to the *porch and set it down.*

A bulky man pulled himself out of the palanquin. He was dressed all in grey-green cloth, in cutaway jacket and breeches, with a straw hat that he kept one hand to as he took large steps to reach the porch. The other hand held a packet. He did not run though, unlike the bearers who raced for the poor shelter of the pomegranate tree. Perhaps he could not run because he was quite elderly, or so he seemed to me. He had large English features, especially his nose, but eyes that were soft and sharp at the same time. They were blue. It was no trouble for me to discover this because they were fixed on me in a very direct way.

I was the first person to greet the famous painter Mr Hickey, therefore, though I did not know who he was. He handed me his damp hat.

"Child," he said. "Pretty child. Is Mr Bristol at home? Not expecting me, but I've come anyway. Being in the area, and his my next undertaking."

I set the hat down on a small table and did a namashkar for him, as my mother had trained me to do. But what startled me was his voice. He spoke in the same accent as my father though his way of talking was gruff.

"Sahib, I will find him. Please step into the hall."

But Mr Bristol had already arrived though no servant had gone to fetch him. He must have been looking out of his window at the traffic that was braving the sudden rains.

"Mr Hickey. What an unexpected pleasure." Then, to me, "Anila, run and tell your mother to join us in the salon. At once."

Upstairs, my mother paced our room, furious.

"I am wearing rags," she said, "and no jewels except this bangle. How does he expect me to present myself at once?"

She was wearing a kurta pyjama of dove-grey silk, with a white scarf that seemed to be made entirely of cobwebs, so fine was its lace.

"Ma, you look beautiful," I said. "Come now, please."

I didn't believe this Mr Hickey would be impressed by fineries. His eyes were too clever for that.

She freed her braid from its fastening and let it hang, woven through with a white silk thread. Then she took a sweet-smelling bela flower from the bloom vase she kept on our bedside trunk, and clipped it into place just in front of her ear. She draped her scarf over her loosened hair, drawing its fine ends over her shoulders. Then she followed me down to the salon.

Mr Hickey stood up from the winged chair when she came in.

"Afternoon, my dear lady," he said.

All at once there were so many busy eyes in that room! Mr Hickey's did what they must. Mr Bristol's kept count like a Company policeman. Mine were a spy's.

What I saw was this.

Mr Hickey was looking at my mother just as any proper gentleman would, not at all like Mr Bristol's usual friends with their furtive habits. He did not offer to kiss her hand – I was sure he knew better. But he bowed to her.

"Be so good as to step towards the window," he said to her. "How are you named, good lady?"

She smiled at him, a warm smile, such as Mr Bristol himself rarely received from her. I wondered if he noticed this, but sneaking a look at him, I could see that he was pleased with the event so far. He was hugging himself like a child offered sweet things.

"My name is Annapurna," she said.

She stood in the window where the green light of the creeper and the grey of the clouds and rain threw soft dark shadows on her face. He asked her to turn this way and that, and, finally, to let down the scarf, "Hope you don't terribly mind, dear. My work."

There was his accent again. To hear my father's tones unsettled me. I wondered if my mother had noticed those echoes too.

He asked me then to fetch the packet he had left in the hall, and when I brought it to him he took from it some pencils and sheets of paper. He motioned to my mother to stay as he had placed her, and then, while we all watched as if this were a puppet show, he made swift marks on his pages. I could not see what he was drawing and I thought it rude to move closer, but I was struck by the speed of his hand.

When he had finished his observations, Mr Hickey asked my mother to sit down, but she remained standing. Then he asked Mr Bristol if he might tour the downstairs apartments of the house. The two of them left us there for some moments. I did not dare move. I felt we were all under some kind of spell that I did not wish to break. Besides, he had taken his drawings with him.

They returned. Mr Bristol was looking a little cross, I thought. But he was the one who spoke.

"My dear Anna," he said. "Mr Hickey feels that he will do a very fine portrait of you but the lighting in our house is not sufficient. At least it is not properly to the north, he says. He has a room set apart in his own house where he would like you to repair for sittings. Mr Hickey's daughter has done the service of chaperone in this situation several times before without objection. So I think, though it is regrettable to put you to the trouble of travelling, that you will oblige us both by consenting to this arrangement. I have looked upon Mr Hickey's first drawings and I am confident that we will all be happy with the outcome."

My mother merely bowed her head, but I could only just prevent the huge smile I felt inside from reaching my face.

Mr Hickey bowed again, clicked his heels and left us with a rush of the short remarks that seemed to be his personal language.

"Good-day ladies," he said. "Our next meeting, then. In Garden Reach. My pleasure, entirely."

Before a word to forbid it could be uttered, I ran after him, as far as the porch. The bearers were just outside with the palanquin but Mr Hickey groaned when he saw that the monsoon had not obliged him by stopping. He put his hat on, hunched his shoulders although he was still safe inside and pushed his drawings further down into the packet he carried. He gave me a long look, sighed and removed one of the fine sheets.

"For you, then. The best of today's work."

He winked at me. "Conceal it," he said.

Then he was gone again, into the rain, to face the struggle with the durwan and his locks that accompanied every exit from our house.

In my hand was what my father had been searching for, so long and so in vain. His Annapurna was there on the cream-coloured page, from the tip of her head to her slender waist, drawn in charcoal and a touch of red chalk, and all the beautiful lines that my father could never make, despite all his attempts. Mr Hickey had found her soul.

THE DOOR
BETWEEN HOPE
AND FEAR

THUNDERSTORMS AND TOWERS CRASHING down, galloping hooves and groans in graveyards. In story-books these are the kinds of noises people hear when they get news that shakes their bones. For me, oars squeaking and straining in their locks will sound for ever like the oldest door in the world.

We two have come through the oldest door in the world, Anila, the door between hope and fear. So, little one, don't look back. It's closed behind us now.

Without sail, Benu and Hari were rowing the big boat as best they could, just the two of them. It was heavy work but Madan had told them they didn't have to take us far, just to the next stout tree on the bank side, for tying up.

"That's what has to be done. Move the boat upriver so no one can tell that the sahib and I have started our journey from this place."

He did not explain the need for secrecy but waited until we had begun to move. Then he tied a brown cloth wrap on his head and jumped off the boat and joined Mr Walker. It seemed they were going on a walk through the rice fields. Nobody else was wanted along with them, that was clear, not Carlen to carry, nor Anila to draw. I wondered what Mr Walker would do now if he were to meet his great unknown bird tiptoeing through the mud.

We had already seen a bittern in those quiet parts, away from the boats and the shouting on the river. Bittern was Mr Walker's word, for I had never before seen this bird with a beak like a bayonet. Madan called it the veena bird, and its deep sad voice really did sound like the low notes a good player can pluck from his veena. But this bird was smaller than her kind, he said, and he had before never seen a veena bird with such short wings and a head that appeared to be dipped in honey. That had made Mr Walker very happy. He liked my sketches too.

"You have her sitting on her nest as if it were a throne. My Eveline would love this golden-feathered lady."

Perhaps Mr Walker merely wanted to get away from the river for a while. For my part I loved the freedom I felt on the water, where the world changed by the moment and the people in it too.

Except for one. Silent as a cat, Carlen had come to stand beside me. I continued to stare outwards until my eyes ached to close but still I knew his gaze was only on me. He rested a knee against the gunwale and blew his breath towards me.

"So, here we are again, hinny."

Hinny.

Mr Walker had raised his eyebrows when I asked him what that word meant, a night or so ago.

"Hinny, Anila? Where on earth did you hear that

good old English word? You get a hinny when you cross a donkey mare and a horse, a mule if it's the other way round. But most people say mule for either."

Not Carlen the countryman of course. Now that I knew what he was calling me, I ignored him. But my heart raced. Benu and Hari were occupied up front and, in any case, Carlen was their senior. There was nobody else I might call on if he laid hands on me again. I felt the tip of my pencil and thought it was quite sharp enough to do damage to his fine face.

"You're looking for your father, hinny? The dark horse? Or maybe I should say the pale horse, considering everything. I know where he is."

There he was, with his sleek hair and his close-fitting clothes, moving now to stand beside me. He was so close I could smell the mint that he chewed every day, dried mint he kept in a neck bag just as poor Hari kept his precious betel. He held his arms behind his back as if there was something he was guarding from me. I had seen him a couple of times taking food in the cabin when nobody else did, rice and nuts that were already running low. Greedy guts. He was not fat, though, he was lean as a leopard.

Now I wanted to push him into the water. How dare this foul Englishman say he knew anything about my father when even the Company men claimed they had no knowledge of him?

"You're lying. You couldn't possibly know. You know nothing about him. He would never be around you. He'd know what you were like, a bully, a filthy bully."

Carlen laughed.

"The kitten has a rough tongue too! But you see, my

puss, I have a good memory for facts. I store the things I see as if they were hooks and ropes and shot powder. You never know when they'll be needed. One green eye and one blue? Yes, I know where your sire is though I didn't know that he was that the times I saw him. Let us say you're not all donkey, Miss Tandy, no matter what's on view in this pretty picture."

"*Don't* do that! Please be careful!"

He was holding my mother's picture out over the river. If he had been nearer to Benu and Hari their oars would surely have splashed water onto the fine paper until it softened and the chalks ran. But they were up front and straining hard, the oars rasping in the oar-locks, and even my shout didn't reach them.

"Please give it to me."

He took the drawing back out of danger and I reached for it. He shook his head. The only consolation was that he was holding it carefully, not bending or twisting the paper, not pressing his thumb down on my mother's innocent face. Then I saw where he was touching her. He knew I saw it too. He smiled his cat smile and caressed her as I turned my head, sickened. Then abruptly he spoke.

"I like 'please'. It's good manners. But that's not enough for such news as I have, is it?"

"You can't have news! It's years since my father left the city and nobody has had any report of him. He would never stay away so long without a reason. So you could never have met him. You must have heard people talk of the way he looked, for everybody liked him, and you're trying to threaten me with what you've heard."

"I'll say it once again, then. One green eye, the left, one blue eye, the right. Hair straight and thin. An Irish speech, rude as they come. But you know that, of course."

I would not let him see what he had done to me. I would not. I stared hard at his neatly trimmed finger-nails. They had huge crescent moons in their pits. Perhaps because of all the nuts he ate.

"So then, is the handsome hinny going to take a gamble on my news? And what about this precious picture of yours, what's that worth in a boat with such dirty wet water everywhere around? Or why not bid for picture and story together, like a wild pledge at Newmarket? Depending on your assets of course. Mine are here."

He tapped the side of his head, as if to show me where he kept his image of my father. Then he raised up the drawing of my mother again and fanned himself with it. He was smiling.

"And yours are, where exactly, hinny?"

I looked at him miserably. Yes, he knew himself well, this man Carlen. He might store his information like knives but his real power was his silence. If I were to tell Mr Walker what he had done today, or before today, nothing would protect me from his silence. He knew I knew that.

"I'll give you this ring. But please, you must tell me what you know. Only tell me what is true. Tell me some other thing so I can believe you."

"So small a ring? That gets only a paper mother, not a living father."

He took Miss Hickey's tiny gold ring without a

word and dropped it into one of his waistcoat pockets. The picture was safe in my hands when I thought how easily I might have arranged for Mr Walker to ask me to show it to him again, and have the theft discovered that way. But it is an easy thing to drop a paper, or tear it, perhaps, or step it underfoot into the mud and call it an accident. As Carlen had said, it was just a gamble, for him as well as for me. And, either way, the stakes were higher for me.

His eyes, so very blue, stayed on my face. Did he have the right way of it about my father's eyes – that the left one was the green? What a thing to be sure of! I had to close my own and picture how my father used to hold me before I could say the same thing with certainty.

He knew what I was doing with my eyes shut, I swear it. He decided to throw me another line.

"Your father used to draw too. But not birds. Ship's wheels and sails, roofs and riggings."

Ship's wheels?

I suddenly thought of my gold mohurs, stored at the bottom of the leather case, and wondered if he'd already found them. My heart jumped and fell back down. What else might I bargain with if he had?

"Where did you see my father? When? Is he in good health? Please tell me."

Up front Hari squawked suddenly as our boat bumped hard against the bank, and then swung its broadside out again into the flow where a large boat was coming fast downriver. Benu dived off with a rope and scrambled through the reeds until he could stand up on the bank and pull us alongside, hauling the lead rope taut round the trunk of a chopped tree.

The boat was full of red-coated soldiers. Most of them were standing but a few were leaning over the prow. These ones whooped when they saw Benu's brave jump and then, when they saw me, they shouted and pointed and called out like monkeys. I pulled my scarf up over my face and turned away and their noise passed downriver with them.

But in those few seconds Carlen was suddenly gone, as if he'd never been standing close beside me, never been dripping his poison into my ear, never defiling my poor dead mother.

Any other time his disappearance would have made me glad. That we could journey on without him, whatever it took, I'd begun to pray for that. But now! If what Carlen claimed was true, that he had seen my father, no matter when it was, or where, this was the only news anybody had ever brought of him.

I'd had two different lives since Papa had left us, one at Mr Bristol's house, one with the Hickeys. How many lives had he had? Was he really, truly, still alive? All along I'd beaten that question away because it could be answered in two ways and I would accept only one of these. I needed to believe my father was out there in the world, just separated from me by a spell that would be lifted when I could work out how to do it.

Perhaps I should have been more faithful to my little Durga, as my mother had been all her life. Now Durga was rewarding my neglect by sending me Carlen as a guide. He was the last person I would have chosen but I needed him.

THE NEEM TREE

CARLEN WASN'T IN THE CABIN. He wasn't on the riverbank. Nor in the water anywhere near the boat, which was as well, because he did not swim. Not in our Ganga at any rate. He said it was dirty. I knew too that he laughed at the small offerings of rice and fruit that Madan and Benu cast into the waters each morning before we set out.

Yet my gold mohurs were safe, still wrapped in the purple scarf at the bottom of my case, along with the peacock locket. Perhaps he'd been too pleased with what he'd found to poke further. All the birds were there too, and my box of paints and pencils was untouched. But I guessed that Carlen would not dare harm anything that concerned Mr Walker's business.

Benu shouted that there was fish on the pan and he and Hari looked at me with surprise when I said I would prefer to take a walk instead, to look for birds. My mind couldn't rest and the thought of food made my throat close over. I packed my notebook and pencils into my bag and left my slippers on deck for I thought the paddy fields would be all a-squelch.

"Will you be safe, Miss Anila?" Hari asked anxiously. "Perhaps there are snakes."

"You have your pencils today?" Benu held up his fingers and pretended to count all the items I should have. "Your notebook? Your chalks?"

"And my eyes, Benu, two of them in working order." I smiled at them. But where was Carlen? They hadn't seen him go, they said.

The clay path was baked hard for the most part but at times my feet were sucked into patches of warm mud where water was coming through. Small brown frogs skipped out of danger as I put my toes down. I had never seen so many frogs but, for all the plenty, the paddy birds patrolling these muddy parts drew themselves up like temple guards as I passed. They saw only a robber.

I came level with a line of trees planted beside a little waterway. I was glad of the shade now for the sun was high, and even gladder to see that one of the trees had a clever arrangement of branches. It was a neem. Even here, away from Calcutta, there were friendly neems.

Climbing to the first fork was easy. On the next level of branches there was a hole in the trunk and outside it some soft tan downy feathers were sticking to the bark. I was tempted to put my hand inside but this winter season was the time for owl babies. Not even if these might be unknown owls for Mr Walker would I disturb them.

My tunic had streaks of green across it by the time I made it to the second lookout branch. I sat there with my right arm round the trunk and felt a little of what it must be to be a bird, cool, high up and scanning for its dinner.

Where were Madan and Mr Walker? I thought per-haps they had gone to look for a temple, one with the kind of paintings or statues Englishmen liked to look at. My mother told me that Mr Bristol's friends used to make up hateful stories about these temple works, even about the goddesses themselves, though of course they did not understand the first thing of what they saw. But surely Mr Walker was not of their kind.

There was no sign of a temple anyway, no matter what direction I looked, just narrow stripes of water picking their way in lines across the flat green fields. I decided I would climb a little higher.

It made a difference, that extra little trip up into the sky. What I could see now was a huge square dug out among the fields, quite close to the main waterway that drained into the river. It looked like one of the city water tanks, deep and sunken, but we were in the countryside where tanks were small, like ponds. Nor did it seem to hold any water, but it glinted all the same, all along its bottom. It sparkled.

There were people inside the tank. I could count ten or more. Some were walking around, tiny stick figures I could just make out by squinting. Others were bent over like bandicoots, lifting and hauling.

I turned to look back at the river. There it was brown and strong, stretching ahead of our tied up boat, beginning to curve like a dagger. I could see another boatful of soldiers coming along.

I took a deep breath, preparing myself to twist round and climb down the tree when the astonishing thing happened.

Great brown wings arrived underneath me, out of

nowhere it seemed, without even a flap. They were sails, sails come out of the sky, sails of feather and muscles, with all their power spread along the delicate tracery. They brought a draught with them, and a sharp smell of blood and water that rose up beyond my nose and into my eyes.

Only afterwards did I think that what I saw was like a fairy tale, like my mother's kind of story, where a giant bird, brave as Jatayu, arrives to work magic, to rescue somebody. But when it actually happened, the magic was all in the suddenness, the hugeness of the bird, and the thrill I felt all along my skin.

She had such a fine balance. Her huge claws gripped the edges of the nest hole and she made little shifts to her back and her head when she needed to reach in to her babies. Her wide wings were as smartly folded up as an umbrella in a shop. I knew the babies were feeding on what she had brought them, fish chewed up and dripping.

She was there only minutes and then she rose up again and glided away.

I sat back against the trunk and drew everything I could remember of her wings in flight and at rest. I wrote down my colours, the flashes of black and gold and white in all the brown. I made ten sketches. But my best one was the quickest one, which showed the mother bird's round head bent back against her body, with just a little curve of owl cheek showing and her two long ears flattened into her head feathers.

Down along the water track three figures were moving away from the strange tank. One was thin, one was broad, one was fair. That much I could see, and that much told me who they were.

How had Carlen known to find the other two? Why had he rushed away as he did?

It was only a short walk back to the river and the boat, and I was sitting with my back against the tree trunk watching Hari and Benu play a silly game with the neem sticks I had brought back when the three men arrived. Mr Walker had a flushed face and a bite on his cheek that looked sore. Carlen did not look at any of us but went on board and started to unpack the tents.

"We did not mean to be gone so long," Mr Walker said. "Did you find anything new to draw?"

Without saying anything I handed him the notebook. I watched his face as he took in exactly what it was I had done. He passed the drawings to Madan.

"Where did you do this work, Anila? How did you think of drawing the fish owl in this way, from above? These are intriguing pieces."

I pointed at the neem tree in the distance.

"I climbed right to the top. I could see for miles. The nest was halfway up the tree and she came to feed them while I was there. It was the most wonderful thing I have ever seen, that pencha feeding her babies underneath me."

Madan's eyes were full of measurements as I sang this story out like a child.

"And what else did you see?" he asked. "Did you see the sahib and myself?"

"I saw all three of you. I saw a big tank like the Lal Dighi tank with people moving around inside it. And I saw two big boats with soldiers in them on the river but they went right past. I saw frogs too, lots of them, and paddy birds eating them as if they were fruit."

I could hear my own voice, as if I were reciting a rhyme. Perhaps it was that silly way of speech that was making me think like a child too, for I truly had to bite my tongue to stop myself saying that the only thing I had not seen from the top of the neem tree was my father.

I stood up then and moved away, with everyone's eyes on me. Carlen had my tent up so I went inside it and sat there, my knees up, my chest heaving. I felt like a fool. It was not my business what Mr Walker did when he left my company. I only wished he could help me find my father. It certainly was not his fault that he could not. Worst of all, Carlen had seen me behave like a spoilt child.

It was dark outside when I heard Mr Walker's polite cough outside the tent.

"Anila, will you come down the river path a little way with me?"

The little slice of moon was high in the sky and we could see quite well as we walked. I saw three figures wrapped up in the cabin. But Carlen had laid his bedding outside on the deck away from the others. I fancied that his light eyes followed us down the path, warning me not to tell tales on him.

"Anila, are you vexed with me?"

I shook my head. But he waited for a proper answer.

"No, Mr Walker. How could I be? You are always kind and thoughtful."

"But something has upset you today, am I right?"

I could say something that was true, at least.

"I keep dreaming about my father. He shrinks and shrinks until he disappears."

Mr Walker tut-tutted at that.

"Och, that is a hateful thing. But it means nothing, such a dream, you know, except that finding your father is your principal care and so it preys on your mind. Only the likes of our murdering old King Macbeth would have dreams that tell the future, not good people like you, Anila. And his dreams were only a story anyway."

He stopped walking and faced me.

"I know you must think I deserted you today, and without a word, too. But I simply did not wish to put you in possession of uncomfortable knowledge."

If he only knew.

"You know I have official business here, Anila. And you know I have my passion for the birds, to discover what I may of them. But since I came here I have discovered other things about India. I have found out that the Company, the English, whatever we call ourselves here, are committing an evil deed in Bengal and probably all over."

The evil was all about salt.

"Everybody needs salt, Anila, birds, animals, humans. Especially in a hot country where we all sweat in the heat and lose our own salt. When salt leaves your body you must find more or you will die. Or at very least you will get sick, even if you have food and water. And it is the little ones who die first."

The Company was making huge profits from making and selling salt, he said. Nobody else was allowed to do this, on pain of death, and the salt prices were high even in a famine year, when crops were poor.

"What you saw today was an outlaw salt depot. Madan's cousin maintains it. He collects and sells the salt that people manufacture further down the river. His price is fair, his risk is immense."

"But all I saw was a tank in the ground!"

"Yes, for it's easy to disguise that way with vegetation, and the beauty of it is you would have to be an owl to know it was even there. Unless you were a tree-climbing species like a certain Anila Tandy, of course."

I did not smile at that so he continued.

"Do you know that it was Carlen who first found out about this business? It was when he came to hire our boat that he heard the men talking. Until this trip I did not know that Carlen had any knowledge of Bangla but he does. Knowing my concerns, he instructed me as to what questions I should put to Madan. I have Madan's trust now, I am proud to say. He understands that I want to do something about the matter. He told me about the river salt trade and the men told me of the dangers they run. My intention now is to raise the question of the tax when I return to England."

And Carlen, good and brave Carlen, had rushed away to warn his master that soldiers were passing by on the river. This Carlen who had read out my Bangla words as if they were monkey language.

"But I thought that Carlen ... well, he mocks Madan and our religion, and I cannot think he cares about the welfare of poor people in Bengal."

I was afraid to say more.

Mr Walker sighed.

"Carlen is a strange mixture of a man. He saved my

life the year I came down to England as a troubled young man inclined to brawl, and he has been in and out of my life since then, as suits both of us. He often pretends to be what he is not but I cannot say why such is his way. He has many masks and some of them are unpleasant."

Then he looked at me as sharply as he could in the darkness.

"He has not been disrespectful to you, I hope, Anila?"

For a long time, I could not think what to answer.

"Anila?"

"He does not seem to like me, so I find it difficult. That is all."

"For that would be unpardonable and I would not pardon it. Do you understand me?"

I nodded. That was some knowledge to bank indeed. But I thought to myself that my gold mohurs were the best hope I had of making Carlen tell me what I needed to know.

ALCHEMY

OUR FIRST TRIP TO Mr Hickey's house was made in a carriage, as there had to be space for Mr Bristol to accompany us. Besides, a palanquin could not travel all the way from Old Court House Street to Garden Reach.

Mr Bristol was curious to inspect the arrangements for making the painting, I knew that. But it was also true that he never missed an opportunity to inspect other people's houses, their furniture and rugs, pictures and silver.

Now, as we jogged along, he told us more about the other gentleman's portrait of his bibi, the beautiful one that had spurred him to have my mother's likeness painted by the same hand.

"She cannot hold a candle to you, my dear Anna, though it cannot be denied that she is very fine and her champion is a noisy fellow around the city. Why, it would be criminal not to have your worth known similarly, no matter the cost to me."

My mother shifted along the padded seat, a little closer to me, and sighed. She was wearing his choice of clothes that day, of course, but nobody could deny that he had a good eye for an outfit.

Her sari was a very fine green China silk. Mr Bristol

claimed it was the very green of the mulberry leaves that gave birth to silk itself. Underneath the sari she wore a jacket of peacock green, crafted by the lady from Kashi, and there was a matching jade insert in the circlet that bound her hair. Her fingernails and toenails were polished with a lustre coating. Round her neck was a string of tiny river pearls and her earrings were dainty leaf shapes of fine filigree silver.

Of course Mr Bristol had not said a word about anything as lowly as feet but that morning my mother had sat patiently on our bed while I carefully traced a design of feathers on her soles with red alta paint.

"They won't know any better about such things, but you and I do," she'd said.

Our ride was so long that Mr Bristol began to huff and puff that he had not hired a boat instead. But at last we found ourselves rattling past spacious houses, each one set down in a garden of great size.

The carriage pulled up outside a white house, which had no gate, even though it lay quite close to the roadway. Instead of tall walls there were bushes that guarded a small lawn, bright green from the rains. The house had a verandah running round its upper storey. I thought how wonderful it would be if we had no gates and no durwan but a viewing place like that where I could watch the world pass by.

Mr Hickey was on the entrance steps to greet us. Unlike us, he had not dressed up and his rough cloth trousers and canvas smock already had spatters of paint on them.

"Welcome, everybody!" he said, and he shook Mr Bristol's hand. "Now, inside, please."

We moved into the hall, which was not at all like Mr Bristol's dark hall. Light streamed though a round window of coloured glass. A stone staircase led out of the hall and at the *foot of it stood a very small lady dressed in a dark blue English dress.*

She stepped forward and shook my mother's hand and then took mine. I could feel that her hand was delicate and dry, even in the summer heat. It seemed such a personal thing to do, to take a person's hand, but I found I did not mind. This lady, who must be Mr Hickey's daughter, was greeting us in the English manner. But I noticed that she merely bowed her head to Mr Bristol, who was already stretching his neck in every direction. He was quite shameless.

"My dears, you will be stuck with me for some time while my father prepares his worst," Miss Hickey said to my mother and me. Then she laughed, so that we might know she had made a joke.

She was pale and she had her father's blue eyes. She wore her straight fine brown hair bundled up into loops on either side of her head, a style I had never seen. When she was not speaking or smiling her mouth had a slight twist that was not at all horrible. I wondered if this was a natural thing or something nervous in her. She was older than my mother, I thought, but I could not really guess what age she might be. I had never met an English lady before.

"You must be Anila," she said to me. "My goodness, it is a shocking thing to confess, but I have not met anybody of your age since I came to Calcutta and I do so miss my young cousins who have so many interesting things to say at all times. We must have a long chat together during the days when this important business is going on."

Her eyes were dancing, as my father's used to. I decided I liked Miss Hickey for her kindly welcome and I smiled back at her. So did my mother, with her rare wide smile that I used think, when I was small, made the birds sing louder. She slipped her arm through mine as she did when we were alone.

I realized then that my mother had been nervous about this meeting because she, too, had never before met an English lady. I think she had expected a different treatment.

"This way, this way," said Mr Hickey.

He led us to the back of the hall where we stepped into a wide room that faced out onto an open porch. This had the same fat smooth columns that stood in the front of the house. In the distance we could see tall palms that followed the line of the road. Here the light was like water.

In front of the columns, but still in the room, a low day bed had been positioned and spread with a fine rug. Mr Hickey told my mother to sit on it, and to stretch her legs out.

When she was settled, he told her that he would be making an oil sketch that day.

"Next time, there'll be something to hold," he said. "An Indian thing. Not to worry, I'll choose it. And wear the same fine clothes, please. Of course, you know this."

I could feel Mr Bristol's pride like a sun ray in the room. He had plumped himself down onto a battered wing chair and of course he had done this without noticing that Miss Hickey was still standing.

Now Mr Hickey set up his canvas on a support with wooden legs so that he did not have to hold it at all. There was a small roughly made table alongside him, with brushes and pots and saucers laid out in no order at all.

Miss Hickey motioned to me to help her draw up a broad stool from the open side of the room so that we might sit together on it.

"My poor music stool," she said. "It has an idle time of it here, I'm afraid. It has just seen off yet another poor harpsichord with the ague."

I looked at her, baffled.

"This climate gives the best of instruments the shakes and shivers," she explained. "As if they were humans. But perhaps you would like to go over and see up close what my father is doing?"

I thanked her and went to stand near Mr Hickey. He was squeezing bright colours from little skin bags onto a piece of fine wood the shape of a water lily leaf. His canvas was already painted all over in a dull clay colour, which shocked me. Why was it not the hopeful white of a page as his drawing had been? And nowhere on his wooden plate of paints could I see the sand and pearl colours of my mother's skin, or the many different greens that the light made out of her sari and blouse.

He looked round at me and he must have read on my face every doubt I carried. His eyebrows shot up and he blinked his eyes at me twice. I did not know what to say.

"Child," Mr Hickey said at last. "Painting is alchemy. Matter into beauty. Time into future. Look at the far wall."

Mr Bristol was frowning at me now but somehow I did not think that his painter friend was offended. I went to stand at the darkened wall and saw what I had not noticed before, a painting of two small girls in white dresses, one with a pink sash, the other with a blue. The younger one held a fruit up to her chubby face, and looked out at me, blue-eyed and yellow-curled. The elder girl had a protective hand on her sister's shoulder, and, under her fine, fair hair, you could see that she had a sweet little twist to her mouth. An expression unique to her that had been caught in paint and carried into the future.

OTTERS

SUDDENLY CARLEN WAS THE busiest person on our boat. There he would be, coiling ropes and wrapping sails for Madan as if there had never been a sulk. Or else he was sharing fishing lines with Benu and Hari though he still made as if he recognized none of their words.

Even when I returned from bathing in the morning I never found him on his own. If he was preparing our food he would also make certain to be boiling hot water for Mr Walker's shave and calling out to him in his tent – did he remember this, did he think that, was there ever such a thing. The only person he did not seek out was me. He kept his eyes from me whenever I tried to catch them. Carlen made it clear that, for now, it did not suit him to accept questions from me.

Again I had the terrible dream about my father shrinking to a tiny size and then disappearing from my hand. I tried to think of Mr Walker's wise words but at night in my dark tent they had no weight.

Now Madan was steering us along the centre of the river because by the banks there were so many smaller boats cutting in and about like dragonflies on the water.

As the days passed we saw towns as well as villages and one of these was full of French people, Mr Walker said. Its name was Chandernagar, which means town of the moon. I thought of Garden Reach as we passed by its ghats and wide streets and saw large houses set back from the river, which curved round the town like a young moon growing.

My notebook had a whole navy of ducks now, and owls, darters, geese, swamp hens, egrets and swans. Mr Walker believed our best hope of recording a new species was the little honey-coloured bittern but he also thought the fish owl drawings could be turned into something spectacular when I came to the job of painting.

"Nobody has ever thought to draw a bird in that way before."

I should have been thrilled by his praise but nothing sat well in me. I kept thinking of what Carlen knew, or claimed he knew, and what I feared from him. As my father shrank in my dream, so Carlen grew giant-sized. And still I could not command his attention.

When the towns lay behind us we began to pass through jade green countryside where cane grew, and dye plants. The boats we met now all had a happy air – their sails were brightly coloured and we heard songs coming over the water from them. Our boat had been silent up to this but now shy Benu began to sing from his place by the tiller. His was a spring song about a buffalo herder walking by the river, imitating everything he saw on the way, a sweet and funny song. I think we were all proud that the *Hera* finally had its own music.

The more we journeyed upriver the more I enjoyed my morning bathes because here there were many turns in the banks making miniature coves where the water was quiet. One morning I had found such a place and I was lying on my back drifting, my favourite thing to do in the water. My hair was floating behind me and some bank side herbs were bobbing against my feet.

Then I saw the otters.

A mother otter was leading her babies out of their hole in the bank. She dropped each one close by the water and then returned for the next. There were three in her litter and she held each as a cat does her kittens. They wriggled in her mouth, the furry little babies, and they beat their tiny webbed feet like fists. The babies were still dry but she was as wet as I was.

I did my best to be as still as a stayed stick so that I could see what she was doing and not frighten her. We had spotted these water animals a couple of times already, but only by way of a quick splash and a small dark head swimming away fast. Mr Walker's eyes had filled with tears the first time.

"I know of no other animal that enjoys its life the way an otter does," he said. "Eveline and I once saw them making slides in the snow, dashing themselves into the water and coming out to do it over again and again. And these were adults! She said to me once that she would like to be reborn as an otter if the good Lord saw fit to offer those kinds of arrangements in heaven."

Perhaps this was she. But I could not fetch Mr Walker now. My smallest movement would scatter them.

The mother was showing the babies how it was that

she swam. She dived down and when I raised my head from the flat I could just see her dark shape moving in the water, twisting like a large fish. The little otters were like every other kind of baby in the world. They looked up- and downriver, anywhere but at what their mother was trying to teach them. One little fellow tried sitting up on his hind legs and fell over on his back in the reeds but not before I could see that his whiskers and tiny smudge of a nose were like things alive and separate from the rest of him, they quivered so much.

A grey heron passed over us, gliding on its great wings, heading downriver to find a good fishing place. But there was one fish the bird would never find because that hardworking mother otter had found it first. She hauled herself up onto the bank and dropped her catch, still arching itself, in front of her babies.

I saw a strange flash of coloured light bouncing on the water near the otters. But it was a small fishing boat coming downstream that broke up the little scene. The pole man saw me in the shallows and called out a greeting, staring hard at me as he drove his danr down into the water. He saw nothing of the little water family though, for they had disappeared.

How could I tell Mr Walker what he had missed? That was my bother as I came back along the path. But there he was, standing at the prow of our boat, waving, a great beam widening his face.

"Anila, we saw them, did you?" he called out. "The otters? Carlen had the telescope set up, the fortunate fellow, and he spotted them."

There it was, set up indeed, and truly like the tiny ship's cannon I had first thought it to be, positioned on a chest with its barrel overshooting the gunwale of the boat. My stomach suddenly felt as if there was a glove of red-hot iron in it, grabbing and poking at me from inside. Was this the first time that Carlen had decided to track me and watch while I bathed? Why, he did not even care now that I knew what he had done. His face was turned my way but there was no acknowledgement there, no pretence, just his steely eyes passing over me and away.

I had to kneel down by the reeds and bend my head over my knees, trying to stop myself being sick.

Mr Walker was out of the boat at once, but he came to a halt some feet away, not wishing to embarrass me, I believe. His voice was all concern.

"Anila, my dear. Hari is getting water. Take your time."

The sickness passed after all. I could not take breakfast however and while Madan, Carlen and Mr Walker prepared for another trip to another salt depot I went into the cabin to lie down, away from the sun. Benu was on deck, watching out for the most part, but from time to time I heard loud splashes and knew he was swimming. He called out sometimes too, to boats passing, and to my ears he sounded then just like my old friend Dinesh. I wondered where Dinesh was now and what work he had found and whether he remembered the day the boat with the Englishmen came up our creek.

THE BOY

WHEN I WOKE I knew that something was different. Outside, the light was thick and yellow, even languid. Mr Hickey would call it sulphurous but my mother would have thought of wild cats or jackals. Clouds the colour of mud were flocking round the sun. Perhaps a storm was coming, though it was not the season.

Benu had abandoned his fishing. He was sitting on deck with his crayon and some sketch paper I had given him but he blushed as I came near him and covered his work.

"No good," he said.

But I had seen that he was not drawing birds. He was copying letters, the ornate gilt letters that spelled H-E-R-A. My glimpse told me that his copy was close but I knew he would prefer if I said nothing.

"Benu, I feel as if I can't breathe. I must walk somewhere. Will you come? Perhaps as far as that village?"

I pointed to where a track led from the river path to a small village screened by its bamboos and tall palms, a place the same as dozens we had passed yesterday and the days before.

Just like my grandfather's village. My mother's first home.

"I cannot leave the boat," Benu said. "My father has left me to mind all that we have."

He stretched his arms out, one reaching fore, one aft.

Of course. How stupid I was.

"Then, I'll just go that way myself."

Benu's forehead creased just like his father's.

"It is not safe for you," he said.

"Perhaps on the way then I'll just find another neem tree to climb. One with an eagle in it this time – that will protect me!"

But he didn't laugh and shook his head, his frown unchanged, as I left.

It felt so good to walk, even under the heavy clouds, that it was a while before I realized what was different about this place. Here nobody was working in the fields, not one person, and there was no sign of any human presence, unless you wished to count the huts ahead. Over them the kites were circling, ever so surely.

"When the kite builds, look to lesser linen."

Whenever birds stole pieces of the dhobi's laundry work Miss Hickey would say that verse of her beloved Shakespeare. But here there were no linens drying, no saris stretched like ribbons on the earth, just as there had been no women to scrub them by the water.

I thought for a moment of my mother's stories of enchantments, where people were shaped into wayside rocks or locked away to moan in the clefts of trees until the right person happened along to release them. But Mr Walker's account of the salt taxes was fresher in my mind. Perhaps these village people had gone to work in the outlaw salt tanks, where even the small hands of children might be needed.

The first of the houses was a pukka house, brick-built unlike the others, and it had a high wall round it, also of brick, that seemed to be sheltering a garden or a courtyard. A narrow grassy path led alongside this wall and from the other side I could hear all the insects of late afternoon buzzing. A black fly landed on my neck, then another larger one and they did not shift even when I shook my head in irritation. I had to slap them away.

I looked towards the smaller houses. There was nobody at all abroad in the village, not even a child. Not a goat. Not a dog to bark at me, the stranger.

I felt as if a rough pestle was grinding away in my stomach. But with no people around, surely there was nothing to fear. Except that I might not find the drink I now realized I wanted very badly.

Just where a tall old mango tree hung over the court-yard wall there was a gap at the bottom like a giant mousehole, with all the broken bricks lying where they had fallen. A small lizard lay motionless on one of them but he shot into a crack as I bent down and peered through the hole. Beyond looked green and promising.

On the other side, I straightened up. I was in a courtyard orchard. It was entirely overgrown but you could still trace the elegant brick paths that lay under the weeds and broken stones, and imagine the way the fruit trees must have looked when they were young and clipped and cared for. In the centre of the court-yard a long deep fish tank was set, a tank that seemed to be properly maintained, unlike the trees. Its water looked fresh enough for drinking and as I came up to it I heard a fish plop down into the water after a jump, and then saw the ripples spreading where it had landed.

Further on, past the tank, a wizened peepul tree stood in front of the old house. I thought I saw some drinking gourds lying at its foot and made my way to it.

But my eyes had deceived me.

A boy was tied to the tree. He was sitting on the ground, his back pressed up against the trunk, and his head was slumped down over his chest. All he had on was a filthy torn dhoti, for whoever had done this had used his own thin head wrap to tie him. He was a boy, but it was hard to say more than that about him, not even his age or his true size, because his body was so swollen. His arms and legs were like great soft vegetables and his belly looked like a full water bag, only it was angry and sore. There was a smell of something sweet, something disgusting, all around.

I felt a stinging pain on my own foot and looked down. That was when I saw the ants, the lines of red ants that were marching away from the boy as if he were a city and they the soldiers who had ransacked it. I called out in disgust and stamped my foot but they kept coming.

The boy did not stir at that, did not lift his head to see where such disturbance came from. I looked up in despair and saw the kites again, flapping their wings and making plays earthwards as if they meant to land. That sight made me sure the boy was dead.

There was surely nothing left in my stomach but something struggled up into my mouth nonetheless and

I bent over to retch. No dead person I had seen in my life had looked so terrible. I had known what to do for the person who'd mattered most of all. I'd not been alone then. But this? All I knew was that I could not leave this child's body to be devoured by birds or worse. Benu would just have to abandon the boat and help me bring it to the river.

First I had to cover it up in a safe place. I fiddled with the cruel knots that held the body to the tree and the sweet smell crept from its sticky flesh onto my fingers. I moved the child's arms round to his front. His poor wrists were mangled as if they had been in irons. I thought of how painful it was when blood flowed again after you had been sitting on your hands, hot and darting as if the blood was full of pins and needles. At least he was spared that.

Then the boy groaned, an animal sound, not human at all. He was alive.

"I'll get you some water."

Perhaps my dry mouth made me whisper. Perhaps it was the shock of finding out that the boy was alive not dead. But in the silence of that place I could also hear that my voice quavered like an old person's.

"Then I'll get help."

I had nothing to use except handfuls of torn grass which I dipped into the tank and pressed to his mouth so he could suck the moisture. It wasn't enough but at least they made cool compresses too, to soak on his poor sore flesh. I made several journeys until his arms and legs and stomach were covered with the damp green stuff. The peepul tree had hardly any leaves left so it made no shade. The boy had been left there to face the full sun, and even though clouds had gathered since, this cursed place felt like a furnace.

Tangles of hair hung over his face but he was now trying to toss them back, to see who or what had freed him. I pushed the hair out of his eyes as gently as I could and saw that his face was bruised but not swollen as the rest of him was. The ants had not travelled so high. He looked perhaps seven, I thought, and his eyes were as black and as large as my mother's.

"Don't be afraid, please don't. We will get you away from here to a safe place, I promise."

But even as I spoke these useless words, the fierce light in his eyes went dull and his head again dropped forward. I knew he must have a proper drink though I feared to leave him. And I had to get Benu, or someone else, to help me carry him through the gap in the wall and back to the boat.

I dashed to the tank one last time, pulled off my trousers and plunged them into the water. They easily covered the little boy and I arranged the dirty head wrap as a pillow under his head. He was released from the tree now but otherwise he looked as poorly as he had done when I had found him.

I waved my arms to threaten the kites, still horribly hopeful above. Then I ran, pulling down my kurta tunic as far as it would go, which was not enough. If I met anyone now, I could not think what might happen.

THE CONCH

I WAS LUCKY. No one had come out from the big brick house since I had arrived and nobody came forward now while I ran past one after another of the small rough houses until I found the main village tank. The road ended at the water's edge. Beyond the trees there were only the footfall paths that led away to the fields. I heard a buffalo call out from there, furiously, as if it needed to be milked.

I hated to step inside any of the houses but I had to find a cup. And though they didn't look different from any small village house, it seemed to me that the sweet sickly smell of the orchard hung inside these dwellings too. Perhaps this was a village where only ants lived now? My stomach turned over at the thought but then the buffalo bellowed again. There was no time to be disgusted. That familiar sound reminded me that real people lived here, and they surely included the boy's captors. Whatever sorcery had removed them might restore them at any moment.

Again, I was fortunate – the first house I entered had two things I needed. A brass pot and, underneath it, a dark cotton cloth that I wound like a sari round myself. Even more auspiciously, when I ran to dip the pot in the tank, I almost tripped over a huge conch shell lying in the water grasses. The conch was clean, not dusty or muddy, which meant it had been left there only a short while ago. Who would neglect a valuable conch in this way? Not that I cared who or why, for, if it worked for me, that meant I could call out for Benu without losing the time it would take to run to the boat and back again.

I had never blown a conch before – no girl does. But I had often seen it done. On our lane, Varsha and Bashanti's father blew louder calls than anyone in all Calcutta, they had told me proudly. When nobody was watching we would twist our lips as he did and blow rude noises into our hands.

What a power was in that shell! It turned my breath to thunder. I could surely have blown down the mean houses and walls of this village, if I'd had time. But three blasts were all I allowed myself. Then I threw the conch down by the water's edge and headed back to the courtyard with my potful of fresh water, striding as fast as I could without spilling any.

Benu was at the turn of the path when I reached the brick wall. His face was stretched tight from running but it collapsed when he saw me. If he was angry that I had been gone so long I could not detect it. Only his relief.

"First you disappeared," he gasped. "I was giving you a little while in case... Then I had to wait till two boats passed... But the conch... I thought they had taken you ... that they were going to beat you..."

"Benu, hurry."

I pushed him towards the broken place in the wall, shoved the pot inside and wriggled through once again. I didn't wait for Benu, I knew he was my shadow.

The boy's eyes flickered when I removed the damp covering from him. With Benu on one side and me on the other, we raised him again and let him lean back against the peepul tree. I poured some of the water over his head and face and then put the lip of the pot to his mouth. He drank like a baby then, but in great gulps, swallowing noisily. Benu tried to show him that he should drink slowly. It was no surprise that he vomited, though not food, only white slime that hung in strings over his poor bitten chest. If there were not two of us to hold him up he might have slipped forward and choked.

The boy's black eyes moved from my face to Benu's and back but he said nothing at all while I told Benu how I had found him so cruelly tied up, without a soul on hand in the village to help me or even to tell me what had happened here.

"This place is dead," I said, "and yet it feels alive, as if something worse will happen. So we have to move him now he's had his water and get him to the boat somehow."

"And quickly, before these devils come back." Benu's gentle face was twisted as he spat the words out. "My father can deal with this. He will know best."

It was a difficult passage back to the river. With Benu out front and me behind pushing him, we managed to get the boy through the hole in the wall though we could see that the pressure on his legs and arms caused him horrible pain. What was worse was that he did not seem to understand what had to be done but cried and tried to wriggle away from us and curl up on the grass by the wall. I put my hands to my ears so that I could not hear his pleading. I felt like his torturer and I could see that Benu felt the same.

In that brief privacy I pulled off the rough sari and struggled again into my damp trousers. I left the cloth and the pot by the crumbling wall, not caring if they were ever to be found again.

GOOD FORTUNE

MISS HICKEY HAD SOME *sheets of paper and pencils ready for me when our second visit came round. This time Mr Bristol did not come with us, which was a relief to everyone. Even Mr Hickey seemed happier. He was whistling as he gave my mother a little brass image of Lord Ganesha to hold in her hand. This Ganesha held his elephant trunk neatly to the left so that his man's belly stuck out like a ripe fruit.*

"Found it in the bazaar," he said. "Appealing little thing."

Of course my mother would have preferred to hold a Durga but she took the little god and positioned him until Mr Hickey said she had got everything just so.

I was the lucky one of us two. My mother had to sit motionless and stare out at the view from the porch, where our bearers were sitting on the grass, dozing. I was sitting on the floor near her, drawing a picture for Miss Hickey of the bulbul that used to sing near our house on the lane.

When tea and cake were brought in to us after an hour or so, my mother joined us and told Miss Hickey about my baby drawings on palm leaves.

"She loves birds, just as I," she told Miss Hickey in her

best English, "but she is like nobody. She makes you to see them for always."

When Mr Hickey took up his brush again, Miss Hickey took me out of the room to see the rest of the house.

"Can you perhaps read English as well as you speak it, child?" she asked me. "For, if so, I have books that you might enjoy."

She showed me into a long bright room with comfortable seats and couches. There were pictures hanging everywhere on the yellow walls, piled on top of each other as well as side by side. There were portraits of ladies and gentlemen, soldiers in uniforms and men in black, views of buildings, pictures of fruit and kitchen ornaments. There was even a coloured drawing of Krishna sitting in his tree playing his flute, with the gopis, the herd girls, bathing underneath. All the walls were covered except for one, which was home to a glass-walled bookcase like Mr Bristol's, only this one was larger.

I did not know whether to look at the pictures or at the books. Miss Hickey saw me hesitate and she sat on one of the couches and patted it so that I might join her.

"Tell me about yourself, my dear," she said. "We can pick books in a while. But I would love to hear about your life here in Calcutta and your lovely mother. I have not managed a great acquaintance with India yet, which I feel is a shame for me, and somehow I think you are just the person who will provide the key."

It was a strange business, but in just a little while Miss Hickey had heard from me all about my father and his terrible departure the previous year. I had very little to say about Mr Bristol and our life today. I felt that part of our life was like the road outside, with all its ups and downs on show.

"My mother does not like to talk about him," I said. "I

truly believe that he will come back, that he loves us. But I worry so much that he will never find us."

There were tears in Miss Hickey's eyes.

"And you say he is Irish, not English?" she asked. "Did you know that we are Irish too? Surely we must be able to trace some news for you. We shall make enquiries from the Company and if you would prefer that your mother not be told this at first I can understand."

Mr Bristol had not mentioned that the Hickeys were Irish. I suppose that he did not think it would mean anything to us. But now I understood why Mr Hickey's voice had sounded so familiar and so pleasant to me when I first heard it. Miss Hickey's voice was different. It was light but very clear and chopped, not full of soft endings like my father's. She finished all her words neatly as if she could see them divided up on a page. Now she spoke again.

"A daughter and a father are very close," she said. "My father is like a bear at times but he has a heart of gold and he is a very intelligent and questioning type of person. I would hate to be apart from him now that my dear mother has left us. I have a sister, as you may have guessed, I think —" she smiled — "but she is preparing to be married and lives in London."

She stood up and her face was very stern.

"I feel that I must look after you, Anila," she said. "You are here for a reason and I will not let any harm come to you. You are in a vulnerable position and you have such abilities and talents that would put the rest of our pampered society here to shame."

What might I say to that? But I told Miss Hickey that my mother was also full of talent and abilities, and that she was just as good a storyteller as the Mr Swift who wrote books.

Only she was shy in company and her stories were all in Bengali.

"Bless you, child, I know that is true. That is, I believe you. We are all wonderful creatures if we only have the good earth to root us and the space to blossom."

She forgot about the books for a moment then, and took me out to her garden, which I thought was much more pleasant than Mr Bristol's neat one, especially because you could see the broad river at the end of it, beyond a roughly cut hedge. On the water you could see ships and boats of every size. I thought how I would never be bored if I could only live in such a house.

A mynah with a crooked tail landed on the grass very close to us and Miss Hickey scolded him for refusing his breakfast of oatmeal that morning. He set his head to one side and seemed to be listening.

She took me back into the salon again.

"Did you know the other lady?" she asked. "The other Indian lady that my father painted some years ago?"

I said that we had only heard about her, that Mr Bristol did not bring my mother round to meet his friends in their houses.

"We never meet ladies, only gentlemen," I said. "But the dressmaker from Benares tells us news about them sometimes."

Her little face twitched at that. She did not say, in the way Mr Bristol had made sure to, that my mother was more beautiful. Instead, she told me the other bibi's name and where she lived. She was a Mussulman, I heard, and had worked as a sweeper before the English gentlemen had noticed her fine face. I could see that this bibi was someone Miss Hickey had liked and felt for, someone she had spoken with, someone who was much more than a fine painting on a wall and money in her father's pocket.

She was at her bookcase now, picking books down and flicking through them, returning them to the shelves.

"It's so difficult to pick a book for someone," she said over her shoulder, "and my father has collected quite a few unfortunate ones."

I would have preferred to look for myself but I knew she was determined to make a choice for me so I stayed still and stared at the pictures.

"I think you might enjoy these, Anila." Miss Hickey put three books into my hands.

"The Natural History of Birds, Intended for the Amusement and Instruction of Children, *By Samuel Galton," I read.*

She beamed at me. "Of course the birds in it are the birds of England for the most part, I am sure."

"The Female," *and I stopped.* "I don't know this word."

"Quixote," *she said, pronouncing the strange word as* quicksot. *"A brave but foolish knight-at-arms in an old story from Spain and the lady in the book you are holding is his equal of today. And this last one is* Aesop's Fables, *very old folk stories from the Greek. The animals and birds in them are as human as ourselves, as devious and as cunning. Your dear mother might enjoy hearing some of those."*

When we returned at last to the painting room my mother was standing up, stretching her arms out in relief. She gave me the little Ganesha to hold and I rubbed his belly for luck, before putting him down on Mr Hickey's table of brushes and paints. The painting was secure on its support, and seemed larger than I remembered from the last time. Or perhaps it looked that way because so much had happened on its surface since then.

Mr Hickey had conjured up my mother just as she had sat,

with her arms and her head turned in a graceful way. Every shot and glimmer of her green silks seemed to move as they did in life. He had found the glossy black for her hair, and had worked life into that also, so that you could believe her braid would toss any moment if a breeze came past the pillars on the porch. Her skin, for which I had not believed he would ever find the colours, looked as alive as if there was blood under it.

But he had not yet filled in her face, nor the silver jewellery she wore, and she had no feet. There was no wall behind her and the couch was a shape merely, and went without its fine rug. Lord Ganesha had yet to appear though my mother's right hand was clearly settled round something. I hoped it was our good fortune.

NAMES

FOR ALL HIS GREAT SIZE, Madan had a touch as gentle as my mother's. He and Mr Walker laid the boy out on some cushions in the cabin and Madan produced a jar of dark neem oil from one of his cupboards.

"You did well to cool him with the water," he said to me, his huge hands spreading the salve over the boy's limbs and belly. "You probably saved his life."

Benu had told them everything, or almost everything. My parched throat hurt me and after answering a few questions I felt too weary to speak further. But when I mentioned to Madan that the buffaloes had been calling to be milked he at once left the cabin to stand on deck and stare in the direction of the village. It was dark by then but when he came back inside he reported that there were no fires there yet, no sounds.

We stood around awkwardly, watching Madan's ministry, all of us, that is, except Carlen. He was on the bank fiddling with his fire, but this time I knew he was not being callous.

When Benu and I had stumbled back to our mooring place with the boy, Carlen had been the first to meet us. His face went paler than ever, if that was possible, when he saw the child, and I thought for a moment that he was going to be as sick as he had made me that morning. But no, he came forward and lifted the boy from us as if he weighed no more than an infant. He held him and rubbed his back gently, as if he had a very young baby in his arms. Then he carried him on board the boat.

Now he came in with a clay cup and I could smell his telltale mint in the steam rising from it.

"Get the boy to drink this," he said to Madan. "It will cool him on his inside too; it heals."

Madan saw to it that the boy took a few small sips. He was sitting up now, and we put a blanket round his shoulders, for there was the fear that his fever would give way to a deadly cold. He spoke some words but they were so jumbled we did not understand him.

Only Madan had any idea of what he was saying and that was because of his great knowledge of the different people who lived along the river. But even so his great brow furrowed over and over as he tried to piece the child's halting tale together. It was dark except for the red glow of the fire on the bank by the time we understood what had happened that dreadful day.

"He has no name, he says, none that he remembers. His master called him Slave."

"Oh, Madan, we must find him a name," I said. "We must think of a proper good name."

Madan nodded grimly, but Carlen flinched at my words, I noticed. His hands were clenched tight round the empty clay cup now while Madan was talking but I had seen him touch the soles of the boy's feet very gently once or twice as if he were a baby.

The boy did not know how old he was. He was a tribal boy from a place away to the east, the only one of his people to survive a terrible disease. A great land-owner, a zamindar, had found the starving boy crawling among the dead bodies of his village people and had taken him back to his own home.

"But none of the servants there would let him share their space and so the zamindar gave the boy to his own brother, a crazy man."

This was the man who lived in the tumbledown brick house with the peepul tree and the fish tank. He ruled over the people in the little hamlet as if he were a rajah. He could be kind, he could be cruel, the boy said. But because he was mad, nobody knew which he would be on any day of the calendar.

"He might beat the boy in the morning and give him sweet payesh in the afternoon. He made him dig holes in the orchard one day and fill them up again the next."

Madan shook his head as he told us these things. But there was worse, he warned us.

A little girl in the village grew fond of the boy and had asked him to catch a fish for her family. But he had no skill to do this because he was not allowed to mix with the other boys in the village. Instead one morning he took a fish from his master's tank. The old man had found him standing by the water with the net and the fish still gasping in it. Unfortunately that day – today – was one of the master's bad days.

First the master had locked him inside the house and the boy thought he would get away with a beating.

The master left and was gone a long while.

"When he came back," Madan told us, "he took the boy to the courtyard and tied his arms to the tree. Then he mixed a pot of sugar and hot water and brushed this all over the child with a horse brush. He told him then that he had ordered all the villagers, even the old ones, to the next hamlet, where he had gathered some players to put on a putul naach, a puppet show. They went because they were so afraid of him, even though there was a day's work to be done."

Madan was shaking his head and his voice was a little unsteady.

"Then he hit the boy in the face and went off on his horse to see the puppets himself. If you had not found him, Miss Anila…"

"This would not happen where I come from," Hari muttered. "These are savage people."

Benu looked directly at Mr Walker.

"I would like to kill that man, sahib," he said. His forehead was knotted and a little vein throbbed in his jaw.

"And you think you could run from that family's revenge?" his father said. He glanced quickly at Mr Walker.

"We must be gone from here before it is light," he said.

Mr Walker nodded grimly. "I am of the same opinion, Madan. Indeed, I'm beginning to think we may have journeyed far enough upriver as it is. We have our unknown bird, Anila, or a very good chance of it, at any rate. I've seen the salt trade at work. Perhaps this terrible happening is signal enough for us to turn back.

We are gone, what is it, nine days, Madan?"

Madan nodded but said nothing. My heart quickened.

Mr Walker did not speak for a while. The energy that was such a part of his nature seemed quite absent so that I felt he was almost a stranger. But this night Carlen was also behaving oddly. Perhaps I was too.

"Poor benighted child," Mr Walker said at last. "Well, we have rescued him now and so we must race ahead of any consequences. I will not endanger any person here. The man is clearly and cruelly mad and the people are living in terror of him. And I cannot even report him to Fort William because of all the salt depots around here."

He hit his knee hard. I knew he felt powerless. I felt it myself but it was so much worse for him, being in command of our journey and yet having to watch this evil deed go free of punishment.

"Sahib, the English would support the zamindar and his family members anyhow, because they bring in the taxes." Madan lifted his shoulders and looked round at all of us. "Never mind. Word can be spread along the river. Things can happen. But I believe, as you do, that we should turn back now."

There was a silence. Then Carlen spoke.

"We should call the boy Manik."

We all looked at him and I think everyone was showing a different kind of confusion. Madan, Benu and Hari had not expected to hear a child's pet name in Bangla coming from Carlen's lips. I was taken aback by the softness in his voice. He stared directly at me as he said the name again.

"Manik. It means little jewel. Look at him. He knows you saved him."

The boy was sitting up now and he had a fistful of our spiced rice halfway to his mouth. His swellings had gone down though you could still see the hateful bite tracks the ants had made over his skin. His thick curly hair, clean now, was tied back with a yellow handkerchief that could only have been Mr Walker's for I could see an E and a W on it worked in red thread. The boy's huge eyes took us in, one by one, but they always came back to rest on me.

"Manik is a perfect name," said Mr Walker. "Now we should let him sleep, and ourselves too, so that we can leave here before sunup tomorrow. Nine days perhaps, returning – yes, that's good enough time to meet my dates. Tomorrow we'll head downriver. And, for sure, we are none of us likely to forget this place."

We started for our sleeping places. When I left the boat for my tent Madan was making the boy comfortable in the cabin between himself and Benu. Hari had stayed behind in the cabin too. Carlen was not to be seen but his bedding was spread out on deck.

I hugged myself in the cool air. Truly I felt hopeful that tomorrow at last I might make a bargain with Carlen – he had been almost friendly to me. But one bother stood between me and my sleep, bone-tired and sore though I was.

I did not think I was ready to say goodbye to our life on the river.

THE BOOK OF
SURPRISES

HERONS WOKE ME NEXT MORNING, squabbling and shouting their news to each other, but so early that there was just one thin silver line of light setting out on its journey across the lowest part of the sky. At any other mooring place Madan would have looked around for anything that might disturb our sleep. But he had not noticed the herons' nests last night.

Or perhaps he had, I thought. For the birds had certainly got me up before daybreak. Perhaps I should wake everyone?

I would bathe first. My shoulders still pained me a little and the cool water would be soothing, the live flow like a mother's hands on my skin, kind Ganga.

On the boat I saw a small face peering over the gunwale, looking upriver towards me and I waved. The water would be good for Manik too but perhaps it was not safe for him to venture out until we had left this place far behind. I set out to walk to the spot where I had seen the otters.

"Anila, come back. Now!"

Mr Walker's voice had an edge in it. When I reached

the tents again, he and Hari, Madan and Benu were standing on the bank. I realized then that they had been up before me but there was no fire, no breakfast. No Carlen.

"I don't know where the wretched man has got to, but we will have to leave shortly or goodness knows what wrath we will be facing from that village. Get the tents down and then let everyone get on board, so that we can cast off in an instant."

He stared off towards the dark line of trees that screened the village. Then he gestured towards the fields all around and the river path. But if he were trying to make Carlen appear he had no success.

"He's taken my pistol so he must be looking for a hare or a duck or something to vary our diet. He told me he was sick of fish. But now is not the time for such a pastime."

Benu wrinkled his nose in disgust at the idea of such flesh-eating. Then he and Hari set to dismantling the tents as best they could, though I noticed that they made very rude work of folding them up. Manik was watching everything from the deck but Madan quickly shooed him into the cabin where the Venetians were tightly closed and he would not be seen.

When we had packed everything away Madan looked at me. Mr Walker was still on the bank, pacing the length of the boat, back and forward, always looking towards the village. His face was drawn tight over its bones and his hair looked damp, as if the day was already hot which it was not. He looked ill, I thought.

"I do not think he is gone shooting ducks, do you?"

Even as Madan was saying the words my heart

dropped down. He was right of course. The passion that had seized Carlen yesterday at the sight of poor tortured Manik had not been content to busy itself in caring for him. He had gone now to avenge the cruelty in the way he best understood. That left all of us now in some danger surely but that was not what had shaken me.

"Oh, Madan, Carlen knows where my father is but he won't tell me. And now he's gone."

I hadn't meant to say this to anyone but it was impossible to keep silent now. I pushed past Madan and his neatly wound ropes, jumped up on the rim of the boat and ran to Mr Walker.

"Mr Walker, Carlen has gone to kill that man. You must know that if I do. But I need to talk to him! We must go after him, please, please. Or I'll go myself."

I started away then for he was not answering me. He was too shocked. But he reached out as I tried to run and grabbed my wrist, so tightly round the bones that it hurt and he pulled me back until he could hold me there in front of him. Then he crouched down so that his face was on a level with my own. His eyes looked sore, like green fruits cut open too early. Or else they were angry. I wasn't sure which.

"Anila, you will get back on that boat now. With me. We are leaving directly. Carlen knows we are starting back downriver today. He's clever enough to be able to find us when he gets this madness out of his mind. If he does, that is."

He marched me over to where Madan was waiting to take me back though I was crying out all manner of things that nobody could understand. But when Benu swung the tiller and brought us out into the centre of the river and we felt the strength of the current now bearing us back the way we had come, I stopped babbling.

All of us are borne along on the great river, Anila, even the birds that fly above it and never touch it.

I sat there hunched on a coil of ropes, looking in no direction. Nobody paid me any heed either, though I was certain that Madan had passed on my desperate words to Mr Walker as they sat closeted in the cabin, leaving Hari to tend the ropes.

I felt a touch on my arm, the slightest touch, as if a feather had fallen out of the sky. Manik was kneeling beside me. He had placed one hand on my arm and he was stroking it there, forward and back, forward and back.

"Anila," he said. And then, "Manik takes away the hurt. Like you did."

I put my hand on top of his and we stayed like that for a little while. Behind us Benu began a song and the day filled with one thing after another, with heat and light and the noises of the river and her boats, with smells of morning cooking carried on the breeze, with the jewel colours of saris stretched out to dry by the banks. Women were walking the river paths with damp washing piled up on their heads and at times you could see their water bodies marching along underneath them where the water was still.

Some called out to us and one bold girl shook her bangles at Benu. I could hear his blush in the way he sang his next words. This made me smile, despite every bad thing.

"Will you get my bag, Manik?" I asked, for I would not go inside the cabin.

He came back clutching my flat drawings case looking like a tiny runner, like one of the fleet-footed boys and men who carry mails and messages around the city. I showed him some of my birds and his eyes grew larger. When he saw the owl he laid a finger on the paper and then put it to his mouth as reverently as if it were an image of the goddess Kali herself he had touched.

"You must tell me if you see a bird you don't know, Manik. Do you understand? Any strange bird at all, so that I may put it down on the paper here."

Manik nodded solemnly though I had no notion whether he understood me or not.

And then, just to make it more confusing for him, I started to draw, not any bird at all, but the otters of yesterday morning.

In truth I found this work much more difficult than drawing a bird and I didn't know why. Feathers are just as dainty and intricate as fur, and probably more so. I think perhaps it may be that birds make shapes that are complicated but they all come from the same Book of Shapes. So, if you learn that, as my father did with his buildings, you can draw them all, with practice. But an animal is like a human. There are too many surprises under its skin and all over its face. Mr Hickey said that humans were a never-ending Book of Surprises when you came to draw them. But he had trained with that Book and I had not. I felt my otters lacked life.

At last Mr Walker and Madan came out of the cabin.

"Anila, will you come inside with me, please?"

Madan laid a huge hand on Manik's head as he passed us.

"There's a lad whose fingers will tie the neatest knots," he said. "Come and learn to be a boatman, Manik."

I put my otters into the case and followed Mr Walker into the cabin. The air was fusty but neither of us was inclined to open the Venetians and Mr Walker had closed the door firmly behind me.

"First this, Anila. We are stopping at the next big ghat, which is quite close now. Madan will send some men he knows there back to that cursed village to find out what they may. So, what we will do there is wait. Now you must tell me what on earth it was that disturbed you in such a shocking manner this morning."

I told him then, and it was the greatest relief to tell him everything, right down to the loss of my tiny ring, which no longer felt important.

"I believed him, Mr Walker, because how else could he know such a detail as that about my father? But then he closed down his whole person, his mouth, his ears, his eyes. It was as if he wanted me to suffer more. And I would have given him all my money, my paints, everything, to find out where he saw my father, and when. For he may still be in that place."

Mr Walker had put his head in his hands very soon after I began my story. When I finished he stayed like that for a few moments and then stood up and began to pace the floor just as he had paced the riverbank, though here his head was skimming the roof of the cabin. He looked as white as his very own Mr Minch.

"I cannot explain what exactly was in Carlen's mind

when he was treating you in such a vile fashion. My best estimate is that he was very jealous of your position here, of your talent, of your very appealing spirit, so that he wanted to fashion his little power of exposition into a kind of torture. There is nothing to be said by way of excuse. Nothing. But let me tell you everything I know about the man himself so that you may understand his nature a little better."

Carlen was a foundling child, Mr Walker told me, who had been abandoned by the gates of a stables in the eastern side of England.

"He showed me the country there one time. It was as flat and full of rivers and creeks as Bengal itself, Anila."

The stable people had raised him, but very roughly. They'd given him only the one name, Carlen, to do service for everybody else's two names. I remembered then how yesterday Carlen had had freely betrayed one of his own secrets, the good knowledge he had of Bangla, in order to bestow a fitting name on little Manik.

"They beat him, they did worse. When he was eleven or so he ran away and learned to live on his wits."

Carlen was a young horse thief when Mr Walker met him first, a most dangerous trade because such thieves were always hanged when caught.

"I was spending my grandmother's good money in inns and on horses when I came down to Cambridge but I had no sense of what I was doing, and certainly had no skill for it. For some reason Carlen took pity on me when one of his own gang of scalpers was about to despatch me after robbing me. That was our introduction and it has always given me a duty towards him. In many ways he is a remarkable person though you will hardly credit that, Anila."

Certainly I would refuse to do that! But at that moment I was trying to picture serious, kindly Mr Walker in the alehouses and cockpits that he described and that was an impossible thing. He seemed to know what I was thinking.

"I was full of hatred then myself, for the loss of my sister and my part in that, for my father and his unyielding nature. It took me quite a while to settle, to become a lover of books, of knowledge."

"And birds?"

He smiled sadly.

"I had that always, you see, from my sister Eveline."

Outside Madan roared and we felt the clunk of the tiller behind and the shift underneath us as the boat tilted for the bank.

Mr Walker sat down, as abruptly as a child.

"Here we shall wait, Anila. Let us pray that the news they bear is good."

THE PAINTING

"A CAPITAL JOB, HICKEY!"

Those were the words Mr Bristol used when the big day came and he was invited to have first sight of my mother's finished portrait. They were the same words he used with his gentlemen friends when their deals worked out, or their law cases were won.

For weeks, Mr Hickey had become coy about his work, as we had been warned he would.

"He'll turn it to the wall so you cannot peek, and he will become very short if you ask him anything about it," Miss Hickey told me. "You must humour him, for that is his way always, to wish to surprise the patron above all. And to be honest, Anila, quite apart from that, I think you make him nervous with the questions you ask."

That was true. He had taken to calling me "that little peppercorn", though he was just as generous as before with paper and pens for me, and he would always ask to see what I had been drawing, after my mother stood up from her sofa and stretched her arms. But now these conversations came only after he had carefully turned the painting away from our view.

So, of the three of us who were not Hickeys, I don't know

which one was the most curious on the day of the unveiling. That was what such an event was called, Mr Hickey told me, and he had gone so far as to hang his best black cloak over the painting.

"Patrons. They do like a bit of drama, a fuss," he said. But I could see he liked the same himself.

We were gathered in the painting room. Miss Hickey had called for lime juice and whisky and cakes with cream but they were to stand ready on the long sideboard until the unveiling ceremony was over. Mr Bristol was twittering like a brain fever bird but my mother held herself serene.

Mr Hickey began a little speech.

"Good afternoon to all of you," he said, although he had greeted us already.

"You will think that I state the obvious when I say that the subject of my painting," he bowed to my mother, "is a most beautiful lady. But I have discovered during these past few weeks that she is as delightful in her manner as in her face. That is not always the case."

I wondered if everyone had noticed that Mr Hickey was finishing his sentences. That in itself was surely a tribute to my mother.

"I have learned much from her, for she is a lady imbued with the stories and traditions of her country."

He fixed Mr Bristol with a keen look.

"I hope such things have been expressed in my work as well as every other quality that you might expect to find, sir. I might even remark that my subject's daughter has done excellent duty as a painter's apprentice and you may find some recording of that too."

Mr Hickey cleared his throat. Now that he had launched himself on a sea of fine phrases, it seemed he had more to add.

But Mr Bristol had had enough.

"Remove the cloth, Hickey!" he called out. "Don't hide your talent from us under that black bushel any longer."

He laughed but Mr Hickey did not. He stepped up behind the painting and very neatly lifted his cloak, putting it down on the worktable I had cleared for him.

We all stared at my mother in the picture.

Every part of her was there now, face, hands and feet, all her jewellery on and the little Lord Ganesha in her grip. There was no surprise any more for me to see that Mr Hickey had made her cheeks glow and her huge black eyes drink up the misty world beyond the marble columns.

What did make me gasp now was that Mr Hickey had painted something that was new in my mother, something I recognized now that I saw it underneath the fresh varnish. For I knew my dreams had been painting the same thing for me for some time now, over and over, in dark shades.

My mother's gaze was fixed on another world, one where her gentleness and all her hopes would be rewarded at last. This terrified me because I saw that the painting told the truth. She was drawn towards a departure as some birds are, come their time, to find again the lake where they were born. It was no matter that I jumped up and down in front of her and with all my loudness tried to hold her back.

She was staring at the picture herself now with interest.

"Look, Anila," she whispered to me. "Mr Hickey has painted your face in the little mirror. How clever he is to get us both into the picture."

I went closer to look, though Mr Bristol clucked at me for standing in front of him.

She was right. The tiny hand mirror on the table by the couch was placed at an angle so that it might have caught my mother's face. Instead my face was what you saw, young and bold-eyed, anything but faraway. What I thought was just as clever was that Mr Hickey had copied the design of my mother's foot painting and used it to decorate the casing of the little mirror.

We were admiring these things when Mr Bristol spoke his opinion.

"A capital job, Hickey! You have outdone your last work in this line, no question of that."

I could see Miss Hickey flinch at his words. Mr Hickey merely bowed his head but I could see that his eyes were cold. Mr Bristol's praise was hardly praise at all. He saw little of the craft, or the many choices Mr Hickey had made to compose his picture. I was certain he could not see my mother's soul beating on that canvas like wings.

Miss Hickey clapped her hands and called for the drinks to be handed round, and the plates of cakes and nuts. She herself served my mother to a glass of lime juice and bid her sit down to chat.

Mr Bristol had wandered away into the hall to see what he might see. I went to stand by Mr Hickey and the painting.

"Please may I ask you a question?" I said to him.

He looked startled.

"Yes, my dear?"

"Do you think my mother is sick?"

He passed the back of his hand over his forehead. Then he looked round, to see where Miss Hickey was, and my mother. There were drops above his lip but it was a cool day. We were at the start of winter once again.

"Anila, you must not read so much into what you see on a canvas," he said slowly. "Painters are like poets. Seize an element and make of it something else. Play with it."

He looked directly at me and those blue eyes did not shift at all when he answered.

"Truth is," he said. "I feel sorry for your mother's situation. Perhaps that's what you are seeing. And saying. Our friend there, obviously, he won't see that. Beyond his pale, such a thought."

He shook his head and drew in a breath.

"But look out for her, all the same," he said. "She is a sensitive lady."

He picked my hand up and stretched my fingers out on top of his great ruddy ones.

"The talent you have in this hand, my dear. Must be followed up. I'll speak to Bristol. You could pick up quite a bit from me, if I say it myself. Helena would be glad too. Of the company."

He led me over to the seat where they were sitting, his daughter and my mother.

"Told Anila here they must come back. Regularly. She needs schooling. And you need the river air for your good health, my dear."

He gave my mother a little bow and left us.

Miss Hickey was so pleased with this proposal that she produced little dimples I had never seen before. She pressed cakes on both of us and when we could not take another morsel she took us out into the back garden. My mother gasped when she saw the river. We showed her the crooked mynah and by the time we were called out front again, she had persuaded the bird to eat cake from her hand. Miss Hickey swore she was jealous and said that she would not deal again with the faithless creature, but her dimples were showing again so we had no fear for him.

My mother was quiet on our journey home, though Mr

Bristol would not stop from wondering where he would hang the picture, and whom he would invite to see it, and whether or not he would permit Mr Hickey to place it in exhibition. It was travelling with us in comfort, having its very own seat, while we three sat squashed together facing it.

"To have society see you like this, that would be a fine thing, my dear," he said to my mother. She stared at him without replying.

I knew how she felt about such exposure. But I also knew he was not measuring the expression on her face against the one that Mr Hickey had captured in the picture. He could not. He had no art to see what was under his nose, though that skill was what he most prided himself on possessing.

He may have been blind but I was helpless.

STAR-GAZING

MADAN TRUSTED THE TWO MEN he had sent to the village. But when they had not returned by nightfall he said such things I would never have imagined hearing from him. The ghatsmen had calculated how far it was and how long it would take to go back across the fields and creeks and Madan told us the pair should be well returned by the time we sat down to eat. Mr Walker bought a huge bekti fish to treat us. But the men were not back and that most delicious of fishes tasted like paper in our mouths.

Now Mr Walker had to tend Madan's worries as well as mine, and, of course, his own.

He sat with me on the roof of the cabin, fitting his telescope together. The moon was more than a half now and she was smiling down with all her growing strength, beaming at her own twin in the dark water.

"I was staring at Jupiter last night," he said, "trying to see if there was a message up there in the sky for our saved little boy."

I looked at him in surprise. Was Mr Walker a star-gazer then, like the star-chart makers in the bazaars?

They claimed they could see our fortunes written above our heads in a script that changed each night.

"Some people say the stars and planets are lights for the gods," I said. "but I think perhaps the gods made them for the night birds and animals. Not for us."

In truth I found the night sky a lonely place, too big and too cold for human words and names.

"Look here," he said, and he pushed the golden barrel into my hand. "It's almost two centuries since the great astronomer Signor Galileo discovered that Jupiter had four moons of its own. But though I believe they are up there I've never seen one of them, not with these poor eyes of mine, anyhow. See what you can see, Anila."

I put my right eye to the cold brass. The glass turned even the deepest black cloth of the sky into lace, fine white points that shimmered and bewitched the eye. Surely it was easier to find the great planet without an aid. My father had shown it to me long ago and had told me its name, Jupiter, king of the gods. My mother called it Brihashpati. Brihashpati had his own day, Brihashpatibar, which the English called Thursday. Until now however I had never heard of any moons except our own faithful one, which grew a hare's face when she was full and fat.

I tried my left eye and now I found a difference in what I saw. To one side of the planet I could see a lustre point. It might have been a dim star. It might have been a chip of rock or dust trapped between the two glasses in the brass tube.

But down the length of this telescope that had travelled all the way from the city of London came a light of sorts. Perhaps indeed it was a moon shining down on its own great rock in the darkness.

If that, it was shining too on all of us alive on earth. Wherever my father was, it must shine for him as surely as it did for Mr Walker and me on the river, for Miss Hickey on the sea, for Anoush in the city.

I looked at Mr Walker.

"I saw something – a light so small." I put my little fingers together to show him.

"Bless you," he said. "Sometimes it is hard to believe when you cannot see. But you have always believed your father is out there in the world, Anila. I always found that striking when you spoke of him. Such faith. And I will tell you something else. One of those moons-in-hiding that only you can see tonight is called Ganymede. Ganymede was a servant to the gods but he began his story as a little kidnapped boy like our Manik."

He stood up and gently took the telescope from me.

"So the stars seem good, Anila. You go to sleep now, in the cabin this time. I promise to wake you when there is news."

But he did not have to.

I heard the soft tap that someone's hand gave to the side of the boat and I heard people stirring and then the boat itself felt suddenly lighter as they left it. I parted the wooden slats and saw Madan and Mr Walker following two men away from the ghat steps into the shadows of a shabby godown set back from the river.

When I looked at that little midnight huddle I knew that Mr Walker would wait till morning to wake me, to better prepare me for bad news. I had to know now.

I felt all their eyes on me as I tiptoed up the steps, past men bundled up and stretched out asleep. I came to stand a little apart from the four, outside the godown. I couldn't make out the expressions of the two strange men who stood with long shawls wrapped round their heads and shoulders. Madan was shaking his head slowly. Mr Walker was rubbing the old bite on his face as if he could erase all the bad things that had ever happened in his life.

"Ask Madan for his oil," I said, for it was something to say. "It will bleed if you do that."

Madan looked at me then and there was great sadness in his face.

"The sahib's man is dead," he said. "But so is the boy's master. That is justice along the river."

If Carlen had been content with killing the man he might have escaped easily, it seemed. He had gone to the brick house and shot the master in his sleeping room, for that was where the old man was found afterwards, kneeling on the floor as if begging for mercy. But then Carlen had gone through those miserable huts in the white light of the morning, waving his stolen pistol and forcing the village people out of their homes. Then he threatened them with punishment for their cowardice in permitting such things to be done to Manik.

The zamindar's men had arrived in the middle of the day and had discovered Carlen at the tank, forcing the villagers to immerse themselves, one by one.

"He must have looked like a raving preacher," said Mr Walker, sadly. "Trying to make them purge their sins. Anyway the new arrivals made short work of poor Carlen. It didn't at all bother them that he was an

Englishman. These two men did our respect of burying him, they tell me, when dark fell at last, and I know they must be telling the truth, because look here, Anila…"

Lying on his open palm was my little gold ring, with its hands clasped round the crown.

"I know it is poor consolation, my dear, given the secret that Carlen has carried with him to his grave. But think of this, Anila. When I get back to Calcutta and then to London I should find it entirely possible to trace where Carlen has been in the last few years, for I always took care to log the tasks I sent him on. Arising from his background, you see."

He was pleading with me to have some hope. But I could see in his poor haggard face that he had little himself and also that his own heart was sore for a person and a part of his life that was finished. I had no words to help him there.

I left the group and walked back to the boat. But first, from the steps of the ghat I crouched down and washed my ring in the Ganga water, washed it clear of blood and hate.

I heard Mr Walker and Madan coming back on board and settling themselves on the deck. Or perhaps they were sitting up instead, as I was. I sat till grey light seeped through the cracks of the Venetians. When at last I could see the shine on the cabin's polished cupboards and the soft cushions on the seats became crimson, not black, I reached for my bag. I wanted to look at my mother. Much much more, I wanted to hear her, I wanted her warm touch. But her picture would have to do.

There was a piece of lined paper folded round my mother's portrait, the rough kind bazaar scribes used for their letters. There was writing on it, a small script, neat as a girl's best writing, easy to read. It was addressed to me.

THE ANGEL

MR BRISTOL WAS NO HEMAVATI, that was for sure. But later that year when it became obvious even to him that my mother was not herself he first made huff and puff but the next thing he did was call a doctor to the house. At least he did that.

The doctor was English, quite an elderly man. He carried a hateful black leather bag that he snapped open on the bed so that it folded out like the wings of a great bat. I could see bottles and tiny silver knives set into a cloth inside it. It yawned open and the air from it smelt sweet and foul at the same time.

"She's not sick with a fever or wasting away," Mr Bristol said to the doctor. "Look at her, she's a picture of health, and small wonder with the food they get in this house and no expense spared, ever. But she talks nonsense now, strings of rubbish. Other times she sits there as if she's frozen. She hears nothing and says nothing."

He looked at the doctor the way people look at priests in the temple.

My dear mother was lying in our bed and I sat on the floor beside it, holding her right hand. I tried to make her wash every day and old Rupa brought plenty of water to our room and sometimes stayed to help me, but today we had not yet got so far. I hated my mother to be seen by a man like this doctor, but especially when she was not clean. Mr Bristol was right however when he said she looked healthy enough. She did. Only her eyes and the way she beat her fingers in mine were worrisome. And, of course, her silence.

The doctor asked my mother to lean back against the cushions. Then he put his hands on her eyelids and pulled them up to stare into her eyes, his face just inches from hers. He felt all round her head, moving his fingers like a blind man over a child's face. I bit my tongue because I knew my mother's hair was dirty, full of yesterday's oils and dust and flies. We had sat out in the garden watching the water fall in the fountain, my mother staring into it as if it was a new sight for her.

Then he asked her to stand but she stared at him and did not move. He sought my help then and together we got her legs from under the sheets and onto the floor ready to stand. We heaved her up and then he asked me to take away my hand.

"Walk a little," he said to her, but she simply looked at him. I said it to her too, but in Bangla, and more sharply than I had ever spoken to her before.

She took one step but after that one it seemed that her bones simply turned to cotton because she fell over and stayed there on the gleaming wooden floor, lay just as she fell, with her legs twisted. Her eyes were fixed on the ceiling and did not even seek mine out. I could not bear it.

We got her back into the bed then, and the doctor looked grim indeed. He snapped his bat case shut and he ushered Mr Bristol out of the room. He closed the door.

It was a thick door, but I put my ear to the keyhole and heard what I could.

"Not good, impossible to say, possibly a bleeding stroke or … deadly anyway… Not long in my estimation. Best follow custom when it comes."

Mr Bristol made a noise. When he answered the doctor his voice was hoarse.

"No medicine for this? No surgery? Would pay, you know … if you recommend…"

But whatever was said to those questions must have been with a headshake only because all I heard was another groan or whatever it was. And then, "An exquisite companion… All I could ask for…"

I heard their steps forward and was by the bed in a thrice. My mother had heard nothing or if she had she had closed her eyes against all the words in this house.

Mr Bristol's fleshy face was white and grey like ashes and he would not meet my glance. He went instead to the window where the shutters lay open to the little garden below. I believed he was weeping in his own fashion.

So it was the doctor who told me what must be told to a girl whose mother is dying.

But most of what he told me was not necessary because Annapurna, my dear mother, was wise enough to die in just a very few days after that. She had never troubled anyone in her life and I am sure that was part of the reason her death was speedy. She did not want me to suffer for the reasons the doctor had described. Very near to her end, she closed her fingers round mine and I looked down at our hands that were joined as if someone had carved them in one piece. I knew that in part she would be with me all the days of my life ahead.

Mr Bristol wanted to bury my mother in the big cemetery in Burial Ground Road and he told the doctor he would call for the black-coated funeral men and their dark carriage horses.

But I cried out at that. No, I believe I screamed, until the doctor stood by me and said that my mother's body must be brought to the river instead.

"Do as the Gentoos wish it, or you will be cursed, Bristol, for doing the wrong thing."

For so stiff a man, he was understanding enough, though I thought he was rude and forward when he put a hand on my forehead and felt under my jaw with his pale fingers.

"Poor orphan," he said. "but at least you are in good health."

The durwan arranged everything in the end, and Mr Bristol told him to spare no expense in what he ordered, or what fee he must pay the priest. Rupa and I dressed my mother in a plain cotton sari. We rubbed sandalwood paste onto her feet. Then we bound her loosely so that she was ready for the bier of palms. She would travel by boat up to the private burning ghats. The durwan had seen to it all.

I do not remember much of what happened that day. Mr Bristol did not come with us but he permitted Rupa and me to leave the house with the bearers and travel with my mother so that I could light the pyre. There was no son, no father, no brother to do this, just me, the only family mourner. I found the place so terrible that I did not lift my eyes to right or left but just followed the bearers and the small white shape that they carried. I remember that an old priest sang hymns in a voice that quavered. My mother would have giggled at that, I knew, but I hoped he was saying the right words. Rupa was murmuring her own prayers but I had none to offer. Not then.

A fog was settling in from the river when I touched my mother's body for the last time and lit the fire. Kind old Rupa held me as the shawls of fog and smoke mixed together and we felt both the heat and the damp on our arms and feet and faces. She held me as we made the return journey, something I cannot recall at all. I do remember that the durwan opened the gates faster than he had ever done in all the time I had spent in the house. This man who never wasted a word now looked at me with swimming eyes and I realized that he had probably cared for my mother's presence in his own brooding way.

Mr Bristol himself was at the door to greet us. He asked if everything was done according to our rites, as he put it, and then he went into his study and closed the door. I do not think he meant to be unkind. I think he feared his own emotions and, possibly even more, he feared the effort he must now make to decide my future.

He was spared that anyway. News travelled fast in the English city, as fast as in any bazaar. The next morning the durwan was busy again with his gate locks long before Mr Bristol left for the court. I was upstairs in our room then but all the sounds of the house and garden came in those windows and, above the songs of the sparrows and bulbuls, I could hear the clipped voice of Miss Hickey though her words were not clear.

I did not move from the bed where I had spent the night lying on top of the covers. But if I was playing durwan to my own self, Miss Hickey was having none of that. She was knocking on the door and calling my name and then entering and pulling me up into her arms.

"Oh, my dear, my dear," she whispered. "What a terrible loss. The angel." And then, "She thought you were the most wonderful child she could ever have wished to have. She was so proud of you, Anila. And I can feel free to tell you now that she exacted my promise, as if that was necessary, to take you into our care, if anything should happen to her. That is why I came here at first notice. My father heard the news only *last night and I spent the night waiting for a decent hour to come knocking on Mr Bristol's door."*

She looked at me, my swollen face and my eyes that must have looked as they felt, full of grit, and red as clay.

"I came to your room first thing but now I will go downstairs and talk to him. There will be no problem, none, you may have my word for it."

She left me, with a final hug that smelt of sweet lavender water, and went downstairs to find Mr Bristol. I lay back and closed my eyes. Perhaps I slept then because it seemed to be late afternoon when Mr Bristol himself knocked and came into the room. He looked nervous.

"Anila, my dear," he said. *"You know that the Hickeys have become fond of you and it is an extraordinary circumstance but they have very kindly offered you a home in the aftermath of all this…"*

He waved his hands around, and looked down at the floor for a moment.

"To tell you the truth, I did not know what to suggest to you. I would have consulted your mother but it was too late, by then. And I would not have my reputation sullied by idle gossip. I would perhaps have suggested the church, but now Miss Hickey has made this offer and she believes that you are agreeable. Is that the case?"

I just nodded, lying head down on my pillow, not looking at him.

"All her clothes and jewels, all her money, these are yours my dear."

There! My mother had her answer now.

I sat up.

"Thank you," I said to him. *"But I will just take my clothes and if you would give me her green sari, the one from*

the painting, I would take that. I don't want the painting, you can keep that."

His mouth was opening and closing like a fish landed on a bank.

"But there is quite an amount of money, child, and I would not cheat you of it, you know that. You are all alone now. The painting was not in my offer, by the way."

"You could give the money to Rupa then, or the church, or whomsoever," I said back to him as fast as I could get the words out. "But I don't need it. My father will be coming back some day, and he would not like me to have such money."

I felt badly immediately those words were out, but it was said. He probably thought I was made mad enough by my mother's passing to bring my father to life again.

That evening Miss Hickey came again in the carriage and by then my bag was packed. Rupa cried when I said goodbye to her and left her one of my mother's silk saris. Mr Bristol shook my hand on the porch and then bade me wait a moment. He went into his study and came back with the red-covered Robinson Crusoe.

"Remember me and your time in this house whenever you read this," he said. "You are a clever girl with all your reading. If you apply yourself there must be a position for you somewhere in the city when you are older and you will have my recommendation."

Miss Hickey bowed to him and took my arm. We stepped out into the garden and I looked round it for the last time. Night was falling and the fountain had stopped running but in my mind I could still hear that liquid sound. It had reminded my mother of her river. On summer days when monsoon did not drown it, it had told me something about freedom, even *though I knew its poor noise was false and that the fountain water was as trapped as we two had been in this place.*

The durwan raised his hand in salute and we travelled away in the darkness to Garden Reach, where I have stayed ever since.

The greatest kindness of the Hickeys was that they did not try to erase my mother's memory but spoke of her always so that she hung there like a fixed star in my sky. Beyond that everything they did on my behalf was to offer encouragement and the greatest affection.

Mr Hickey taught me how to prepare a canvas and use paint and schooled me in perspective and shading and other tricks of drawing. Always his joke was that he is protected from bankruptcy by the fact that birds attract me to paint them while humans do not. To that end he even bought for his library some of the famous Persian bookplates that are filled with animals and birds, picked out in gold and colours like jewels. They are not what I paint but they are beautiful.

It was Miss Hickey who taught me the English names of birds as far as she could, and improved my language and my knowledge in every other way. In return I taught her Bengali but she says that I am a better student and she a better teacher.

I am full of my own cares towards the two of them and glad of that, above all things, for it would be lonely beyond measure to be set under the skies on your own. The darkness in my life is the one that grows as an unpaid account does. The years that now separate my father and me are yawning and mysterious.

Miss Hickey kept her word and went to the Company on my behalf, to search for any news of my father. I was young then, and stayed at home, and was not present for the meeting she had with the person in charge of the Writers' affairs. I know that she returned full of fury that her errand had been thrown out by a man she called "an arrant bully". Afterwards she engaged the legal gentleman whose bibi had been painted by Mr Hickey to visit the Company on her behalf but he had no luck either. She intends to make more enquiries in Madras, where all ships to and from England must stop.

That is why I have stayed in Calcutta while my dear friends have gone south. I believe the answer to my father's absence lies here already and I must work harder to find it. Or else it will come one day from abroad, perhaps in a letter or a parcel. Or, best of all outcomes, he will step off a ship one day and when we have found one another we will begin a new life together.

THE STORM

TO MISS ANILA TANDY *in the happenstance I do not return from my mission.*

If you are reading these words likely Ill not be returned though you can find this paper sooner if you are smart and early about your drawing. Its no matter for I have made a mind to tell you these things any case since you saved our little boy Manik from his suffering and death. They tried to crucify him like the Lord.

I cant be other than I am now. I am made twisted though Edward Walker did his best for me and the right ways were easier to find around him always. Then you were there and taking all his best care. I could not have it. I grant I did you wrong. Another thing was that you had parents once for all that you are orphan now. I had none myself but thought I did well enough until you came along. It is hard for the poor to look at the rich.

But you have a father as I told you so you are not really orphan stock anyway. Take heed now lest you lose this paper so learn what I say. You are clever as I am myself. Your father is in Madras living near the place they call the Island. People know his name but he hardly knows it himself. He hears them call him Patrick Tandy but he has no memory of what Patrick Tandy has been or done in his life.

What he did to be like this is something that made me find out his company when I was in that city twice. Though it was not him who told me for he cannot remember it. His story is known in that place and you must have poor friends who could not find it out for you all this time.

When he was in ship from the Cape to Saint Helen he tried to stir the other passengers to speak in anger against the cargo they took on at the Cape. And what was that but a holdful of black slaves fastened down crueller than a butcher would tether an ox for killing. So the captain put him off on a boat at the island for jail but a storm recked that and only two of four men came clear alive on the rocks. Patrick Tandy and another man who had it that poor Tandy cracked his head first and then nearly drowned. From that day he was told his name but who knew the rest of it to tell him? No wife or child in the record. When the bucks on the island saw he could do things with a pencil for he did not lose that gift from

God they rid themselves of him and parcelled him back to India to be useful. They feared the spirit that set him going for the slaves. Now he goes out and draws ships and such things and for sailors sometimes pictures for their girls. Any seafarer in that quarter will find him out for you. He is happy mostwhiles in what he does though he has less of the roopees than I have myself.

It was the name itself Tandy that gave me the nod when you turned up first like a bad dose but you have a strong look of the man too most when you have the pencil going. You are not what I called you a hinny but I was called plenty worse names myself in my life. You did the same for the boy as your father was trying to do for the black slaves. Blood is a strange thing isnt it and you are lucky to have it.

There you have it Miss Tandy and I wish you well after my poor dealings to you. Look after the boy whatever else you do and pray for my soul after your fashion.

Carlen of Horkstow, county of Lincoln, England

I have not written to Edward Walker for that is too hard on me at this time. Tell him he is a good man and a special case and if only there were more of his kind. I am sorry for the pistol too.

THE RETURN
JOURNEY

WE MADE GOOD SAIL downriver for the current was with us and the winds too. Mr Walker took care of the sail when he was needed, which was often now that we were a man short. He wouldn't let Madan take on any new hands, not even the two who had brought us the murderous news, nor anybody from the ghats we were passing.

"I could not stomach that," he said.

He ignored the way Madan rolled his eyes then and blew his breath out. But for all that he allowed the boatman to shout orders and lose temper with him just as he did with Benu and Hari. He simply bent his head down and pulled harder on the ropes.

I did what I could to ease Hari's cleaning tasks but he would not let me help with the meals. On that matter he was closed and I did not know if it was because of my history or because he could best show his devotion to Mr Walker by frying his fish just the way Carlen had done. I told him he had a great talent for fish and so I should cook the rice but he shook his head.

"Lord Dakshin Rai, his is the hand who moves us all."

That was Hari's Lord of the Swamps and Tigers, I had learned, his own home god. But I was left no wiser.

Our quicker motion meant that the nights we spent on the water would be fewer, which felt a mercy to me now. Nevertheless, I worried that each time we moored it seemed Mr Walker was thinner than the night previous. After darkness fell and we had eaten whatever Hari prepared he would make himself busy by lamplight too, in the cabin, writing letters that he filed away in a tin-lined case like my own. He would not say what they were.

"A return journey is always different," he said to me when he caught my eyes following his pen. "But none more than this one, I believe."

Those nights Carlen hung between us like a dark moon.

When I had burst out of the cabin to show Mr Walker my letter, the letter that had brought me such joy and promise, I thought he would surely be glad that the story of Jupiter and his messengers had proved as true on earth as it was in the heavens. Why, Carlen himself must surely be counted such a messenger, I thought. What he said did not speak of gladness, however.

"So, a foul deed has borne good fruit despite all. Perhaps the man is not altogether damned. You will find your father in Madras soon enough then, Anila, and in my company. I guarantee that."

He nodded briskly as if to say, look, we are halfway to the city in the south already, and there is little remarkable about such an outcome. Then he folded the letter and returned it to me. He said nothing of Carlen's words about himself, an opinion that I thought was truly well expressed. Of course he did not mean to wound me or cast me down, I knew that. But it was evident that that was the way he was left himself.

What Mr Walker did not forgive in Carlen I found I could now pass over. On the other hand, while I could not mourn the man as he must do, I could honour him, or at least the struggle he had made to put his good news on a page for me. To me his words were fire and warmth but for all their wonder I could see they did nothing to heal poor Mr Walker's hurt. And so I felt it would be unkind of me to be very light-hearted around him. I set my face as carefully as a priest that morning, and that is how I continued.

But inside how different it was! In the mornings I watched the swallows swoop over the water and felt my heart lift into the air with them. Everything made sense in my life, everything fell into order, everything flowed along, even the sadnesses. My father was alive and well and although he had forgotten us he had never betrayed us. It truly was an enchantment of a kind that had fallen on him. How well my mother would have understood that.

The only person who made Mr Walker smile as we made our journey downriver was little Manik, who liked to sit up front, watching the river traffic through hooped fingers, as if through a spyglass. Now that we were safely away from his village he was as happy as any young creature. His eyes were clear and he sang, both Benu's songs and others he made up himself. He was still a little in awe of Mr Walker but he liked to chop his tobacco for him or find him a good walking stick along the banks when we moored.

Once he brought back some clean bamboo and Mr Walker surprised us all. With his sharp knife he took a slice of the smooth wood and cut some neat round holes in it.

"This is a Scottish whistle now, young man, and so you must learn a Scottish tune. Watch my fingers and copy what I do."

Mr Walker spoke such fine Bangla. But when he put the bamboo to his mouth he blew a tune that a monkey might have done better. No matter. Manik was entranced with this addition to his musical powers and in a day or so he was making his own compositions. Fishermen blew a conch or gave a *wah wah* cheer when they saw the tiny boy piping away at the prow of our boat.

Whenever this happened Benu's eyes would find mine and each time I found myself smiling back so that we surely looked, both of us, as if we were fond new parents preening over their clever little one.

"What do you think will happen to Manik when we arrive back in the city?" I asked Benu one morning. I kept my voice low though Madan and Mr Walker were huddled together up forward, in conversation. "Will he stay with your family?"

"Unless the sahib has a plan my father will decide," he said. "I already have three brothers younger than me. But Manik is…"

Benu paused. He tilted his head back and squeezed his eyes tightly shut and then finished his words in a rush. "He is the sweetest to me."

There was no time to spare while Benu was at the tiller, which was most of the time our boat was under sail. But I wanted to help him draw and make his letters. I had pages left over now in my notebooks, and very little reason to draw any more myself, as all my sketching was done and the finished work, with paints, required to be worked at a desk. So I tore some blank leaves from my notebook and spent a day making an alphabet in English and Bangla for Benu. For each sound I drew a beast or a bird, just as long ago my father had done for me. Except for one. My "B" was a picture of Benu himself, swimming, with his long hair loose in the water. I left the pages and some pencils underneath his red head wrap while he swam.

I had another matter on my mind too as we travelled, and Madan, who had a hawk's eye for all that he was a boatman, must have spotted the way I kept looking to the riverbanks on our right-hand side.

One morning he asked me to sit with him and mind the sail as it swung.

"Two nights ago I sent word ahead to my brother to go to Arjun's house," he said. "Arjun knows that you are coming back downriver. He wept when he heard that his daughter is dead. Then he asked questions, so many questions about you, but all my poor brother could say was that perhaps he should meet you. So it is arranged. We will be there tomorrow."

I hadn't guessed we were so close. I joined my hands in gratitude to Madan. But he looked at me so hard then that I felt he required something else from me. His voice was changed when he continued.

"Perhaps you fear he will not have any place in his

heart for you. Don't begin a tale in your head that hasn't been told yet. That is women's way, always."

I bit my lip. Madan, of all the world, to say such a rough thing!

"You should wear a sari for this meeting with the grandfather, not those."

He jerked a huge thumb at the trousers that had so taken his fancy before, though it was true they had looked more respectable on that first occasion. Now they had all the stains of the riverbank on them, stains that would never wash out. I had no intention of wearing them when I met Arjun. I nodded my assent, my obedience, to Madan but my stomach was biting me. Why was he suddenly unkind?

He cleared his throat.

"I worry about my boy."

He looked away for a moment while I stared at him. Did he mean Benu or Manik? I could not quite judge so I said nothing.

Madan tensed his great shoulders then and I could see the channels of his throat stand out, as thick as his own boat ropes.

"He has a tender heart, you know."

I nodded. At last we were agreed on something.

"He likes to write and draw, as I do, Madan. He has a talent for it and an interest. I could help him, if you would permit me. The skill might bring him..."

Madan brought down his fist on the gunwale so hard that I feared something must have broken, his bone or the polished wood. I flinched.

"I see him following your movements, girl, every one of them, whatever the skill is in that. It is obvious that you are not for him. That is not your fault. But everything you do is dust for him. So."

He gestured with his great arms, a beggar's gesture, with the palms up. Madan was pleading with me to leave his son alone.

I did not know where to look. I felt more stupid than I had ever felt in my life. I recognized the truth in what Madan said. Perhaps I had always known it. Perhaps that was indeed women's way, to seek a brother whenever the boy has a heart as big as the world. But what else might have been done? Should I have run away from that evil orchard and said nothing? Should I have been cold or distant ever after to gentle Benu, my helpmate?

"If we offend, it is with our good will."

For the first time in an age, I thought of Miss Hickey, and missed her quick and open mind. Those were her words. Well, no, they were Shakespeare's, but she had made them hers. She always spoke them with a laugh, to excuse me, or anyone else, who had made a genuine mistake in conduct. Later she showed me how the words themselves were full of mischief.

If there was an answer with no deceit in it for Madan, she would have given it to me. But perhaps there was none.

Nor was he finished.

"And let me tell you another thing," he said. "Because of the child and the dead man I don't know how far upriver I can travel again in safety. The sahib and you, you need never see us again. But a cast stone sends ripples for all time."

All of us are borne along on the great river, Anila. Even the birds that fly above it and never touch it.

I had touched it. I had cast a stone.

I thanked Madan for his words and his advice and moved away to sit in the cabin. I did not look to the tiller once, not even when I heard Manik begin to pick out a new tune on his flute.

That night I went to my tent immediately after I had bathed. I had no appetite. I was sure Madan had not intended it, but now I found I was looking forward more with eagerness than with apprehension to meeting my mother's people. They might judge me, and judge me harshly, for not better resembling my mother. But they would be different company and they would not know all the dark things that we on board knew.

ARJUN

WHEN THE DAY CAME I chose to wear my blue sari. What saddened me as I smoothed down its folds and patted the embroidery into place was that I had not brought my mother's beautiful mulberry-green sari. That would have been a proper splendour to show to her father.

Mr Walker stepped out first when our boat swung alongside the little ghat and he handed me down as if I were a lady arriving on the steps of Chandpal itself. Manik leant from the jetty and plucked a sweet-smelling yellow water flower. To put in my braid, he said. Then he set to running up and down the timbers, laughing as they shook.

"They are coming," Madan said. He pointed.

Along the path from the village a little procession of people was approaching, men and women, with some children dancing along in front and around them. One man was ahead of the others, a short man, lean, very upright.

Mr Walker gave a soft squeeze to my elbow and went to stand some feet away. He reached out for

Manik and held him lightly by the shoulders. Hari and Benu stood by, rooted like sentries. Suddenly Madan was beaming.

"Arjun!" he said.

I thought my head would burst. I walked forward because they were close to us now though I could hardly see one face from another. My eyes were full, ready to spill.

I knelt down to honour my grandfather, touching his feet that were long and thin, touching the soil that he stood on, my mother's own earth.

His hands raised me and I truly did feel the course of our common blood, like a shock along my arms, making gooseflesh in the morning's warmth. He put his hand on my lowered head to bless me and tipped my chin up. We stared at each other, both of us looking for the person who had linked us, who stood there as surely as we did. I could feel her all about, in the soft air from the river, in the breaths we shared as we stood.

I saw a man who was not old, though his hair was white and short-cropped, even spiky. His face was smooth, with fine web lines round his eyes. He was darker than my mother but his face had the same oval shape, the same straight nose and small and perfect ears. His eyes were black like hers and they were full of wonder.

"Anila," he said at last. "You are welcome home, daughter."

Then the group broke and people surged forward to touch me and tell me who they were.

First to speak was Arjun's grandniece, my cousin Meenakshi, who told me that a feast was waiting for all our party in his house. She was older than me, quite a bit older, and some of the children were hers. She pointed them out, laughing at each one's name. She had my mother's even teeth.

She pushed forward her own grandfather, Arjun's brother, my old uncle. He had tears in his eyes when he reached to touch my head.

"Annapurna was the light of the river," he said. "As her mother was before her. And you too, tall like a swan."

I was tall here, I realized. I was even a little taller than Arjun.

The small boys had discovered Manik and they all ran away like rabbits towards the house and the food. Meenakshi called warnings after them. The girls followed them, giddy with the outrage. Only the littlest one stayed, a tiny girl with a covering of wispy curls, shorter than a boy's. I handed her my flower, which she held in front of her as if it were made of china.

"Little Jonaki," said Meenakshi proudly. "We nearly lost her to the fever. But look at her now."

Her name meant firefly. How pretty! I picked Jonaki up and then led my grandfather to meet Mr Walker. They shook hands like Englishmen. But in a moment, Arjun had found Mr Walker's Bangla speech to be an astonishing thing and he called his brother and the other men over to hear it.

"Listen to the sahib," he said to them. "He is better than any of the storytellers who come to the village."

Mr Walker smiled at that, with real pleasure. He told a joke about the English that made the men laugh. He ran a hand across his brow to push back his straying hair and just then he looked as he had done the first time I met him. I thought suddenly, this is what he is good at, this is his work, talking easily so that others will chat to him and share their knowledge. He had done so with Madan, with the saltworkers and, long ago, surely this was what he did to win the respect of the horse thief, Carlen.

He had done exactly so with me.

As we began to walk towards Arjun's thatched house, Meenakshi told me what she remembered of my mother.

"I was seven or eight when she left. They were very bad times so Arjun felt she would have a better life with the sahib who loved her. He always feared she would die like her mother. That was a time of famine. It's better now, we do well enough here. Annapurna was always kind to me, she told me stories and sang songs to me. She was a clever person."

She looked at me curiously.

"All those men! And you are not married? To the sahib? Or that handsome fisherman with you, he looks a suitable boy, are you betrothed?"

My heart jumped. I dared not look round but I hoped Benu was not nearby to hear her, nor his father either. Meenakshi's voice was the kind that carried.

"To Mr Walker? Oh no, Meenakshi, but he is the kindest man in the world. And Benu, why he's no older than I am. You see, I live in the English city now and girls there do not marry so young."

"And your father, he allows you to travel around in this way with men? Or is he dead too?"

She was a little blunt, perhaps, Meenakshi was. But I

told her then some of what I had rehearsed to tell Arjun. It was not indeed so very different from the truth, only in my story there was never a Malati or a Hemavati, never a Mr Bristol, nor any big house in Old Court House Street, only the kindness of our good neighbours the Hickeys after we suffered the mysterious loss of my father, their countryman. My father, who was now to be restored to me, as if in a fairy tale.

But Meenakshi lost the final details of my story because as we ducked our heads and came into Arjun's house she caught sight of her oldest boy with rice in his hand and grains dropped on the clean swept floor. She roared and banished him outside though I begged her not to. I was glad that Manik had done nothing so terrible and I rubbed his head as we settled ourselves on the floor to eat. Arjun insisted I sat beside him. Even the little girls sat, thrilled into silence. Meenakshi would not sit down with such a company of men but she stood close by to hear our stories.

It was a real feast we had, with river shrimps and white fish, rice, spiced vegetables and dal in different colours, bright as paint, with sweet coconut and payesh and lots of creamy milk to pour from neat clay jugs. Mr Walker was given the honour of a bamboo spoon to eat with but he too had a leaf for a plate, like the rest of us. He ate well and looked happy, I thought, and my old uncle had his full attention. From what I could hear both of them were intent on talking about the old tales. They were showing off in their way, I realized, just as the small boys were, all of them trying to capture the eyes of Madan and Benu, the giant boatman and his handsome son.

I told Arjun that I still had my mother's Durga altar, the same one at which she prayed for him, every day of her life. He bowed his head.

"That Durga, I remember it well," he said slowly. "It was her mother's and, before that, her grandmother's."

He heard the story of my father then and was shaken. His face changed and in its lines I could see my mother's rare temper gathering like a storm.

"I have never heard of such a thing. A man to forget his family?"

Mr Walker must have had one ear turned in our direction for he leant forward now.

"With respect, sir, Patrick Tandy acted like a hero," he said to Arjun. He laid out better than I had done, the details of my father's story, the ship, the slaves, the wicked rock that had stolen his memories.

"Only the prayers of your own dear daughter kept him from meeting a hero's death. Her blessings have now restored him to Anila in a way that is closer to enchantment than anything I have heard before in my life. We can only imagine how the poet Kalidasa would have been thrilled to hear such a story told along the great river."

My grandfather sat still for a moment. Then he nodded. But I could hardly keep from reaching out and clasping Mr Walker's hands inside my own. I had thought him unmoved by Carlen's letter but I was wrong. His pain had been too strong at the time and I had demanded overmuch of him.

"Then you have been alone in the world all this time, my child?" my grandfather asked. He reached forward and ran a finger, ever so gently, down my nose, so that I knew he wished to mark in particular this feature that we, all three generations, shared.

But I had not been alone, of course, and Arjun marvelled then when I told him about the Hickeys and their horses and their great garden going down to the river where the ships ran by, day and night, with the tides from the sea.

"You would see budgerows passing by too," I told him, remembering what my mother had told me of her father's ambition. "But the ships we could see are taller than the tallest palms and their sails are like fields."

"Then Annapurna must have thought of me often," he said, sadly. "We loved boats, the two of us."

From my bag I took out the drawing of my mother and handed it to my grandfather. There was not much light in the house but I could see Annapurna's beautiful face quite clearly, for Mr Hickey's outlines were strong.

"You hold it in front for me," he said.

He stared so long at the drawing and so intensely that I thought he was moved beyond speech again. But then he motioned for me to put it away.

"I cannot really see what you are showing me. I know it is there but I cannot say what it is. I think my eyes have been fixed on the river for too long. But don't be upset, child. I see your mother when I look at you."

FROM THE
SACRED PLACES

FOR ALL THEIR WISH to make haste, Mr Walker and Madan were happy to let my mother's people keep them from the river until late that same day. More visitors arrived, more people were fed. Meenakshi spun like a top and lost patience with everyone in the household.

Each person had come to look at me, they said, though for some I suspected Meenakshi's food was the bigger attraction. They all said the same things, that my mother had been good and beautiful and that I was full of good fortune to have grown and prospered as I had. Some touched me as if I were a fount of good luck. I gave up trying to remember their names.

All of my own party cleverly extricated themselves from these ceremonies. Once when I walked outside to bid proper farewell to the most ancient of the visitors, I saw Benu on the path talking with a girl of my age, a girl from the village who had not come inside. Shy Benu was talking! Manik was leaning back against his legs, tired for once, and Benu was stroking his hair. He didn't see me or, if he did, he didn't look my way.

I was not sure how I felt about that.

While I was inside being dutiful an important arrangement was under deliberation outside. Meenakshi heard the first noises of the matter from the small children who ran in and out, panting out their news as payment for a few extra morsels. Each time she sent out a wiser and older child to listen and provide us with more details. How I longed to go out myself!

That was how I heard that Manik, our little Manik, was to stay in the house with Arjun.

"Another mouth for me to feed," Meenakshi grumbled happily. "A real boy for your grandfather to train for his boat. A grandson delivered as a gift from the river herself!"

Mr Walker had hummed and hawed a little about this decision, we heard next. He felt that he should take the boy to the city and have him taught the ways of a scholar, for Manik had shown himself to be a clever child. Or else that Madan himself should take the boy, he said, for the child already loved Benu like a brother.

"But Benu loves him like a brother too!" I blurted out.

Meenakshi narrowed her eyes.

"It is the right choice," she said. "Look again."

We stood under the thatch awning for a while then and I saw Manik running along the paths and climbing the mango trees with the other boys, laughing as he went higher than anybody else. Then I knew Arjun's offer was the right one.

"Now I am dadamoshay twice in one day," Arjun called out when he spotted us. He rubbed his hands in pleasure. "To my own Anila and, as Durga's extra gift, to this little fellow too, though he's not my blood."

Then there was my father. For all that he had done in

error, nonetheless I heard that I must bring him back to the village where he had found my mother. Mr Walker's words had taken root and my father was now a hero who would receive a welcome proper to his kind.

That was easy to say, I thought. I would not think about such a plan until I had found him.

The shadows were lengthening along the path to the river when Arjun finally came inside again and took my hand.

"I have a gift for you, Anila. Come with me."

"I want Anila to come on her own," he said firmly then, for the children were clamouring to follow us. And then, politely, he dismissed Mr Walker too. "It will not be for long, sahib, for I know you are keen now to make good time."

He drew me out then into his little garden and I looked left where the river ran, and then right, up the winding path to the village houses. That was a much larger place than the miserable collection of huts where we had found Manik. It was full of life too. Men and women were working and sitting and talking, in the fields, outside the houses, under the trees, by the water. Human voices were carried on the air like birdsong, though there was plenty of that too because koels and hoopoes were calling from the trees and, as I looked up, a rope of geese passing high overhead snorted like pigs. Somewhere nearby there must be a field that had nothing but white flowers in it in autumn, the field of kash where my mother used to lie and look up at all the birds that had stories for her.

But I knew that I could not live here.

Perhaps if I were Manik's age, or even the age I was

when Mr Bristol had come boating up the creek all those years ago. But I had been changed too much by all that had happened to me in the city and by all the people I had met. Now there were oils and varnishes mixed into my life, plum-cake and Christmas songs, music on a keyboard and bound books on shelves. Even the city's busy streets made a beat in my head, and the river that flowed past the white palaces was so very different from this one. The sight of ships heading south into the far world lifted my spirits. This world had stories much stranger than my own, this world that had swallowed up my father.

I will never know if, that day, Arjun had been tempted to break tradition and ask that I, rather than Manik, stay in his home. If he had been, he was also surely watching my face and reading my mind. He never spoke of it and I was glad for I would not have hurt him for the world.

"Your mother and your father, they loved each other? For all that they were so different?"

I looked at him, surprised.

"Oh, yes, they did."

"And that is why, perhaps, she died, even though there was plenty of food and a strong roof and even her own lovely baby one with her. She could not understand why your father did not come back."

He was puzzling it out for himself, I could see. He felt responsible for he had let her go with my father in the first place. My heart twisted as I saw the story he was making, reading it across his eyes, his brow, his mouth, as well as in his words. It was not a rightful story because he did not know all the circumstances.

He took my hand as we stepped past a cropped prickly hedge and down into a wide water meadow. There were a few buffaloes here but nothing else I could see, except some tall herons in the distance where the meadow turned to marsh. Or were they herons?

"Look, my girl, this is what I want you to see. Watch them as we move close."

And as we did, I saw that the birds were not herons at all. Nor storks, which was my second thought, but a common city stork had none of this bird's slender grace and beauty. Its body was grey and grey-white and made a curve down over its delicate pink legs so that the bird's form was like a beautiful letter from the Persian books. Its head was a deep rose colour under a grey cap.

My grandfather pointed towards a group of four or five.

"They are this year's young ones," he said. "See how their heads are still pale and how they drop their feathers as Jonaki will lose her curls."

There were fifteen birds in all.

Arjun stopped me when we were still a distance away. From the side of his mouth he made a strange call, high-pitched but soothing nonetheless. Then something extraordinary happened. As if they were dancers, the adult birds started to perform for us. First, they stretched their long necks to the sky as if they were saluting Surya. Then they formed pairs, bowed to each other and began to bend and sway in dainty steps.

I had to hold my mouth to stop my exclamations and my fingers tingled to draw what I saw. But the birds broke up their magic circle when one of the young birds who was not dancing decided it was time to sit down. He made it such a slow business, as if trying to remember the instructions for folding himself up, that his parents came away from the others to watch over him. They bent over and linked their necks to his when he finally sat as if they were proud of his work. I thought how lucky he was to have them.

It was only then that the tall birds became aware of us. They started telling each other the news and shifting and some made anxious little runs and looked back again to see if we had advanced.

Arjun had tears in his eyes too as we turned back towards his house.

"Your mother never saw these birds," he said, and I knew that was true for otherwise they would have danced for ever in her stories.

"They first came here to our stretch of the river the winter after she left for the city with your father. The priests say that they are from the sacred places, that they bless young couples because of their own sweet bird marriages. This is the only village all along the river, as far as we travel, where these birds will come. You see, I think Annapurna sent them here. Another gift from Durga."

I took his hand and pressed it between my own. There was nobody but myself and my grandfather in that water meadow and perhaps there was something of another world blowing in the sweet air around us.

We walked back in silence.

Everyone was outside Arjun's house when we returned, everyone except Meenakshi and Jonaki, who was trying in her baby way to help her mother clear the remains of the great meal. I stayed behind for a moment as Arjun joined the others.

"May I give her something?" I asked Meenakshi.

She stared at me, not understanding. I reached into my bag and took out my mother's fine scarf and one of the gold mohurs.

"This scarf was my mother's. If you keep it for Jonaki there will always be a memory of her in the village. You can tell her whose it was. And the gold, that was a kindness from my friend Miss Hickey and I would like Jonaki to share some of it. For luck."

Meenakshi was speechless. But Jonaki smiled at me with her baby pearl teeth and took the two gifts in her sticky hands. That woke her mother, who rushed to wipe them.

We all walked towards the jetty, where Hari stood on board our boat, ready to cast away the ropes. Once again I knelt to honour Arjun. But then Manik, poor thing, threw himself round my legs and cried, for he finally understood that he was staying and we were leaving. Benu crouched down and said something to him, and after a moment Manik loosened his grip. He went to stand with Arjun, took his hand and stood proudly with him. Meenakshi popped something into his mouth, a sweet or a fruit, and his little mouth closed over it.

"I told him he was to protect his new dadamoshay and that Madan and I would be back very soon to race him in his new boat," Benu whispered to me, as we went on board the *Hera*. He went directly to take his tiller seat and I noticed that his father did not call on him to help cast off, as was his custom.

What I saw then, for the longest time, as we set sail

in the low evening sun, was the bright purple of my mother's scarf, twisted round little Jonaki's head and waving like a ship's pennant in the breeze that was carrying us down to Calcutta.

NEWS

WHEN I WALKED INTO Mrs Panossian's shop the day after our return to the city I confess that I felt as smug as the Female Quixote herself. Nobody could have better news to tell. All our adventures and excitements, these were my clutch of golden eggs.

I could count them off, right hand, left hand. Good things like discovering the incredible story of my father. Meeting my grandfather and walking in my mother's world. And, every day we were away, learning the ways of birds, the sweetness of the river, the kindness of Madan, Hari and Benu.

And the bad things. Carlen. No matter that he'd been essential to me, or that his death had made him seem noble, Carlen still had the power to twist a knife in my belly. There was the terror of Manik's life before we rescued him. And, though it must be counted in lesser degree, there had been the hardship of saying goodbye to Madan and Benu only yesterday, outside their riverbank home.

Oh yes, that was fresh in my mind.

While we waited for a carriage, Madan asked his

wife, Aparna, to bring us some food. I offered to help but this tall woman, still pretty in her red-bordered sari, drew back and sucked in her breath so that she would not have to share the same air as me. When she brought out her bowl of spiced rice and hot brinjal slices she placed it farthest from me, the unclean spirit. She moved inside then, and I was sorry because she did not see what happened when the carriage came.

Mr Walker, Hari and Madan stood up but Benu stayed. He laid a folded leaf in front of me, tied up with a thin strand of rope as if it were a fancy box.

"For you," he said. But he would not meet my eyes.

I opened the leaf flat on the stone. Inside was a page of my drawing paper on which the English letters A-N-I-L-A were written, as neatly executed as any script I had ever made. Sitting on the paper was a tiny pearl, the size of a nose-stud, a black pearl with a sugar sheen. It was beautiful.

"I found it in the river the day you found Manik," he said. "I could not give it to you before even though you gave me your gift. But it was for you always. To remind you."

He stopped.

"Benu, it is beautiful. When I see you again I will have had it made into a ring. I will always keep it. And your writing, you must…"

His face twisted. Then he was up on his feet and running away, to be useful with the other men. He stood back and did not catch my eye when everything was loaded on top and we gathered at the carriage door to say our farewells. That was as well because my own eyes were dangerously wet. But I was glad to see that

Mr Walker sought him out and slipped some coins into his hand.

Madan clasped my own right hand in one of his and then took Mr Walker's in the other. I wanted to touch his moustache, to reach up and stroke his shining head. If only Madan could be a maharajah of all the world, I thought. A child's thought.

"We will hear from you again," he said, simply. "We will hear good things."

And so we had left them, left our river behind, even though we made our lumbering way beside it for the most part. When we reached the city's broad streets the white world slipped back around us like a glove.

The little pearl had gone back into its leaf and joined the other precious things in my bag. I had it with me now to show Anoush.

The shop's bell gave me away at once. I would have preferred to have stolen unannounced to the end of the counter where Anoush was sitting on a stool, head bent over the ledger and a long pen in her hand. There was nobody else in the shop.

"Anila! I can't believe what I see! You're home again, safe!"

She lifted the hatch in the counter and came out to me. She hugged me so hard that I could feel her laugh underneath like water on the boil. She smelt of lemons and ink.

"And I have so much to tell you! I can't believe what I have to tell you," she said. "My life has changed in just a few weeks. But you, look at you. You've changed too. I can't say how exactly but it's in your face."

Gently, she touched my cheek.

"Anoush, I've found my father."

She stepped back and her mouth made an O just like the little hallelujah boys of St John's.

"Well, not quite, I've not come upon him yet but I know where to find him. All that is needed is to book a passage to Madras and Mr Walker is doing that right now."

I tried to make my story brief, in case Mrs Panossian or the shop boys disturbed us. But that only served to leave Anoush with more questions, so then I had to start over again, and fill in the gaps until she was satisfied. One bearer came in with an order but he was gone in quick time and I could get back to recounting exactly how Benu and I had rescued little Manik. For after she had grasped the events concerning my father, this was the part of our adventure that thrilled Anoush most.

"And Manik is now with your grandfather. So, he is like a little brother for you."

I hadn't quite thought of that. Suddenly another notion came to my mind. Suppose my father had found another woman, perhaps even married one, since he knew no better? Then indeed I might have a little brother, or a sister. But Carlen hadn't mentioned such a thing and if it were the case he surely would have, to plague me with more misery.

Anoush sighed with pleasure. She hadn't noticed my silence.

"Anila, we both saved little boys by accident and look what has happened to us. Now I must tell you my news. I'm to marry. Look!"

She held out her left hand. A golden bronze stone set into silver made a star shape on her pale finger.

"To *marry*? But who, when? What happened? It's only a few weeks since I saw you! Anoush, what do you mean?"

My friend was pink but she was not giggling in her usual fashion. She touched the star ring to her mouth as if to check it, as a blind person might, and then looked directly at me.

"It's not a secret, so it doesn't matter who interrupts us now. We marry at Easter. Do you remember the picnic we had on Christmas Day? The horseman who helped me up?"

I nodded.

"He so much wanted you to speak to him. He was tall and very pale and you made him a namashkar because you wanted him to know you were not English so he might add that to your limp and reckon all your disadvantages at once."

That was what she had told me afterwards.

Anoush's blush deepened.

"Yes, well, he came to the shop the next day because, remember, you shouted out my name and the Panossian name, and indeed he says Anila Tandy is responsible for everything since then! He came again the next day, and the next. And he was so pleasant always that in the end I said I would let him walk home to the Seropins's with me. He bought me a new sari that day because he said it was his fault that my pink one was torn. It's so beautiful, with gold thread, Anila, you will see it."

Of course, Mrs Panossian detected something in the

air, Anoush explained. Or perhaps Gabriel or Mesrop told her about the young officer who would be served only by Anoush.

"Mesrop was a little jealous at first, I believe. But Philip," she blushed again, "his name is Lieutenant Philip Tilling and he is from the city of London, he has shown Mesrop so many new mathematical calculations that now I think Mesrop prefers him to me."

"Anyway, one morning Philip came in and insisted on telling Mrs P what happened on the green and that same day Mrs Herbert – you remember, the little boy's mother? – came in with a basket of English soaps for me and she added the family to the customers' books. So Mrs P thought I was a kind of saint. And then Philip brought a buggy on the Sunday and we took a boat to the Gardens just like you did and that was where he asked me to marry him. Of course he had to ask Mrs P when we returned here but she was not difficult at all, Anila. I couldn't believe it. She said she was glad she had no longer to put effort into thinking about a match for me. But I never thought she did, anyhow. People surprise you, don't they?"

She looked so eager and happy. I perched myself on the counter and smoothed down my cotton trousers as if I might iron them that way.

"He's so kind, Anila. I truly believe we will be happy because I know that from the first he has known about my weakness. He says it makes him love me more. Look, my ring stone is only onyx. He says he will buy another later but I love this one, don't you?"

She wanted me to say something but I was truly confused. Through my soft bag I felt my own little pearl, still wrapped in its leaf bag. I could not show her that now, it was quite another thing altogether, as unfinished as I was myself. My Anoush married? But yes, she was several years older than my mother had been when she left her father's house. She was old enough to marry, nobody could say she was not.

"Anoush, anybody could see how that soldier looked at you that day. He saw everything good about you. I am very happy for you. It's just such a sudden thing to hear about and now I wonder will you be moving away, to England perhaps. I couldn't bear that."

Anoush wrinkled her nose.

"Oh, but I won't," she said. "Philip has only just arrived here. He wants nothing more than to spend a very long time in India, he says. He loves it."

Then she poked my knees gently with her ring.

"Anyway, look at you. You will probably be in Madras always now, by the sea, what with your father *and* the Hickeys. Oh, Anila, do you think you might come out with us on Sunday? To show Philip the little garden house, perhaps?"

Of course our peace could not last. The door from behind opened with a click and Mrs Panossian stepped through, her dress a full black sail.

I jumped down and did a namashkar for her.

"Anila! Well, you are returned to the city as a proven matchmaker if nothing else," she said. "You have heard my young cousin's news?"

She was smiling so broadly her eyes seemed to disappear into her cheeks.

"You will be our welcome guest at the ceremony, of course. You've never been to an Armenian wedding,

I'm sure. But first of all, a clever girl like you will understand that since you have caused Anoush to be stolen from me you must now undo the damage and take up her duties."

I could say nothing for opening and closing my mouth like a fish.

But Mrs Panossian laughed at my confusion.

"Have no fear, girl," she said. "I never doubted that your spirit and mine would be soon at odds behind my counter. I make a jest. Besides, there is great competition for your person. Have you told her, Anoush?"

Anoush clapped her hands to her mouth.

"Mercy, no, but I think it's no matter now, Auntie. Anila has discovered where her father is!"

I might as well have been closeted with a gentleman of the law then, for all the questions that I had to answer, though of course Mrs Pan got only a certain version from me. Had I told her that I had slept in a soldier's tent I believe that detail might have compromised me off the premises. Or that the salt she sold in her store had a rival trade up the river, with no tax to pay.

Anoush had to leave us time and again to deal with the late customers but when she closed the door at last she came back to us.

"Anila, what I forgot to tell you was that the day Mrs Herbert came here with her gifts she was asking about you, most especially. She wondered if you might care to live with them and teach their boys. They cannot find anyone to suit them in all Calcutta, they say, and you impressed them so much with the way you spoke."

But I had been so bold that day. And they so kind.

How strange it was.

Anoush giggled. "Of course you were wearing a sari that day, not your boy legs."

Mrs Panossian looked stern. "They are a fine family and we have a very satisfactory order from them now. You would do well with the Herberts, my girl. Their house in Alipore is as fine as any in Garden Reach, I hear. But who knows what is round the corner for any of us? So I wish you well in your quest and please convey my respects to your dear Miss Hickey when you see her."

She left us then, first running her finger down the counter to test it for dust. Anoush wrinkled her nose but said nothing. When the door had closed behind Mrs Pan she reached into one of the underneath drawers and drew out a white card.

"Mrs Dust-it-down doesn't know about this but I might have forgotten it without her talk of conveying respects."

She slid the card across the counter.

"It's strange, but only yesterday Doctor Herbert came in by himself. He left this here for you, Anila. He said it was not at all to do with the position in his house but that it was important. Privy to yourself, he said."

NEWS FROM
THE PAST

MR WALKER WAS EXCEEDINGLY LATE returning to the house that night. When the moon rose Chandra tried to tempt me with hot water and soft towels, and a boiled chocolate drink for afterwards, for I looked wretched, he said, and should retire to bed.

"The sahib says this chocolate makes him sleep better than his whisky," he said. "But he does not know I sometimes put sleepy leaf in it too, just a little."

He laughed, a mouthful of broken teeth. But when I refused any of his kind offers he went off to his own room with a face on him like a toad in dry weather. Then it was just a sleepy Balor and I who waited for the master to return, the parrot swaying on the back of Mr Walker's easy chair, muttering his puja prayers.

Outside, the moon was turning herself into a baby once again. I didn't know where Mr Walker had stowed his telescope but even if it were on the table in front of me I think I would have feared to look at Jupiter again, in case his hopeful messenger moon would no longer be visible to me.

"Anila!"

There he stood in the doorway, and in the dim light coming from the hall behind him he looked like a boy, a very tall thin boy, with his hair undressed and his lace stock coming adrift round his neck.

"Goodness me, do you know the hour?"

I had not heard him come in.

"Oh, but Mr Walker, I had to wait up to hear about the passage you have found for me. And I wanted you to see this."

He took the white card that Anoush had given me and examined the embossed print.

"But it's just a calling card," he said. "'George Herbert, physician, late of London, now of Providence House, Alipore, Calcutta.' Now who is that?"

He turned it over.

"'For the attention of Miss Anila Tandy. Please call to our address at your earliest convenience. This matter is important.'"

I had told Mr Walker before about our Christmas Day adventure but perhaps he had forgotten.

"Anoush told me today that the Herberts wanted me to teach their boys, you remember the little one she saved from the horses? But she said that this message was about something else, something that the doctor was bothered about."

He blinked a couple of times. He ran a hand through his hair, making the damage even worse. Then he sat down, being careful not to disturb Balor, who was now snoring.

"Anila," he said, gently. "I can't think about that right now. I can answer your first question however. Today I booked passage for both of us on an Indiaman to leave in a seven-night. We have benefited from a few burials, it is true, to be able to have these accommodations so late. Our ship is called the *Dublin*, would you credit that? She'll stop at Madras, of course, for you, and then I'll travel afterwards to England."

The *Dublin*! My first thought was that Durga must have truly forgiven me to send a boat with that name to bring me to my father. But why then was Mr Walker looking so glum?

He poured himself a whisky from his cutglass decanter and drank it half down.

"Well," he said. He sighed.

And that was all.

"Mr Walker, is there something wrong? I'm sorry if you wanted to retire at once. I'll leave you be now. Are you hungry? I can fetch something for you."

I stood but he motioned me down again.

"Anila, I have discovered some other things that will disturb you."

"My father?"

"No. Well, not in the way you mean."

His face suddenly twisted with disgust. I said nothing but my blood was thumping. I felt like an animal brought to a butcher's stall, waiting for the cruel chop.

"Anila."

His voice was very gentle.

"At the Company offices today, I discovered that your father left in place a firm arrangement for your mother to be paid from his savings. Every month she was to collect these monies from a clerk at the Writers' Building. It was a little stipend, not much, but enough probably to feed a woman and a child. But after a couple of weeks the entire amount was collected by a person who claimed she was Annapurna, your mother, wishing to return to her village and thus in need of the full security. She had a pretty little girl with her of the right years. The man remembered the child dancing round his desk for him."

"But that is nonsense. My mother took no money. We had no money. And she was very sick, remember I told you? We never went to the Writers' Building then."

Mr Walker nodded. His face looked carved and ferocious, like a stone idol from the top of a temple.

"And I remember too that you told me that a person called Malati vanished from the house when your mother became ill."

There was a quick sour taste in my mouth. I put my fist to my teeth so I would not retch.

"Malati! But she had no child…"

Then I stopped. I thought of Bashanti and the proud way she wore the dancing anklets she made, with nutshells for bells, even after her father beat her for it. She envied me my house shared with such colourful people. Perhaps she had been eager to go with Malati, to pretend to be me, to take part in a game.

Little one, tell Malati why the poorest grey pigeon wears jewel colours round her neck. She might put your story into her dance.

"Anila, the story does not end there. The reason I am so very late is that I have been to find your old friend Hemavati."

Of all the things I expected him to say this was not one of them. But I had run out of gasps and gapes. I just waited for him to continue.

"Yes, and it was a merry dance in the gloaming, that," he said. "Finding your old house was quite a discovery when all I had to guide me was your descriptions of an old temple filled with monkeys. Oh, and a palanquin maker. But that last was the clincher."

"You found Hemavati?"

"She was not inclined to talk to me at first but eventually she could not be stopped. She knew nothing of this money arrangement, that was clear. She was full of tears then about her own hard judgement of your father, which she pressed on your mother at the time. She put it down to her own bad experiences with Englishmen. But from her I learnt more about Malati."

On the chair back Balor opened his good eye, as if he had been following the story all along and was impatient now for the end of it.

"One day Malati's soldier, Robert Sedge, was brought to your house in the lane in shackles. He'd been caught supplying shot to a merchant in the bazaar. Anyway, before they stood him for court martial he also confessed to murdering his girl for some monies she had hidden from him. They searched your house for it but it was never found there or anywhere else, nor Malati either, if it was she that he meant. Hemavati never knew what kind of money it was they were talking about, or, she swore, she would have searched the city for you and your mother to tell you."

And all the while we were behind the locked gates of the house with the fountain in Old Court House Street. I thought of the summer's day by the creek and how I had led Mr Bristol to my mother, even though I had not understood then the cards that were being played. For my sake she had consented to a life with Mr Bristol that disgusted her. All the good fortune that had come to me since that day had come about because she had accepted a cruel fate. Of course she would never wish to hear me talk of my father's return. She had believed completely that he had betrayed her, discarded her.

Mr Walker sighed again.

"I gave Hemavati your best regards and a bag of rupees. Poor thing, she did not appear well."

"Poor Hemavati," I agreed.

But deep inside, a tiny part of me, even though I did not intend to allow it, was thinking, "Poor Malati." Her greed had made her do a terrible thing to us, to my mother who had always been kind to her, to me whom she petted whenever she cared to. And it had brought her nothing, only a terrible end.

I was so weary. I longed to be picked up like a child, although I was a child no longer, and carried to a soft bed where the badness in the world could not find me. I got up slowly and thanked Mr Walker and went to my bedroom.

AT ALIPORE

MR WALKER HAD ALREADY LEFT when I rose the next morning.

"To order supplies for ship," Chandra said. "For you, too. Lady clothes. Soap and basin for sickness."

He made a pantomime of getting sick and rolled his eyes. Chandra did not approve of sea journeys, I could see that.

I knew I should begin my paintings. My river sketches were not enough for Mr Walker to bring to his beloved Royal Society. Unless she had a proper portrait, like a young lady going to her first ball, it seemed that the golden-headed bird would stand no chance of being presented at that place of scrutiny. I also wanted to do justice to my brave fish owl and the birds my grandfather had shown me in the water meadow. Mr Walker had not seen them and I had great hopes that they might be unknown birds.

But I could not get Doctor Herbert's scribbled words out of my mind. What might the matter concerning me be that had drawn a privy card from him?

I mixed as many browns as I could make, from pale

honey to black molasses. They glistened on the palette like so many sugared sweets on a tray. Outside, the mali was cutting back the hibiscus, which had ended its blooming. I could hear the clip of his blades, and koels calling from gardens further down the street. But my mind kept turning on the thought that prosperous Alipore lay just beyond the maidan, much closer than Garden Reach. If I were clever about it I might get there and back before the afternoon was over.

I closed my paintbox and left my notebooks on the desk in the parlour room.

Chandra tut-tutted when I told him I was going to Mrs Panossian's shop.

"It's only a few streets away, it's perfectly safe, Chandra. Please tell Mr Walker, if he returns before me, that I will work late into the night to make up for this time I'm taking."

By way of reply Chandra banged down the brass doorknocker that he was polishing. Of course that set Balor off inside, making a twin boom, and I had to run in case I would add my own laughter to the disturbance.

Mrs Panossian's shop was full of people, bearers and even some English servants, forming lines in front of the counter. Anoush was too occupied to manage more than a wave to me, and a quick smile.

Outside the shop a cart was being loaded with baskets and boxes that were lined up neatly on the freshly swept pavement. Mesrop was doing most of the work, shouldering his way through the passers-by. He offered no excuses but people made way for him as you would avoid a boulder on the move. I picked up a basket of herb sachets and went to stand by the horses so that he saw me.

"Mesrop, is this delivery going to Alipore? For I have a message from one of your customers to go there myself. The Herberts, do you know them? I could see that your packages to that family arrive safely."

Mrs Pan would not have cared to hear *that* for she prided herself on the shop's reputation for delivery. But Mesrop stared hard at me and then peered back into the shop as if he might catch Anoush's eye.

"Anoush says it's permitted," I said to him, desperately. "But you can see how busy she is."

He reached out his huge hands then and just picked me up as if I were another piece of grocery. He placed me up beside the driver, a little Armenian man wearing a livery of brown and gold, the Panossian colours. Veena bird colours, I thought, with a dash of guilt.

The driver merely shrugged. Behind us two coolies jumped up and settled themselves on the different packets and baggages as best they could. The driver lifted his reins and within minutes we had joined the traffic on the road to Chowringhee.

It was mid-morning and packet boys and coolies with heavy loads ran alongside the carts and carriages, palkis and chairs, sometimes darting between them, at great peril, for all that the road was so wide. There were elephants abroad too, two together, slowing the traffic behind them, both carrying English ladies who squealed with excitement for every sway of the howdahs. I kept my head down when we passed the top of the street where Mr Walker's house lay. If Chandra were to see me!

Only when we had reached the area of Burial Ground Road did the delivery cart begin its work. We must have stopped five or six times for the coolies to drop down and carry one basket after another inside gates that were held open and then banged after them. At least those houses were visible. But when we arrived at last among the green lanes of Alipore, I began to wonder how I might know Doctor Herbert's house. Here every dwelling was important enough to have its own long avenue of palmyras to keep it out of sight, except for glimpses of whitewashed stone.

I need not have worried.

"This is last order," the driver said to me, in a mix of Bangla and English. "House of new doctor. Many herbs for here. Fruits too."

He spun the cart, now so much lighter, so that it ground deep tracks into the sandy area in front of the house. The door opened and two little boys raced each other to greet us, followed by two house servants. A fair-headed lady with no bonnet or hat came out to stand on the steps. I recognized Mrs Herbert.

She clapped her hands to her mouth when she saw me.

"Oh, mercy me. It's Anila, is it not? Come in, you must come in. John, take Miss Tandy inside to the salon while I see your father's herbs delivered to the surgery room."

I thanked the driver, who nodded, without saying a word. The two boys grasped my hands and pulled me inside, little Kit just as boldly as his brother. He bore no trace of his injuries, I was glad to see.

They took me into a large bright room, so plainly decorated that it put me in mind of our salon at Garden Reach after everything had been taken from it. There were no oil pictures or mirrors on the walls here and only a clock and some brass instruments were displayed on the one sideboard the room contained. A round cotton rug adorned the floor but this was severely rucked up by a bamboo pen that stood proud in the middle of it. Inside the pen was the lovely little girl I remembered. She beamed at me, more gums than teeth.

"Georgie can walk now so she has to be kept in the crib," John told me. "Are you going to be our teacher? My aunt is tired of giving us lessons."

"Hush, John. Bring the cushions for us, you and Kit."

Mrs Herbert herself was carrying a tray with glasses of lime juice. She bent to set it on the floor and must have seen surprise in my face for instantly she said, "I love the Indian way of hospitality. Come sit with me, Miss Tandy. My sister-in-law is away visiting today, a welcome respite for her, I think."

John and Kit staggered forward with big calico cushions for us to sit on, on the floor just as we were. They came again with another for themselves, on which they perched like little blond princes until they started to slide off and giggle.

We drank in silence for a moment. Then I spoke.

"Anoush gave me a message from your husband, just yesterday. That is why I came and I am sorry if it is inconvenient. You were very kind to think of employing me. I could think of nothing I would like more except that, you see, I shall be setting out for Madras in a week."

Mrs Herbert's gentle face looked strained for a moment. For all the world I did not want her to think I felt myself above the kind position she had offered me. So, while the boys grew bored with their cushion and moved away to play, I told her I would be joining my guardian in Madras.

"I understand, of course," was her response. But if anything she looked more concerned and I did not think this was merely because her little daughter had begun to cry. "It was a great hope we had, that is all."

She rose and lifted the baby out of her pen, making ready to nurse her. I had not heard that English women fed their babies so.

"My husband will be home shortly for dinner," she said. "He attends the Company in the mornings, and in the evenings all persons are at liberty to come here for the treatment he offers. You must stay to eat with us and George himself will tell you about a separate matter."

THE
DOCTOR'S
TALE

THROUGHOUT OUR DINNER I marvelled at how gentle the doctor and his wife were with their children. After a grace was offered, all three were free to talk and babble as they wished. There were no reprimands for their small failures in table manners. When little Georgiana in her highchair started to throw rice at her brothers her mother simply distracted her with a jelly sweet and asked the boys to wipe the grains up themselves. I saw no ayah for the baby, but the table servants were spoken to as if everything they did was a kindness and much appreciated.

They asked after Anoush and Mrs Herbert clapped her hands in delight when she heard of the outcome of Christmas Day.

"Such a brave and lovely girl," she said. "And so obliging, whenever I see her. Oh, she must have a wedding gift from us, George."

For my part, I did not tell them anything of my own story, or Carlen's end, or even of the rescue of Manik, for the boys were too small to learn about such cruelty. But I told a little of our river adventures and Mr

Walker's quest for an unknown bird. I wished I had my notebooks with me to show them what I had been employed to do, my one true skill. But that thought brought another twinge of guilt with it.

The doctor stood up when we had finished.

"Come into my surgery room, Miss Tandy," he said. "Not of course that you are anything other than the picture of good health, but the boys will not disturb us there."

I followed him into his quarters, a small room to the back of the house. There were cabinets all round this room, their shelves crammed with labelled jars and pots and strange glass utensils in vegetable shapes. A brown delph bowl and pitcher stood on a table by the window. This looked onto a lawn where there was a latticework gazebo, pitched slightly askew. I thought suddenly of my little iron tea house and wondered if I might ever see it again.

I was offered a small armchair and the doctor himself went to sit behind a desk as large as a bed and piled high with ruled notebooks. He took from a drawer a pair of round spectacles and put them on. With these and the straight grey hair that he wore long, he was the very picture of a Persian wizard that I had imagined from the stories.

"I am very glad you received my message, Miss Tandy," he said. "I was concerned how I might reach you when I found I needed to consult with you. You see – a situation has occurred."

I was puzzled for Mrs Herbert had already told her husband that I would be travelling to Madras, that I could not be the children's teacher. But I could see he had a method in telling his tale and in this he would not be hurried.

"I work for the Company and I also work for myself, hoping to do what good I may here and also to learn as much as I can of medical practices that exist outside Europe. You may have observed that I bring here many of the native herbs for trial."

I nodded for I was listening properly, but I confess I was also beginning to calculate how long my journey back to the city would take. The impulse that had brought me here had now used up almost the day and I feared greatly that Mr Walker might be hurt by my neglect of his work. Clearly, there was no urgent matter here for me at Alipore.

It was while the Herberts waited in Madras for their sailing to Calcutta that the Company charged the doctor with his first case on their behalf, he told me.

"I was called to give an opinion in a case of amnesia."

Was that a kind of fever? I had not heard of it.

"Amnesia is a loss of memory," the doctor explained.

My heart turned over.

"Now let me be direct, Miss Tandy. When we made enquiries of Mrs Panossian about the possibility of employing you as a tutor to our children, naturally she gave us your name and a little of your history. Do not worry. I did not share any information with her but I had to ask myself if perhaps there might be a link between you and this patient. You see, he bears the same name, and it is not such a common one. If there were a connection, well then anything you could tell me about his background and circumstances might assist me. Especially now that you are leaving the city."

He looked at me over his spectacles, enquiringly. But I was too shocked to speak. Outside in the garden the boys were shouting, running, but their clear high voices were fog in my ears. I felt as though I had been thrust down a deep well. I was cold.

The doctor clapped his hand to his forehead.

"Oh, Miss Tandy," he said. "I have given offence. I should of course have told you that the patient's condition is not a disease. He acquired it as the result of an accident. There is no cause for worry, should you be kin. He—"

"Doctor Herbert, you are talking about my father," I interrupted at last. "Oh, please, he is not ill? Please don't give me any bad news, not now, not when I travel to meet him only next week."

But what could *please* ever do?

The doctor flushed a deep red. For a horribly long moment, he was the speechless one. He took out a piece of white linen from his waistcoat pocket and wiped his brow. Then he spoke, almost in stutters.

"But, my dear girl, Mrs Panossian, she told me, that is she told us, that your father was dead, she was assured of it, she said. I thought that this patient I had met might possibly be a brother of his, or a cousin, you know. The desire to travel to distant lands often runs in families. I would never have spoken so—"

"Is my father all right? Please, that is all that matters to me."

He sighed.

"He *is* ill, Miss Tandy, but at the same level of illness that he has borne with courage for some years, apparently. Your *father*? Well, of course you must know, but…"

As briefly as I could, I told him what I had not spoken of at dinner-time. Carlen's revelations, Mr Walker's discovery of my father's plan that we should have our own little income, my own beliefs and fears ever since my father's departure. The doctor was completely disarmed by my story, I could see that, but I was entirely impatient to know his. After Carlen, here was the last person to have met my father. And so recently!

He put up his hands, finally, to stop my questions.

"Miss Tandy, my wife always tells me that I wear seven-league boots to tramp over a story, and she will be confirmed in that, doubtless, this time. But I know that what I should tell you first is this. I have committed this patient, your father, to my care. And, since my care cannot be in Madras, Mr Tandy is, even now, travelling with an orderly serjeant to Calcutta. There was no passage for him on the ship we took ourselves. I expect him here at Providence House any day, you see."

He went to the delph jug and poured water into a cup which he handed to me. My fingers brought it to my mouth but I hardly knew how this happened.

"We seem to take turns astonishing one another, my dear," he said, gently. "Your prime question, whether your father be all right, is answered by my yes, my qualified yes. But now I will tell you the way of it all."

"But why did they call you, a doctor, to see my father if he is not very ill? Why can he not stay in Madras? You say he is not any worse than Carlen's letter told me?"

He nodded.

"Best I can tell, my dear," he said. "Nonetheless, what the Company wanted me to do was to recommend that Patrick Tandy be incarcerated for life in a lunatic asylum. And, since no proper such place exists here yet, what they required was that he be returned to England, posthaste, to an institution called Bethlem, or Bedlam, as people call it. A most fearful place where medicine treats mad people as if they were monkeys."

"No!"

My dream suddenly came to mind, that vision of my father shrinking to nothing. Perhaps some things were worse than death. Was this how it would end after all?

"You are right. He is not mad," the doctor said, his voice steady, as sound as I could wish. "But you see, even the king himself is not protected from receiving cruel and improper treatment when such an infirmity is suspected. For the royal mind has suffered so in recent years. I take a special interest in such malady, you see."

He tapped a pile of his books. I could read titles handwritten on the spines of some of them. *Melancholia. Mania.* But no *Amnesia* that I could see.

"I could clearly see that your father is a man of sensibility and honour. That he is respected, even venerated, by those he consorts with. That he can still work in a fashion far more useful than many in this city can and do. That he remains, in short, a person with a purpose who—"

"That is exactly what Carlen wrote in his letter," I said, cutting him short.

Doctor Herbert looked puzzled. As well he might, for of course now I couldn't remember exactly what were the details I had blurted out only minutes before.

"When Mr Walker's man met my father in Madras he said that he made money painting pictures of ships."

"Indeed so," said the doctor. "I watched him at work. Look at this."

He reached for one of his notebooks and turned the pages until he found a slip of drawing paper. He held it up so I could see a small sketch of a fishing boat pulled up on the shore, lying to one side.

I got out of the chair and took the drawing from him. I ran my fingers down the fine lines of the boat, and over the bold tiger eyes my father had made to stare from its bows. I wanted to touch the perfect little boat to my cheek. Oh, there was such joy in that simple slip of paper!

When I looked up again the doctor was watching me, as thoughtful-looking as if I were one of his patients.

"Another matter was this," he said. "There was an unseemly urgency about the Company's request, which made me certain that it was intended to benefit them at the expense of the patient. The person I was dealing with was bound for London himself and keen to oversee this proposed removal in person. A man called Crocker. He took a fury when I told him that I could not in conscience export the patient, your father, to Bedlam."

Crocker! In the Gardens, so long ago it seemed now, Mr Walker had called this man an apocalypse. How right he had been.

The drawing paper slipped out of my hands and as I bent down to pick it up I heard frogs begin to croak outside, a sign that evening was approaching. I placed it on the desk and the doctor smiled at me but I was too stricken to respond. I was shivering. He came round his desk then, and took up my right hand into his two warm ones, pressing it firmly.

"Forgive my clumsiness, Miss Tandy. That name seems to mean something to you. But you mustn't worry. This Crocker did not win his case, far from it. Not only is your father now my patient but his transport and his care are to be entirely at the Company's expense. They had to accept this condition or lose my services."

I could hear the clip-clop and crunch of a horse and carriage arriving at the front of the house. I started up, half in hope, half in terror, but Doctor Herbert spoke quickly.

"That will be my sister returning. It won't happen in quite that way, Miss Tandy. There will be messengers from the Company, from the ship, all kinds of documents and visitations before your father is released here, take my word for it."

"Doctor Herbert, it is so hard for me to believe that my father is coming to Calcutta, after all. This changes everything I was intending to do."

He nodded.

"Of course. Though now you understand that I was ignorant of everything when I asked you to come here. I knew nothing of your travel plans, nor, most wonderfully, of your family situation. I merely thought there was a chance you might help me, as if with a puzzle."

"But I can! More than ever. And you can help *me*!"

Miss Hickey would be shocked at my boldness. I took a breath. "I'm sorry. I have been a little afraid, you see, of what I might find."

He shook his head at that, firmly.

"There is nothing to fear, I promise you. Now, Miss

Tandy, you must come and stay with us, after your father arrives. I don't speak of any duties. That is another matter. But your presence will be invaluable in attempting your father's restoration to health. And if we cannot quite achieve that, at least we can all assist in his happy maintenance until another solution presents itself."

All those unlovely words – restoration, maintenance, solution – were hitting my brain like the black keys that can make the harpsichord sound so sad. Suddenly I wanted to jump up and sing hallelujah. Perhaps the doctor believed he had found my father. But I saw it differently. My father was coming to me – and whatever was the mechanism in the universe that had made this happen, it did not matter a jot. All that it had required was keeping faith, as Mr Walker had said. A door must always be kept open.

If I had not stayed in Calcutta how ever might I have met the spiteful Crocker, or Carlen, or indeed the doctor, for that matter?

To give him credit, the doctor was beaming as he slid the little boat sketch across to me once again.

"So, Miss Tandy, your first step might be to ask your good friend Mr Walker to offer your ship's passage to the next bidder. I understand that you have your paintings to finish in the meantime. I will, of course, have you informed immediately your father arrives in Calcutta."

He stood then, came round his great desk and offered me his arm.

"Now, let me call the carriage for you. And we'll both tell my dear Charlotte that I did not do so badly with my trample-all boots, shall we?"

ARDEA ANTIGONE

MY RIGHT HAND FELT as if it had been crushed underneath an enormous palanquin with seven fat ladies stretched out in it, each one decked in heavy gold jewellery. My poor wrist had forgotten how to turn itself. But in just four days I had finished all my drawings and paintings. They were Mr Walker's now, to bring to London with all his other business.

"Anila, you will be famous in these circles whenever it may be that you come to London," he said, smoothing each piece tenderly before he packed it in gauze paper and placed it between hard covers in one of his sea trunks. "You might become famous everywhere if only we can have a book made of these."

He made me sign each one in the bottom left corner, and write in my neatest script underneath the signature all the names we had for the birds. So I copied these in Bangla, in English, and in Latin words whenever we could find the proper match in Mr Walker's books.

As for the beautiful birds that my grandfather had shown me, Mr Walker had already discovered their name in his tattered copy of Mr Linnaeus's *Systema Naturae*.

"Here we are: *Ardea antigone*, he calls your rosy-headed crane. But here in India it's called the sarus. The Emperor Jehangir loved the bird, I've read that."

I shook my head. I had never heard that name, nor had my grandfather mentioned it. I could not help feeling a little disappointed that Mr Walker's sister had to depend on the honey-brown veena bird to carry her name instead of the tall beautiful dancing bird of the riverbank. But Mr Walker did not seem to share my feelings. Antigone was the name of a Greek princess from long ago, he told me.

"That particular Antigone was brave like yourself, Anila. She stood up to a tyrant and she's remembered for ever for it. But your bird is named for a princess of Troy, I believe. The goddess Hera was jealous of this other Antigone and turned her into a crane."

"Hera, like our boat?"

"The very one. Wife of Zeus, and together they made a great bundle of trouble. No, I am happy that our veena bird will have no such bad blood in her name. She will be an *evelina*, of the bittern family, a lively, happy denizen of the river, just as her namesake was. I hope she will, at any rate."

He touched my wooden chair back for luck.

It had been worthwhile to be so busy with my pencils and brushes because I found I could not think of anything else while my hands were delivering birds, and all at such speed. Whenever I stopped drawing, however, I heard every noise on the street loud and close as a small mouse must hear everything sound from behind his wainscot. Every horse clipping by, every carriage, every footstep passing, carried a message for me from Alipore, I felt sure. But it was not until the evening before Mr Walker's departure that it came.

We were sitting at the little table where I had had my first breakfast with Mr Walker, all those many weeks ago. On the table was my mother's Durga. Hari had brought her from the garden house, only that afternoon.

"Hari's report is that your little house is all grown over again with greenery," said Mr Walker. "It seems the spiders and their colleagues have seized back their rule like the good river pirates they are. But he took the goddess away from the jungle."

Poor Durga looked ever more like a plain clay cup. I decided I would paint over the faint traces of her many arms and her knowing smile. I picked her up and at that moment the doorbell clattered.

"At this hour?" Mr Walker said, almost to himself.

Chandra bustled in. For Mr Walker's last day he had put on a white English shirt which he wore over his dhoti, kept in by a black waistcoat that was much too large for him. He carried a plate, only a tea plate, but sitting on it was a small white card. He put the plate on the table between us and stood there, breathing importantly. Mr Walker handed the card to me.

This is to inform Miss Anila Tandy that her father has arrived today at Providence House, Alipore.

Mr Walker let out a long breath, almost a whistle.

"I am very glad, Anila, so very glad to know this before I leave," he said. He leant over and shook my right hand, as the English will do, and then he jumped up and shook Chandra's hand too, for good measure.

Above us Balor squawked with some emotion of his own. For my part, there were tears running down my face.

"Oh, Mr Walker," I said. But I could say nothing else. There were so many things I wanted to say to him and none that I could. I would have to write them later in a letter, a letter as thick as the one he now bore in his trunk with his promise to hand it to Miss Hickey in person.

There was no end to his kindness. For instance, he had insisted I keep the clothes he had bought for my voyage to Madras though I begged him to send them back.

"And upset Anoush, who helped me choose them?" he said. "Bad enough that I will lose your company going south, Anila."

Anoush had done me proud. There were two new saris, a golden one and another in a shimmering colour that was between pink and purple. There were long tunics, one of green silk, one of blue cotton. There was an English gown, a beautiful blue like Dutch delph. Best of all she had known to order two pairs of men's breeches in soft white cord.

As well as bearing that expense, Mr Walker had declared that I could stay in his house under Chandra's care for as long as it might be. Balor would be doubly glad to have two slaves to serve him, he said.

But now the word had come that answered that invitation.

"You must sleep well tonight, Anila," Mr Walker said after our supper. He had made me consent not to rise at the same hour as he must, before dawn, for, he said, he hated partings above all things. I was glad to agree.

"Tomorrow will such be a strange occasion, no matter how happy, so you must have a proper care for yourself. I will be thinking of you all the time I am rolling around the deck, trying to find my sea legs. You cannot imagine how keenly I will await your news in Madras. Good night, my dear."

He made to leave the room, Chandra ahead of him with a night-light, having left one for me on the table. But at the door he stopped.

"You know," he said, "I was thinking all along that when the time came that I must urge you most particularly to be guided by the doctor, for he seems a fine interpreter of maladies as well as a good man. But on reflection, no. I say now that you should listen to your own heart's prompts first of all, Anila, for they are what have brought you all this way."

Hearrrt's prrrompts. Then he was gone.

I sat up late in my little room, fingering the few precious items I would show my father. As well as Durga, I had Mr Hickey's drawing of my mother. There was my tiny peacock locket, his saddest gift, and there was my own bulbul drawing. That had been made after Papa had left us, but he had known the bulbul itself for it was a long-lived bird, fed in plenty by the people on our lane.

We had a jackdaw at home as bold as that fellow when I was your age, Anila. My sister Cecilia fed him best bits of bacon rashers when my mother wasn't around.

These were all I had to nudge Papa's mind back to his life with us in Calcutta. I regretted now that I had left my mother's purple scarf for Jonaki. She was welcome to have it, but its beautiful bright colour might have been the very thing to best challenge my father's memory, as it had come from him.

Finally I laid out my mother's green silk sari. Though he had never seen it, I would wear it to meet him. I would tell him how his Annapurna had been painted in it and that people spoke of how lovely a sitter she was. Like a lady by Raphael, they said.

After that, there was only my own face he might stare at for clues. There was a little glass in a frame standing on the washstand in my room. I held it close and examined my each feature just as I thought he might need to do.

My watchful eyes stared back at me from the glass, brown like most people's, not the dark black zest of my mother's eyes. My mouth however was set well enough, like hers, and yet it had a determined line, like his. He could not miss that – how often had he remarked it himself? I combed my hair out and fingered it into the childish way he had always liked, in two braids down my back.

When I did sleep that last night in Mr Walker's house I dreamt of a boy on a horse. The horse was black, the boy was fair and he crouched low over the horse's neck, steering it faster and faster over a land flat as a chessboard, jumping over creeks and narrow tanks that stretched out as far ahead as the sky, with not a tree in sight. He did not show his face.

A PASSAGE
TO JUPITER

I HEARD PAPA BEFORE I saw him. He was singing.

If to France or far-off Spain
She crossed the watery main
To see her face again the seas I'd brave

That sad sad song about the pearly girl! How he
loved those kinds of songs and he would sing them all
the louder if Malati or Hemavati were in the house so
that he might drive them away even if only for a little
while.

I rounded the back porch of the Herberts' house,
which gave onto a lawn, the same lawn that was visible
from the doctor's surgery. There was the open gazebo
on the grass, its iron latticework painted white. A man
sat at a sloping desk inside it, staring off into the trees at
the end of the park, singing.

And if it's heaven's decree
That mine she'll never be
May the Son of Mary me in mercy save

I could not remember the words that came next. But I could hum the melody and I did, making an equal music with his voice, loud enough for him to hear. He stopped singing, twisted round in his seat and stared at me where I stood, just outside his little station. A moon to his Jupiter.

He was thinner, darker in skin than I remembered, and his sweet fine hair was cut very short. In one terrible place it did not seem to grow at all. But I would have picked him out from a shipful of men, at any distance, even though I was not close enough yet to distinguish his eyes.

He leapt up and beamed at me.

"Who are you, beautiful girl in green, that you know my song which nobody else seems to know? Is this a dream and if I blink will that polite little boy appear in your place, bringing more instruments for me to draw? I hope not."

He stood up and gently took my bag and set it down on the floor of the gazebo.

"Please take my seat and talk to me for a moment, for the day is long, you know. Tell me who you are."

I bit my lip hard.

"My name is Anila. Anila Tandy."

He looked confused, uneasy. Then, as if remembering his manners, he bowed his head in a way that called attention to the deep gouge above his temple. I forced my eyes to remain steady.

"I was going to sail to Madras to find you. But then you came back to Calcutta instead. Just like you promised."

My voice shook a little on those last words. I wondered if I'd been too sudden, said too much. But his face cleared.

"This is Calcutta, that much I was told yesterday morning. I am to live here now. It seems a fine place. Perhaps the air is a little clammy. Madras is somewhere else again. Like the island with the houses clinging to the mountainside. They're all somewhere else but it's best to stay put in one place and put some memories down the way I've been doing."

"You are Patrick Tandy."

How peculiar it was to say those words to my father. But the doctor had advised me to speak like this. *Be very clear*, he had said. *State simple truths even if they seem obvious to you. Be prepared to say them again and again.*

Papa was staring at me, as children do, with no shyness or embarrassment

"And Patrick Tandy has a daughter. You have a daughter."

He smiled at this information, with none of the discomfort he had shown when I said my name. Then he shook his head, slowly, even politely.

"Well, now. I wasn't expecting you to say that, you know, such an odd thing. They tell me all the time that I forget what happened before I came here, no, not here, the other place. But I remember some things, not only songs. You'll call me foolish but I think it used to be cold enough for four, five blankets, imagine the weight of that, and then a big white cat would come and sit on top of the pile."

I could not hear that without letting him know he was right.

"Oh, Papa, that was when you were a boy in Ireland. You told me about the cold that makes the leaves fall from the trees, and about the cat white as snow. Papa, I'm your Anila. And you're not foolish, not one bit."

There – I had said the wrong things and now I could say no more. My throat was full. He reached out and took my hands in his, staring first at them and then at my face.

"I remember a lot of girls I played with in a garden. I don't think you were one of them even though I see the ring you're wearing and I know it. But I'd surely remember such a lovely face."

I looked down at Miss Hickey's little ring, with its golden handclasp. *That* one I hadn't counted upon to work on my father's memory. But it gave me courage again.

"Papa, the song you were singing. How do you think I knew it?"

Again, he looked baffled. He let my hands go and rubbed the side of his head where the wicked scar lay.

"You look like a clever girl. I suppose that's how. Do you know these lines?"

O long expected to my dear embrace!
Once more 't is giv'n me to behold your face!
The love and pious duty which you pay
Have pass'd the perils of so hard a way.

He spoke the strange words with his eyes closed and his head tilted back until he finished. I had seen Mr Hickey recite verses in just the same way.

I shook my head when he looked at me for my answer.

"I don't recognize the words, Papa. But I like the

sound and they make good sense."

He seemed disappointed.

"Of course you don't know them, they don't belong to the song at all. But they came into my mind just now, somehow. I thought you might be familiar. See, I'll write them down in my notebook."

He reached under his drawing papers and found a small black notebook and a pencil. I stood up to watch him write his lines down on a page that was crammed with jottings and small drawings. His script was still the same, neat, with small, well-formed letters.

He snapped the book shut before I could distinguish any of the other entries.

"The doctor who lives here said I should write down anything that came to mind that I couldn't explain. He said it might all make up a pattern one day, like knots in a carpet."

He laughed.

"I had a meeting with a rock in the sea. That's what took my sense away, they tell me that every day so I can remember it."

"Papa, I heard that you had an accident, that you were very brave."

"Oh, they say this and that. Some people even come to see me for the novelty. But I don't think anybody has ever said to me what you did. Now, isn't that a strange business that you call me Papa and I don't mind it? And yet I have forgotten the name you gave, my dear, though I do know you said it."

"Anila. It means blue like the skies, Papa."

"You see," he said, holding his open palms out towards me. "I would not deserve a daughter. But what

in the world is it anyway, do you think, that has con-
spired to set us two people down here this beautiful
morning, like birds in a cage?"

He stretched his arms out to touch the latticework of
the gazebo and he was smiling at me, even though
I saw tears washing out of his eyes. One blue eye and
one green, the green with speckles of gold in it, dancing like atoms in sunshine.

I wanted to sing my own sad song, a song that had
no rhymes.

*Oh, my dear papa. You are not become foolish. For that
has been my chief fear. No, you are full of a life that begins
every day afresh, as birds do, or brave beasts, that have little
care for what has happened to them or what may yet befall.
But your Annapurna and I, we are your pearls, mired in that
watery main of yours, down deep, farther than anyone knows.*

Sad, but I could make it into a song nonetheless. For
somehow at that moment I knew that it would be all
right, that I would find the courage to face my father as
a friendly stranger, day after day, for as long as it would
take. It might take wisdom or patience, or perhaps it
might only take a lucky chance, to find the right words,
the right pictures, the right knots, that might mend his
broken life together in some fashion.

Now I could see how clever my mother was,
all along.

To be the teller of a story you must begin and end it,
yes, and if you decide to leave for another day what
comes before or next, that is your choice. I was right
about that.

But my mother, the queen of storytellers, had the
real truth in her hand when she drew that never-

ending line on the stone she picked from the fountain. She knew that every story, every life, is as round and complete as a moon that lights up the sky with its own perfect face. But just as a moon turns dark and mysterious half the while, so a story cannot tell you everything you wish to hear, nor can a person. You must discover the rest with your wits and your senses and, most of all, with your heart.

To be alive, and to see that, what could be better or braver or more wonderful?

Glossary

Bengali words whose meaning may not be clear in the text.

anna – one-sixteenth of a rupee
Asarh – the fourth month of the Hindu year, divided between June and July

bibi – a lady, but also used to mean mistress
bombazine – fabric of cotton and worsted wool
brinjal – aubergine

charpoy – a light bed
chikan – embroidery, especially from Lucknow
coolie – labourer

dacoit – armed gang robber
dadamoshay – maternal grandfather
dhoti – length of fabric tied at the waist, worn by Hindu men

East India Company – The English East India Company (there were also French, Dutch, Swedish, Danish and Portuguese EICs) was chartered to trade by Elizabeth I in 1600. By the late eighteenth century, the Company ruled a considerable part of India in governmental style, with presidencies in Calcutta, Madras and Bombay. The British crown took over after the widespread rebellion of 1857.

Ganga – the Ganges river which divides itself to flow

into the Bay of Bengal. One of its delta rivers is the Hooghly, the river of Calcutta.

Gentoo – a term for Hindu, used only by foreigners

ghol – a yogurt-type drink

godown – warehouse

gur – unrefined sugar solid made from sugar cane or date palm juice

Holi – Hindu spring carnival in honour of Krishna

Ikri-mikri-cham-chikri – a finger game played with children

jheel – floodwater pond

kash – tall grass with white flowers, grown for weaving

kerseymere – fine wool twill

maidan – park-like open space; parade ground

mohur – gold coin, worth, at this time, sixteen rupees

Mussulman – Muslim

paan – a popular concoction not unlike chewing gum, made of betel leaves, lime and areca nut paste

palki – short for palanquin, a box-like personal transport carried on the shoulders of bearers

panchali – Bengali folk songs

payesh – a sweet rice pudding

puja – Hindu religious ceremony; also prayers

pukka – well-made, proper, reliable

pukka mix – mortar made with molasses, brickdust and lime

rupee – standard unit of currency

sindur – red powder that married Hindu women apply to their hair parting
syce – groom or stableman

tiffin – light meal, lunch

veena – stringed instrument like a lyre, used in Indian classical music

Gods and Others

Annapurna – the celestial benefactress who fills the rice pot
Dakshin Rai – god revered in the Sunderbans mangrove delta; friend to tigers and to man
Durga – mother goddess and consort of Shiva, often depicted with eighteen arms and riding a tiger
Ganesha – elephant-headed god of wisdom, son of Shiva
Hanuman – the monkey god who helps King Rama find his wife Sita
Jatayu – the vulture that witnesses Sita's kidnapping and dies attempting to rescue her
Kali – another, fiercer, manifestation of the mother goddess, much celebrated in Calcutta
Kalidasa – India's classical poet and playwright of the first millennium, who wrote in Sanskrit
Krishna – a human incarnation of the god Vishnu,

whose adventures are told in the *Mahabharata* story cycle

Lakshmi – goddess of fortune and wealth, and consort of Vishnu

Radha – a gopi or cowherd beloved by Krishna

Rama – King Rama and Queen Sita are lovers separated by evil and magic, whose story is told in the *Ramayana* epic poem

Ravana – the king of the island Lanka, who captures and imprisons Sita

Saraswati – goddess of learning, music and poetry, and consort of Brahma

Surya – the sun god

Songs and Poems

The song Anila's father sings is "The Snowy Breasted Pearl", an eighteenth-century Irish love song.

The lines he speaks are from *Aeneid Book VI* by Virgil, in John Dryden's verse translation. After many difficulties, Aeneas (who is alive) has found his father Anchises (who is dead) in Hades, the Underworld.

Birds

All the birds that Anila draws are real except one. Mr Walker's bittern, the "veena bird", is a fictional bird. Sadly, the beautiful pink-headed duck is today almost definitely extinct: no sighting has been recorded since 1935.

The Painter and the Paintings

Thomas Hickey (1741–1824) was a prize-winning art student at the Dublin Society Drawing School. Being adventurous, he travelled widely and worked as a portrait painter in Dublin, London, Rome, Lisbon, Calcutta and Madras. He was also chief expedition artist on a diplomatic mission to China. His two daughters came with him on his second tour to India. He died in Madras after spending a total of thirty-four years in India. These are facts. But all the events described in *Anila's Journey* are entirely fictional.

The two paintings described on pages 190 and 209 are actual paintings and can be viewed in the National Gallery of Ireland in Dublin. *An Indian Lady* (the cover painting, dated 1787) is believed to depict the bibi/ mistress of the lawyer and memoirist William Hickey (no relation). She died in childbirth. The young sisters in *Portrait of Two Children* (1769) are not named.